BURIED IN THE BACKYARD

A couple of pieces of rusted pipe went flying over the fence, followed by some broken flower pots and a length of garden hose. She carefully laid the quilt square on the back of the chair she'd been sitting in and then started stacking the trash Tripp was clearing out into a neat pile along the edge of the yard. When he finally unburied the piece of plywood, she asked, "Do you need me to come in and help lift that?"

"No, I've got it."

The board bowed almost to the breaking point when he tried to lift it, but she could see more of the familiar pattern underneath the straining wood.

"That's my quilt, all right." Then she gagged as the breeze shifted in her direction. "Good grief, what's that awful smell?"

The words were no sooner out of her mouth than Tripp dropped the board and jumped back, looking a little green himself. She started forward, but he waved her back. "Abby, don't come any nearer. In fact, take Zeke and go wait in the house. I need to call Gage."

It took her a second to recognize the name. "Gage Logan, as in the chief of police? Why do you need him?"

Unfortunately, her mind had already connected the dots to come up with the obvious answer. She froze, unable to advance or retreat. "Tripp? Is that what I think it is under there?"

His dark eyes stared into hers as he gave her a grim nod. All business now, he pulled out his cell phone and punched in a three-number sequence. "Yes, ma'am, I need to report a dead body . . ."

DEATH
BY
COMMITTEE

Alexis Morgan

KENSINGTON BOOKS
KENSINGTON PUBLISHING CORP.
www.kensingtonbooks.com

KENSINGTON BOOKS are published by

Kensington Publishing Corp.
119 West 40th Street
New York, NY 10018

All Kensington titles, imprints, and distributed lines are available at special quantity discounts for bulk purchases for sales promotion, premiums, fund-raising, educational, or institutional use.

Special book excerpts or customized printings can also be created to fit specific needs. For details, write or phone the office of the Kensington Sales Manager: Attn.: Sales Department. Kensington Publishing Corp., 119 West 40th Street, New York, NY 10018. Phone: 1-800-221-2647.

Kensington and the K logo Reg. U.S. Pat. & TM Off.

First Printing: February 2019
ISBN-13: 978-1-4967-1953-9
ISBN-10: 1-4967-1953-0

ISBN-13: 978-1-4967-1956-0 (eBook)
ISBN-10: 1-4967-1956-5 (eBook)

10 9 8 7 6 5 4 3 2 1

Printed in the United States of America

Chapter One

Abby McCree sighed. Loudly.

The only one who appeared to pay any attention to her was Zeke. The huge mastiff mix was dozing in his favorite puddle of sunlight on the hardwood floor. He raised his head long enough to see if she had a treat for him. When she didn't, he gave her a reproachful look before dropping his head down on his paws to drift back to sleep.

"Sorry, boy."

Doggy disappointment was the least of Abby's problems right now. She hadn't been a landlady for very long and didn't know what all the rules were. However, she was pretty sure that saving her somewhat irascible tenant from a gaggle of grannies wasn't on the official list. Still, she felt some obligation to shoo the ladies away from her front window, especially because whatever one of them had just whispered had the other two giggling like schoolgirls. Had none of them ever seen a shirtless man mowing a lawn before? Evidently not one built like Tripp Blackston, but even she had to admit the man was totally ripped.

She set down the tray she'd carried in from the kitchen. It was clearly too much to hope that a plate full of freshly baked cream cheese brownies and sugar cookies would be enough to lure her guests back to their seats. "Ladies, we'll never get the plans for your garage sale finalized today if we don't get back to work."

Two gray heads and one impossibly red one briefly turned in her direction. Glenda, who clung to the mistaken belief that everyone really believed her hair was still the same vivid shade of red now as it had been when she was a young girl, acted as spokesperson for the trio. "We were just thinking that Mr. Blackston looked awfully hot out there."

Another pause for more giggling before she continued. "We think you should take a plate of goodies and a glass of that fresh lemonade out to him. Surely that young man deserves to take a break after working for hours in the hot sun."

They stared at Abby with a hint of accusation in their expressions, as if it was somehow her fault that the early spring day had turned unexpectedly warm. When Abby didn't immediately leap into action, Jean spun her walker around and marched toward the table. "Never mind, dear. I'll take it out to him."

Jean's best friend, Louise, joined her to pile a paper plate high with brownies, while Glenda filled a glass with lemonade. "I'll carry his drink for you, Jean. Abby, be a dear and get the door for us."

Defeat tasted bitter, but Abby knew when she'd been outmaneuvered and outmatched. It was obvious all three women had decades of experience in wielding guilt to get their way. She snatched the plate and glass out of their hands. "Fine. I'll take these out to Mr. Blackston. You three sit down and enjoy your drinks."

On her way to the door, she paused to look back at her elderly friends. "But when I come back, we need to get down to business. While I'm outside, why don't you think about where you want to hold the garage sale?"

Louise winced and then immediately offered up an apologetic smile. "But your aunt always insisted we have it here, Abby. Sybil has . . . *had* . . . the biggest yard and parking is plentiful on this street."

Darn, she should've known they'd play the Aunt Sybil card, a reminder that this house and everything in it hadn't been Abby's for very long. Before that, it had belonged to her aunt for over sixty years, starting from the day she moved in as a young bride and lasting right up until she died just over a month ago. A fresh stab of grief over the death of her favorite relative hit Abby hard. The pain of her loss had yet to fade in the least.

"I wasn't thinking. Of course, you can have it here again this year."

When they finally turned their attention to the brownies she'd baked earlier that morning, Abby headed outside to flag down her tenant on his next trip back in her direction. She knew the instant Tripp spotted her, because he stopped to frown at her from over by the fence. Finally, he guided the mower over to where she stood and shut it off. At least he wasn't going to make her shout over the sound of the engine.

"Did you need something?"

She held out the plate and the lemonade. "The ladies inside noticed how hot you looked out here."

Judging from the way he grimaced, she should've phrased that differently. Then again, the statement was true no matter which way he chose to interpret it. Almost any woman with a pulse would have noticed. Luckily, she wasn't that type at all.

Yeah, right.

Time to get down to business. "I . . . well, actually, they, thought you might appreciate a cold drink and a snack."

He glanced past her toward the large picture window on the front of the big Victorian behind her. From the way he tightened his grip on the lawnmower handle, she didn't have to look to know that the ladies were back at the window. At least he managed a small smile as he nodded in their direction and finally accepted the glass. He chugged down the lemonade in a matter of seconds and then shoved the glass back in her hand.

"Would you like some more?"

"I'm good. You can leave the brownies on the steps. I'll pick them up when I'm done mowing." His dark eyes bored into hers. "And for the record, I don't need an audience when I'm working."

He walked away before she could do more than sputter. The man was insufferable even if he was right. The agreement he'd had with Aunt Sybil was reduced rent in return for doing odd jobs around the place. He was entitled to his privacy.

That didn't keep her from muttering, as the lawnmower roared back to life, "Maybe people wouldn't stare so much if you kept your shirt on."

Abby set the plate down by his discarded T-shirt. As she rejoined her guests inside, Louise said, "The lemonade must have cooled him right down. He's putting his shirt back on, although he certainly doesn't look very happy right now."

Abby's cheeks burned. Had he heard her? If so, he must have the hearing of a bat to pick up her comment over the roar of that engine. Well, she hadn't said anything but the truth. Rather than discuss the matter any further, she sat down and reached for a brownie and her own glass of lemonade. After a brief internal debate, she added a second brownie to her plate. It had been that kind of a day.

"We were talking while you were outside." Louise patted Abby on the hand. "It's not fair of us to assume that you would host the garage sale just because Sybil always did. We were thinking we could ask Dolly Cayhill if we could use her place."

Jean didn't look convinced that was a good idea. "Is Dolly even back from Arizona? I sure haven't seen her around. Normally she lets me know when she gets back in town."

"Do I know Dolly?" Abby tried to put a face with the name. "I'm sure I've heard the name, but I don't know that I've ever met her."

Glenda reached for another cookie. "Maybe not. She and Sybil weren't close."

When Jean snorted as if smothering a laugh, Glenda shot her a dark look before continuing. "Dolly is a snowbird and always leaves town right after Christmas. She stays gone until the weather warms up here. Having said that, I haven't heard that she's back yet."

There was no use in dragging things out. Abby eyed a third brownie but decided against it. "Seriously, I don't mind having the sale here this year. Just let me know what I need to do to get ready and when you want to have it."

An hour later, Abby helped the ladies back down the front steps and got Jean settled into the backseat of Glenda's sedan. After tucking Jean's walker into the trunk and shutting the lid, she stepped back out of the way and waved as the car pulled away. As much as she enjoyed spending time with Aunt Sybil's friends, sharing both memories and laughs, she was ready for some alone time.

It seemed as if her life had been in a constant uproar for the past six months or more, and moments of peace and quiet had been rare.

The only problem was that there was so much she needed to be doing. Before heading back inside, she paused to study her new home. She'd yet to decide if she was going to live in it for the foreseeable future, or if she should get the place ready to sell. Either way, the house needed some serious upgrading. At least Aunt Sybil had had it painted top to bottom, inside and out, just last year, so that much was done.

The large yard was a whole different matter. Her aunt had always been an avid gardener, priding herself on having garden-tour quality landscaping. But over the past few years, the flower beds had definitely gotten out of hand. A lot of the trees and shrubs needed to be pruned or even taken out altogether. Blackberry brambles had gradually taken over one entire corner of the backyard and were slowly creeping closer to the small mother-in-law cottage where Tripp Blackston had recently taken up residence.

Speaking of the man himself, he'd finished mowing and was now edging the flower beds along the side of the house. He might not be the friendliest person she'd ever met, but he was certainly a hard worker. She quickly moved out of sight. This was her house and her yard, and she had every right to stand anywhere she pleased, but the last thing she wanted was to get caught watching him again.

She glanced down at her silent companion. "Zeke, I'm going upstairs to work again. You can stay out here with Tripp if you want."

When the dog stared up at her with his soulful eyes, she gave him a good scratch and a couple of treats that she'd remembered to stick in her pocket. "He knows to let you back inside if you get tired of following him around."

Zeke gulped down his goodies and then thanked her with a slobbery lick. Out of consideration for his feelings, she waited until he ambled off in Tripp's direction before wiping her hand on her jeans. The big guy meant well, but yuck.

The day was getting away from her, and it was past time to get to work. Heading back into the house, she still had to wonder what Aunt Sybil had been thinking when she'd picked Tripp to be her new tenant. Granted, she'd always rented the place to a student from the local university, but he wasn't a typical college freshman. Although never exactly chatty, he had mentioned that he'd recently retired from the army after twenty years. Best guess, that made him a few years older than she was, somewhere in his late thirties or maybe even his early forties.

Glenda had told her that he'd served at some point with Gage Logan, the local chief of police. In fact, it had been Chief Logan who had introduced Tripp to Aunt Sybil a few months back, when Tripp had been in town to register for classes. That was the sum total Abby knew about the man. She guessed she couldn't complain as long as he paid his rent on time and kept up with the list of chores she updated as needed.

For now, she left the yardwork to him while she concentrated on the inside of the house, a major job in itself. Aunt Sybil hadn't exactly been a hoarder, but she had managed to accumulate quite a bit of clutter over the years, not to mention the added contributions from the two generations of her husband's family who'd lived in the house before her.

After grabbing a bottle of water, Abby trudged up to the third floor to pick up where she'd left off the day before. Aunt Sybil had used one of the three small bedrooms on that level as overflow for the stuff she couldn't fit in the attic. At some point, she'd had the wall taken out between the other two rooms, opening up the space for her quilting. One entire wall was covered with built-in shelves, which held the rainbow of quilting fabrics she'd collected over the years. Another held batting, a rack of threads, and bolts of the neutral colors that she used as backing for her quilts.

A complicated sewing machine held pride of place in front of the large window that overlooked the front yard. A stack of patchwork squares sat on the table next to the machine, some already sewn into long strips while others still waited to be joined together. The pattern was a relatively simple one, done in vibrant shades of red and blue, the style of quilt that her aunt had often made to be auctioned off by one of the charities she supported. Maybe someday Abby would try to finish the quilt herself, but not yet.

There was a quilt top stretched on the quilting frame in the corner, another project that needed to be finished. This one was a double-wedding ring pattern done in pastels. Who had it been for? Maybe Glenda or one of the other ladies would know. Abby ran her fingers across the fabric, loving the textures and soft colors. It was tempting to do a few stitches, but she couldn't bring herself to pick up the needle and thread that were still attached to the fabric right where her aunt had stopped working.

But then she hadn't been able to bring herself to touch anything in this one room that was so quintessentially her aunt's. Closing her eyes, she breathed in the fading scent of Sybil's perfume and whispered, "I miss you so much, Aunt Sybil."

Having paid homage to the woman who'd had a profound effect on her life, Abby crossed the hall to the other bedroom and prepared to wade through the day's allotment of boxes. She'd originally shoved everything to one side of the room to give herself space to sort everything into one of three categories: stuff to keep, stuff to donate, and trash.

Choosing the correct designation for some items turned out to be far more difficult than she'd expected, which had resulted in her adding a fourth category—undecided.

On some days, it was that last one that garnered the most additions. It didn't feel right to throw away family pictures, but she didn't know what to do with the ones in which she didn't recognize the people at all. For now, she just left them piled in boxes. It was tempting to sit and read a few more of the letters she'd unearthed yesterday, but she limited herself to skimming just a handful, which had dates spanning more than the past century. The entire collection went into the pile of things she planned to save.

Her primary goal was to pare down the sheer amount of stuff in the house, but she also needed to make room for her own things. For the most part, her belongings still sat in boxes piled in a small room in the back of the house. There wasn't much she'd salvaged from her marriage, but using all of Aunt Sybil's things made it feel as if she were a guest in this house, not its new owner.

Sorting also gave her something to do with her time, while she figured out what came next in her life. At this point, she'd expected to still be half of the couple, Chad and Abby Ohler, who maybe had two kids and a dog. Instead, she was back to being Abby McCree, alone and starting over on her own.

Enough of that. She wasn't going to sit there and wallow in what-ifs and where-did-I-go-wrongs. She'd done enough of that, starting immediately after she'd confronted Chad with her growing suspicion that he was having an affair. Unfortunately, her instincts had turned out to be right on target. Water under the bridge and all that. His loss.

The burn of tears trickled down her cheeks, no doubt the result of all the dust she was stirring up. Ignoring them, she got busy. Never sure what she'd find, sometimes it felt like she was on a treasure hunt. From what she could see, today's boxes contained old Christmas decorations, some hand-embroidered table linens, and a set of canisters decorated with pictures of mushrooms done in shades of yellow, orange, and green.

She held up the smallest one and grinned. "You're all going in the donate pile for the quilting guild's garage sale. I'm betting someone will want to revisit the seventies."

The Christmas ornaments went in the same pile, but she set the linens aside to take downstairs to be laundered. Unlike the family photos, someone had taken the time to pin a note to each piece, indicating who'd done the embroidery and the approximate date it had been done. Even if Abby never had kids of her own, she did have some distant cousins who might like to have a piece of the family history to keep.

There was one thing she'd yet to find. Years ago, she'd come to spend most of a summer vacation with Sybil. The two of them had made a quilt top from clothing belonging to at least three generations of their family. Unfortunately, they'd run out of time before they could finish it. Sybil had promised to pick up where they'd left off the next time Abby came for a long visit. But upon returning home, Abby had learned that her parents had filed for divorce. After that, thanks to the custody agreement, Abby had spent all of her summers with her father's new family in Oregon.

Any further visits with her aunt had been rare and too short to work on a major project like the quilt. Eventually, Sybil had promised to finish the quilt by herself, but it would still be Abby's someday. There were other quilts in the house that were nice, but she wanted this particular one because of the good memories that it represented.

Having completed her self-assigned number of boxes for the day, she dusted off her hands and stood up. Judging by the angle of the sun in the sky, she'd been up there for several hours. If that hadn't been enough of a clue about how much time had passed, the way her back and legs protested from all the bending and lifting would've also told her.

It took a few stretches to get everything loosened up and moving again. She turned off the lights and headed back downstairs with the box of linens. At least she and Zeke had taken their daily walk early that morning, so she could, in good conscience, zone out on the sofa with a book after dinner.

"Zeke, I'll get you fed and then see what I can scrounge for my own dinner."

He hustled ahead of her to assume a position near the container that held his kibble. The phone rang just as she finished filling his bowl. She considered ignoring the call, knowing her friends and parents wouldn't use the landline. No doubt it was a wrong number or someone wanting to sell her something. On the other hand, most of Sybil's friends still used her home number, even though they wanted to talk to Abby.

She reluctantly picked up the receiver. "Hello?"

As soon as she recognized the voice on the other end of the line, she wished she'd ignored the call. "Abby, this is Glenda. I meant to remind you about tonight when I was there earlier today. I'll pick you up at six-thirty sharp. We don't want to be late."

Late for what? Rather than admit that she had no idea what the other woman was talking about, Abby hustled across the kitchen to check the big calendar on the wall. Well, drat. How had she missed seeing the note about a meeting at city hall? Especially when Sybil had underlined it three times for emphasis.

"I can see that Aunt Sybil had intended to attend, Glenda,

but I don't think I need to go to a city council meeting.
I've spent the afternoon clearing out stuff upstairs, and
I'm covered in dust. Besides, I haven't lived in Snowberry
Creek long enough to be up on current events, so I probably
wouldn't even know what they're talking about."

There was a heavy silence coming from the other end of
the line.

"But you have to go, Abby. Everyone's expecting you."

A feeling of impending doom washed over her. She
knew—*just knew*—she was going to regret this, but Glenda
had left her no wiggle room.

"Okay, I'll bite, Glenda." She drew one deep breath and
then another before she could gather up the courage to ask
the one question she already knew she didn't want to have
answered. "Why?"

And just as Abby feared, Glenda shared the bad news.

Chapter Two

"I'm sorry, but I thought we'd already told you about the meeting. Last spring, the mayor herself asked Sybil to take over as chair of the town's Committee on Senior Affairs, which reports directly to the city council. They even did an article in the paper about her appointment, with Sybil's picture and everything. It was quite an honor for her. We all thought so."

"I'm sure it was." But what did that have to do with Abby? On second thought, she was pretty sure she didn't want to know.

Unfortunately, Glenda wasn't done talking. "The mayor heard that you had stepped up to take your aunt's place in the quilting guild. She asked us if we thought you'd be willing to fill in on this committee as well. You know, just until she can find someone else to take over. Considering Sybil's term of office would last for only another four months, we were sure you wouldn't mind. We were right, weren't we?"

Who was this "we" Glenda kept talking about? Not that it mattered. No one had the right to volunteer Abby for anything without consulting her first. Fighting back the urge to rip in to the older woman but good, she forced herself to count to ten before responding.

"I'm sorry—" no, she really wasn't "—but I don't have time to take on any more commitments right now. I only agreed to help with the quilting guild because I at least have some experience in that area." If picking out fabrics for one quilt nearly twenty years ago actually counted as experience. "However, I have no expertise in assessing the needs of senior citizens. I'm sure there are any number of people in town who are far more qualified to do that."

Glenda laughed. "You're right. There are a lot of us who have experience in being old. What we don't have is the organizational skills and business experience that you have. Sybil was always going on about how successful you were in the company you and your husband built from the ground up. How you coordinated everything and kept it all running so smoothly."

Abby pinched the bridge of her nose to ease the first hint of an oncoming headache. Yeah, maybe she did have skills, but what had they gotten her in the long run? She did take some small pleasure in knowing that Chad, her ex, was struggling to keep the business afloat all on his own. He'd bought out her half of the company as part of the divorce settlement. While he'd been the public face of the business, she'd worked just as hard as he had.

Evidently, he'd learned the hard way how much she'd actually done. When he started calling her for advice, she reminded him what he'd said in court regarding her role in the company. Something about him being the real force behind all of their success. In fact, he'd told the judge that Abby had been little more than a glorified file clerk and didn't deserve fifty percent of the fair value of the company. Luckily for her, the judge hadn't believed him.

But back to the matter at hand.

"I'm sorry, Glenda, but—"

Before she could finish, the other woman interrupted. "It's okay. I understand, but here's the thing. I hate to ruin the surprise, but the mayor is going to present you with a plaque honoring Sybil's service to our town. I suppose I can accept it on your behalf."

Great. Now Abby felt like she'd been kicking puppies.

"No, in that case, I should go. Don't worry, I'll be ready."

"That's great. Like I said, six-thirty sharp."

"Got it."

"And don't forget to act surprised."

"I'll do my best."

She hung up the phone and glanced at Zeke. "Dog, do you think I just agreed to do more than smile and say a few words about the plaque?"

Her furry friend woofed softly and leaned against her leg while she patted his wrinkly forehead. "Yeah, that's what I thought."

The next morning, Abby was convinced there wasn't enough coffee in the world to clear the cobwebs out of her head. She'd come home from city hall last night too agitated to fall asleep easily. After tossing and turning for two hours, she'd given up and gone back downstairs to read until the wee hours of the morning. All told, she'd managed about four hours of sleep. It was a good thing she didn't have anything on her schedule today other than to go through more boxes. However, that could wait until after lunch. For now, she was going to soak up some sunshine while she took her frustrations out on the blackberries in the backyard.

All in all, last night's meeting had played out pretty much as Abby had expected. The only positive thing she could say about it was that Rosalyn McKay ran her meetings efficiently. The usual call to order was followed by the presentation of various committee reports. Next, a handful of local citizens expressed their displeasure on various issues in town. The mayor had politely thanked them for their input and then referred each of them to the correct department in the city government to see what could be done. Finally, she ended the meeting with a brief ceremony honoring Aunt Sybil, ending it with the bombshell, "And we want to thank her niece, Abby McCree, for agreeing to serve out the rest of her aunt's term."

Abby had almost bolted for the door. Instead, she'd accepted the small plaque. She could only hope that she'd sounded more gracious than she'd felt. The situation was hardly the mayor's fault, and she figured there would be plenty of time after the official part of the meeting to clear up the misunderstanding about the vacancy on the committee.

Not so much. While Mayor McKay was apologetic, none of the remaining members of the committee were really in a position to take over the helm for the final months of their tenure. One gentleman was definitely on board for taking over when the new committee started up in September, but he was scheduled for a hip replacement that would limit his mobility for the next few months.

In the end, Abby had given in. On the way home, she'd told Glenda in no uncertain terms that this was the last one of Aunt Sybil's commitments she was willing to assume. Her aunt had always relished being involved in a large variety of groups in town, but that wasn't Abby's style. Not at all.

Glenda had the good grace to look guilty and promised

not to volunteer her for anything else without talking to her first. That was great, but she still had a garage sale to organize and a committee to run. Mayor McKay had suggested that Abby make an appointment with her office in the coming weeks. Her assistant would be happy to bring her up to speed on what the Senior Affairs group was currently working on.

Rather than think about it anymore, Abby stuffed a few of Zeke's favorite treats into her pocket and headed out to the toolshed to grab a pair of heavy duty gardening gloves, the pruning shears, and a shovel. Zeke trailed along in her wake and flopped down beside her feet while she considered the best plan of attack for clearing out the heavy growth of blackberries and other weeds. But that wasn't the only problem.

"Well, dog, I'd have to guess that Aunt Sybil used this part of the lawn as a dumping ground for anything that wouldn't fit in a trashcan."

Zeke studied the offending bushes and junk with grave concern. Abby understood how he felt. From where they stood, she could see some half-rotted plywood, a bunch of old pipes, and a rusted-out wheelbarrow, all buried under a thick layer of vines and thorns. No doubt she'd have to pay someone to haul it all away once the plants were cut back to a manageable level.

"I guess I'd better get started. Those blackberries aren't going to prune themselves."

Zeke gave a soft woof and stretched out in the grass to supervise.

Two hours later, Abby was ready to concede defeat. Between their thorns and stubborn roots, the blackberries were clearly winning the battle. Despite her best efforts, she'd only managed to reclaim about a foot of the lawn. She wiped the sweat off her forehead with the sleeve of her shirt and wondered what to try next. Heck, it wasn't as if she'd ever had a yard of her own to care for. She and Chad had lived in an upscale condo on the east side of Lake Washington. The only plants she'd ever owned were a couple of orchids she'd kept at work. Come to think of it, they hadn't fared all that well, either.

"I hear people around here rent goats to take out blackberries when they're out of control like this."

Abby jumped and nearly lost her balance, which would've sent her stumbling forward into the blackberries. Two strong hands caught her shoulders and held on just long enough to make sure she was steady on her feet before dropping away. As soon as she was free, Abby whirled around, her heart pounding in her chest as she punched Tripp on the arm. Wow, those muscles were every bit as hard as they looked. It felt like she'd hit a brick wall, the blow no doubt hurting her fist far more than its intended target.

"Darn it, Tripp, don't sneak up on a person like that. You scared ten years off my life."

To her surprise, he grinned at her. It was amazing how much a smile softened all the hard edges of his face, making him look younger and more approachable. Tripp jerked his head in the direction of a large pile of brush not more than thirty feet from where she stood. "I didn't sneak anywhere. I've been pruning those rhododendrons for the past hour. Zeke's been dividing his time between the two of us. I figured you would've noticed I was there."

"Obviously, I didn't." She was also willing to bet that hitting a tenant ranked right up there with ogling on the list of things a landlady wasn't supposed to do. Meaning an apology was in order. "I'm sorry I hit you."

His smile only widened. "That's okay. I barely felt it."

Even though she'd already figured that much out for

herself, it still made her mad. She'd put a lot of oomph behind that punch. Stuffing a lid down on her temper, she aimed for a more reasonable tone of voice. "Did you say something about goats?"

Tripp nodded. "I had to pick up some more fertilizer and weed killer yesterday. While I was at the lawn and garden center, I asked the lady what the best way was to get rid of blackberries, especially in an area this large. She suggested renting some goats. Evidently, they love to chow down on the bushes, thorns and all."

When she tried to picture it, the image didn't quite come into focus. But what did she know? "Huh, I've never heard of such a thing."

"Me neither. I asked her for the names of people in the area who do that sort of thing. You know, in case you were interested."

"Did she say how it works?"

He shrugged. "Evidently, the goat owner puts up a temporary fence around the area and turns the goats loose inside. They charge by the day. The owner, that is, not the goats. I'm pretty sure they'll consider this a free all-you-can-eat buffet."

"Very funny."

Actually, it was. Even if Abby couldn't quite picture how it all worked, she was game. It paid to hire experts to get a job done right. If she had a problem with the pipes or the wiring, she wouldn't hesitate to call a plumber or an electrician. This wasn't any different, even if these experts had four legs and strange eyes.

"Give me the numbers, and I'll call them right away. It's worth a shot."

Tripp pulled a couple of business cards out of his wallet and handed them to her. "Let me know if there's anything I need to do before they come. I've got classes this afternoon and one in the morning. Otherwise, I'll be around if you need me."

"Sounds good." She picked up her yard tools. "Guess I'll go see a man about a goat."

Tripp laughed again as he pulled on his work gloves. "I bet that's something you never thought you'd find yourself saying."

"True enough."

Two days later, she found herself once again standing shoulder to shoulder with Tripp as they watched the goats start chowing down. She normally didn't hover while a contractor was working, but the goats didn't seem to mind having an audience. Even Zeke seemed to find the whole affair riveting.

Joe, the goats' owner, had made quick work of setting up the fencing the previous afternoon. He'd come back today and turned a small flock of goats loose inside. Once everything was under control, he'd left to go meet with another potential client, promising to check back within a couple of hours.

Tripp smiled as he glanced in her direction. "Gotta say, they sure got right to work."

Abby had to agree with his assessment. "I can already see a big difference. At this rate, they should have the whole area cleaned out in a couple of days."

"Once they're done, I can start hauling all that trash out of there. Any idea what you want to do with this corner after that?"

"I've been giving it thought. I'm thinking something low maintenance would make the most sense. It doesn't get much direct sun, so I was looking online for plants that thrive in partial sun or full shade. It sounds like hydrangeas might do well here." At least she hoped so. "Before I make any firm plans, I thought I'd take pictures and ask someone at the nursery for advice."

Then something caught her eye. "What is that black and white goat chewing on?"

"Which one?"

She pointed toward the back corner. "The one with no ears."

Tripp leaned forward to get a better look. "Looks like he's gotten ahold of a piece of cloth. That can't be good for him. I'd better try to take it away before he swallows it."

He let himself into the makeshift pen and waded through the other goats to get to where the animal in question was still tugging hard on the fabric. From where Abby stood, it appeared to be part of a larger piece sticking out from under a piece of plywood. The material ripped free just as Tripp reached the goat. He quickly pried the fragment out of the goat's mouth and tossed the soggy mess over the fence to Abby.

"There's more under that board. I'll pull it out of there before one of the others decides it looks tasty."

Abby held the fabric by one corner, not sure if it was slimy from the goat chewing on it or because it had been out in the weather for a while. Probably a disgusting combination of the two. She held the soggy fabric out at arm's length to study it. It appeared to be part of a patchwork square, one that looked vaguely familiar. As soon as she spread it out to get a better look at it, she knew why. The dark blue plaid had been part of a dress she'd worn when she was ten, one of several she and Aunt Sybil had cut up to make the quilt she'd been hunting for.

Her pulse kicked it up a notch. "Tripp, I think this might be from one of Aunt Sybil's quilts. I've been looking all over the house for it, and I can't imagine why she would've left it out here."

"Only one way to find out." He gently shoved a couple of goats out of his way. "It's under a bunch of junk. Give me a minute to unbury it."

A couple of pieces of rusted pipe went flying over the fence, followed by some broken flower pots and a length of garden hose. She carefully laid the quilt square on the back of the chair she'd been sitting in and then started stacking the trash Tripp was clearing out into a neat pile along the edge of the yard. When he finally unburied the piece of plywood, she asked, "Do you need me to come in and help lift that?"

"No, I've got it."

The board bowed almost to the breaking point when he tried to lift it, but she could see more of the familiar pattern underneath the straining wood.

"That's my quilt, all right." Then she gagged as the breeze shifted in her direction. "Good grief, what's that awful smell?"

The words were no sooner out of her mouth than Tripp dropped the board and jumped back, looking a little green himself. She started forward, but he waved her back. "Abby, don't come any nearer. In fact, take Zeke and go wait in the house. I need to call Gage."

It took her a second to recognize the name. "Gage Logan, as in the chief of police? Why do you need him?"

Unfortunately, her mind had already connected the dots to come up with the obvious answer. She froze, unable to advance or retreat. "Tripp? Is that what I think it is under there?"

His dark eyes stared into hers as he gave her a grim nod. All business now, he pulled out his cell phone and punched in a three-number sequence. "Yes, ma'am, I need to report a dead body. Please tell Gage Logan and whoever else you think should be notified. Yes, it's in the farthest corner in the backyard. I'll wait for him there."

Abby held strong while Tripp verified the address and agreed not to touch anything else until the police arrived. Sirens began wailing in the distance, or maybe that was just the roaring in her ears. She was pretty sure Tripp was yelling something, but his voice sounded as if it came from a long distance away from where she stood.

The next thing she knew, the ground came rushing up at her as the world around her swirled and then briefly went dark. A pair of strong arms swooped in at the last second to prevent her from hitting the ground. Her thoughts cleared a little as Tripp stomped across the yard, carrying her over to the back porch. Instead of dumping her on the steps, he sat down and settled her in his lap before shoving her head down between her knees.

"Breathe. Take it slow and easy."

He sounded so mad, but she couldn't figure out what she'd done to anger him. After she'd sucked in several deep breaths, he released his hold on her and helped her sit back up. She blinked several times, trying to clear her head and make sense of a world that had gone all topsy-turvy on her, even if she didn't immediately remember how or why.

Tripp glared down at her, looking as if the last thing he wanted was to be helping her, even though he made no effort to shove her off his lap. "Darn it, Abby, I told you not to faint."

She might have mumbled "Sorry," although she couldn't be sure. The squeal of tires and tense voices told her the two of them wouldn't be alone for much longer. But for the moment, she wasn't too proud to lean into Tripp's strength for a few more seconds.

"Tell me that was a dead animal buried under that board back there."

His grim expression softened just a little. "I really wish I could, Abby, but I try not to lie to my friends."

She didn't know what shocked her more: that there really was a dead body in her backyard or that Tripp Blackston might actually consider her a friend.

Chapter Three

Abby pulled the collar of her sweater higher up around her neck. "I suppose it would be in poor taste to find it entertaining watching the police trying to corral goats to keep them from eating a crime scene."

It wasn't actually a question, but Tripp answered her anyway. "Yes, it would, but you're not wrong. By my count, that's the third time they've had to wrangle that same brown one out of the blackberries."

She could only imagine Joe's shock when he'd returned to find out that his flock had discovered a corpse. The goats might not have been traumatized by the experience, but their owner sure was. Right now two of the deputies were busy helping him load the goats back into his truck. Somehow she doubted he'd be coming back to finish the job anytime soon.

Abby shivered and turned away from the window when a pair of men in disposable coveralls wheeled a stretcher across her lawn. Maybe it was cowardly of her, but she had no interest in seeing what came next. "Was Chief Logan able to tell you anything about the . . . about who was out there?"

"No, but I didn't really expect him to, at least not until

he has a chance to get a handle on things. I'm sure there are procedures he has to follow in cases like this. I know Gage well enough to know he'll do the job right. Snowberry Creek isn't a very big town, but I'm guessing the county or even the state will have resources he can draw on if he needs to."

Tripp poured himself another cup of coffee and topped hers off at the same time. She really didn't need any more caffeine, but the warmth of the cup felt good to her hands. Although it was a nice day outside, she had been chilled to the bone ever since Tripp had left her sitting on the porch steps while he went to meet the police.

She should've been the one to handle the situation from the beginning, but she was grateful that Tripp had been willing to step up to bat until she'd gotten better control of her emotions. By the time Gage Logan had arrived on the scene, she was back up on her feet and reasonably sure her legs wouldn't collapse again.

Tripp stepped away from the window. "Looks like he's headed this way."

For reasons that weren't clear even to her, that announcement spurred her into piling a plate high with cookies. After all, when guests came to visit, one offered baked goods and beverages, no matter the occasion. By the time Gage knocked on the door, refreshments were served. A bit of hysterical laughter threatened to burble to the surface. Aunt Sybil would be so happy to know that all the old-fashioned rules of etiquette she'd taught Abby had finally paid off.

Tripp gave her a wary look, no doubt worried she was about to go into another meltdown. Straightening her shoulders, she stepped forward to invite the police chief into her kitchen. "Please come in and have a seat."

She gestured toward a chair at the kitchen table. "I thought you might like a cup of coffee about now."

Without waiting for a response, she pulled out the opposite chair for herself. Tripp hesitated for a few seconds and then took the seat on her right.

Gage removed his hat and tossed it on the counter before sitting down. "Coffee does sound good, Miss McCree."

"Please call me Abby."

He pulled out a small notebook and a pen. "I've already heard Tripp's version of things, but I need to take a statement from you as well if you're feeling up to it. Otherwise, you can come down to the station later."

She didn't want to talk about the situation at all, but putting it off wouldn't make it any easier. As if sensing her distress, Zeke appeared in the doorway of the kitchen. He ignored the two men as he crossed the room to lay his head in Abby's lap. Gage's eyebrows shot up, and his mouth quirked up in a big grin.

"That's some dog you've got there. What kind is he?"

Abby gave her furry friend a quick hug. "Aunt Sybil adopted Zeke through the animal shelter in town. She said he was a mixed breed, but the vet's best guess is that he's mostly mastiff. He has the right build and coloring."

She covered Zeke's ears. "I don't want to hurt his feelings, but it seems he's a bit on the small side."

The two men exchanged quick looks, clearly questioning anything about Zeke's size could be called small. "It's true. He only weighs ninety pounds. Male, purebred mastiffs can easily top out at sixty pounds more than that."

Tripp shifted in his chair, drawing Gage's attention in his direction. He patted Zeke on the head before speaking. "So what can you tell us?"

All vestiges of good humor disappeared from Gage's expression as he instantly switched gears back to a lawman with a case to solve. "Not much other than the victim was female. There was a purse wrapped inside the plastic tarp with the body. We did find a wallet and a driver's license. However, final identification will have to wait until the coroner completes his examination. All we know at this point is that the body appears to have been there for some time."

"You said 'victim.' I'm guessing you suspect a crime has been committed, that it wasn't an accident." All right, that wasn't the smartest thing she could've said. There was no way that body had accidentally ended up wrapped in plastic and a quilt under that sheet of plywood. "Forgive me. I wasn't thinking straight. Of course something bad went down back there."

"There's nothing to forgive." Gage looked sympathetic. "Most people never encounter a murder victim in their entire life, much less stumble across one in their backyard. All things considered, you're handling things pretty well."

Another wave of chills washed over her. Tripp looked as if he wanted to ask Gage more questions, but she really hoped he wouldn't. He might be curious, but she had no desire to learn any of the gruesome details. Still, it was her yard, which gave her some sense of responsibility.

"Is there anything I can do to help, Chief Logan?"

"Like I said, I need to take a statement from you. Other than that, we'll be cordoning off that part of your yard as a crime scene until we've had time to collect any possible evidence. We may also ask the state crime investigators to take a look around, too. I should also warn you that as soon as news of this gets out, people are bound to be curious. If it turns out to be a problem, give my department a call, and I'll post an officer here until we clear the area."

She'd already noticed several of the neighbors lurking

out front. So far, none of them had ventured any closer than that. "Thank you."

Gage took another sip of his coffee and then set it aside. "Are you ready to get started?"

No, what she really wanted to do was crawl back into bed and pull the covers up over her head. "Sure, where do you want me to begin?"

"Tripp has already told me about Joe putting up the fence yesterday afternoon, so why don't you start when he arrived this morning with the goats, and go from there."

"He arrived right at eight o'clock just as he promised he would. I kept Zeke in the house until the goats were unloaded and in the pen."

She closed her eyes and let her memories of the morning play out in her head like a movie. Gage probably didn't need to know how many cups of coffee she'd had to drink or that she'd ignored a call from her ex-husband. He didn't complain, though. Maybe he didn't mind the worthless information if it meant that by going into such detail, she wouldn't miss telling him something important.

Half an hour had passed by the time she'd finished telling her version of the events and then answered the few questions he had for her. Most had to do with the quilt she thought she'd recognized from the scrap the goat had been chewing on.

"I could be wrong about that, though. At first glance, it certainly looked like one of the squares the two of us had made that summer. On the other hand, it has been nearly twenty years since I last saw that particular quilt. Even then, we'd only finished the quilt top itself. We hadn't sewn on the backing or done the actual quilting. We'd planned to finish it the next time I came for an extended visit."

She stared into her coffee cup, lost in the past. "However, because of my parents' divorce, I never had a chance to spend another summer vacation with her. Any visits after that were only a day or two long. When it became obvious that I would never have enough time to help her with the quilt, Aunt Sybil finished it on her own." Tears burned her eyes as she added, "She promised I could have it someday. She knew how much it meant to me."

Abby drew in a slow, calming breath. "Having said that, I know we didn't completely use up all of the fabrics I picked out of her stash, so it's possible she used some of the same ones in another quilt. In fact, the members of the quilting guild often trade fabrics, so it might not be one of hers at all."

And here she sat rambling on and on. "I'm sorry, Chief Logan. I'm guessing you're not interested in the ins and outs of quilting."

"Not a problem. You never know which details will make or break a case." He stood up and retrieved his hat from the counter. "I'd better check on how things are going outside. Once an identification has been made, and we have some idea of the time frame involved, I'll get back in touch."

Tripp went outside with him, the two of them stopping to talk for a minute or two before the chief continued on back to where his team was still hard at work. Tripp glanced back in her direction before disappearing around the corner, most likely heading for his own place. It was only midafternoon, but it had been a long day for both of them already.

"Zeke, why don't you and I go upstairs and work on those boxes?"

The dog didn't often follow her all the way up to the third floor, preferring to sleep in his favorite sunbeam in the living room downstairs, but she was glad he made the effort this time. He gave the room a good sniff and then settled in for a snooze on the twin bed in the corner next to the open window. Meanwhile, Abby picked a box at random and got to work. It didn't take long to sort through the old paperback books and add them to the donate pile. She opened the next box, but she ran out of steam before she'd delved very far into its contents.

The murmur of voices from the backyard drifted up through the open window, making it hard for her to concentrate on the job at hand. What were they doing out there that took so long? Only one way to find out. She sat down on the far edge of the bed and gave Zeke a good scratch while she watched the technicians and a few cops still hard at work. She didn't envy them having to search for clues in that overgrown mess.

A movement on the other side of the yard caught her eye. Tripp had gone back to pruning the rhododendrons. She had to give the man credit for being diligent. On the other hand, maybe the morning's events had left him feeling restless and in need of something to take his mind off whatever horrors he'd seen underneath that sheet of plywood. He suddenly straightened up and glanced around as if sensing her scrutiny. She ducked back out of sight and turned her attention to her furry companion. "Zeke, tell me I should finish at least three more boxes before giving up for the day."

The dog snorted, making his opinion on working that hard all too clear.

"Easy for you to say, big fella, but these boxes won't empty themselves."

Zeke was back to snoring contentedly before she emptied the box she'd already started. When she'd gone through two more, she decided she'd earned the right to quit for the day. Granted, they were two of the smallest cartons, but they still counted. When she closed the window, several of the people working down below looked up at the sound. What were they thinking? Had they found anything that would point a finger at the person or persons responsible for the woman's death? Abby hoped so. Like anyone who had lived in a major metropolitan area, she was no stranger to the existence of violent crime.

That didn't mean she'd ever brushed up against it personally, and the realization that she'd been living so close to a dead body was creeping her out big time. Time to switch gears and do something else to keep her mind occupied.

"Hey, Zeke, what do you say we bake some bread to go with the soup I put in the slow cooker this morning? I'm also getting low on cookies in the freezer."

When he didn't immediately abandon his comfortable position on the bed, she went for the big guns, calling back over her shoulder as she headed downstairs. "And I thought I'd make another batch of those Zeke's Treats that you like so much. But if you're too busy sleeping to keep me company while I work, well, maybe those treats can wait until another day."

The big dog could move fast when he was motivated. He rushed past her before she reached the first landing. He waited at the bottom of the steps, his tail wagging furiously. She patted him on the head when he fell into step beside her. Once in the kitchen, he stopped in front of the counter where his treat jar sat just out of his reach.

"All right, two treats and that's all. I don't want to spoil your dinner."

He accepted them with great dignity and carried them over to his bed in the corner. It felt good to lose herself in the familiar routine of baking. Maybe if she kept busy, she'd be tired enough to forget about the yellow crime scene tape festooning her backyard and be able to sleep. One could only hope.

It was three batches of doggy treats, a double batch of peanut butter cookies, and two loaves of bread later before she finally crawled into bed. Even then, sleep hadn't come easily. Most of the time she found the sound of Zeke's snoring soothing, but not this time. It was hard not to resent the rumbling reminder that only one of them was asleep. She'd quit looking at the clock after midnight when exhaustion had eventually won out over worry, and she'd finally drifted off.

One good thing about being unemployed was that she could sleep in until noon, and no one would ever know or care. She didn't have to live by anyone's schedule but her own. Well, except for Zeke's. After venturing out of her room long enough to let him outside, she filled his water bowl and served up his morning ration of kibble.

As soon as he completed his rounds, she locked the back door and prepared to dive right back into bed, even though it was already after nine o'clock. She'd barely made it to her bedroom when someone rang the doorbell three times in rapid succession. A few seconds later, a heavy fist started pounding on her front door. It was so, so tempting to ignore the determined summons. Despite her current state of exhaustion, her conscience was still working well enough to point out that it could be Gage Logan needing to talk to her. Or maybe it was Tripp. He never bothered her without good reason.

Deciding sleep could wait a few minutes longer, she trudged back down the steps. At least she was decently covered in her oversized T-shirt and flannel pajama bottoms. Her hair was probably a mess, but if her uninvited guest wanted fancy, he or she should've called first. She peeked through the narrow window to the right of the door to see who it was.

A man she'd never seen before immediately spotted her and held up an ID badge to the glass. "Miss McCree, I'm sorry to bother you so early, but I'd really like to talk to you about what happened here yesterday."

She squinted at the writing, her mind slowly making sense of the words, which read, REILLY MOLITOR, *SNOWBERRY CREEK CLARION*.

Good grief, he was a reporter. That was the last thing she needed. She ducked back out of sight, wishing like crazy she'd ignored her conscience like any intelligent person would have and gone back to bed. Before she could decide what to do next, the knocking started again. The man obviously wasn't going to leave anytime soon. Well, she'd open the door just far enough to say she had no desire to talk to him.

But not before she called Zeke to her side, knowing he'd give even the most stubborn of people second thoughts about sticking around where they weren't wanted. With the dog's reassuring presence right next to her, she cracked the door open.

"I'm sorry, Mr. Molitor, but you'll need to talk to Chief Logan if you have questions."

The reporter started to crowd closer to the door but backed up just as quickly when Abby opened the door far enough for Zeke to stick his head out.

Molitor immediately gave the dog a wary look. "Boy, I'm not sure if that's a pony or a dog. More importantly, is he friendly?"

"Not always," Abby lied. "Now, as I said, take your questions to the police chief. He's better qualified to answer them."

"Oh, I've already spoken to him, Miss McCree, but I have a couple of simple questions just for you."

The reporter offered her what he obviously thought was a charming smile, but she knew a shark when she saw one. She also knew she wasn't going to like the questions, not one bit. Before she could slam the door closed, he blocked it with the palm of his hand. The deep rumble in Zeke's chest would've made a lesser man retreat, but evidently Reilly Molitor was made of stronger stuff.

"Fine, ask your questions. I won't promise to answer them. Either way, you'll leave then, or I'll be calling the police myself."

He held up a small device and pushed a button, making it likely whatever she said next would be recorded for posterity. She stared at it with growing dread.

"Miss McCree, am I correct that you're the niece of the late Sybil Rollins?"

She nodded. When he held up the recorder, she gave in and answered, "Yes, I am."

"That's great." His eyes glittered with growing excitement. "So, tell me, Miss McCree, do you have any idea how your aunt's archrival, Dolly Cayhill, came to be buried in your backyard, wrapped in one of Sybil's quilts?"

Chapter Four

Abby blinked and shook her head. Had she heard him right? Had the murder victim really been Dolly Cayhill? If so, that would certainly explain why none of the woman's friends had heard from her for months. She shuddered at the thought. Glenda and the others would be distraught over the loss of their friend. And what did he mean about Dolly being Aunt Sybil's archrival? Did ladies in their eighties even have such a thing?

She suddenly realized the reporter was still waiting for her to answer, his stupid recorder still shoved in her face. What did he expect her to say? Especially considering she hadn't even heard who the victim was until he announced it, not to mention that she'd never met Dolly Cayhill and knew next to nothing about the woman.

Finally, she did the only thing she could think of—she stepped back and shoved the door shut in his face. He immediately started knocking again. It was hard to ignore him, but she wasn't ready to face a barrage of questions she couldn't answer. It was a relief when the pounding stopped. There was no use in trying to go back to sleep again. Maybe a jolt of strong coffee would clear her head and help her face what was bound to be another stressful day.

No sooner had she padded back toward the kitchen than the knocking started up again, this time at the back door. Great. Even if she ignored him, he would still be able to look through the window in the door to see her standing in the kitchen. She really wanted that coffee, but she didn't need an audience while she waited for it to brew.

She was about to give up and head upstairs to shower when her cell phone started vibrating on the counter where she'd left it to charge. Feeling ridiculous, she did a mad dash into the kitchen to grab the phone and immediately retreated back out of sight into the hallway. When she saw who was calling, she debated whether or not to answer. Finally, she gave up and swiped her finger across the screen.

"Hey, Tripp. What's up?"

His voice came across the airwaves all loud and grumpy. "You do know someone has been pounding on your door. In fact, he still is."

Well, yeah. She was just hoping the guy would simply disappear. "Yes, I do."

He sighed. "Any reason you're not opening the door? I've got a test tomorrow, and all that racket is making it hard to study."

"I did answer when he was around front. He's a reporter from the local newspaper and wants to ask me a bunch of questions I have no answers for."

"Like what?"

"Like how my aunt's 'archrival' ended up buried in my backyard. What am I supposed to say to that?"

The knocking stopped briefly, so she risked a quick peek into the kitchen. When she realized Reilly Molitor had pressed his nose up against the window to get a better look around her kitchen, she jumped back into the hall. Darn him, he was keeping her from reaching the coffeemaker, and she really, really needed caffeine.

Tripp was still talking. "I didn't know her all that well, but I've got to say that your aunt didn't seem the type to have an archrival."

She hated that hint of a chuckle in Tripp's deep voice, but she agreed with his opinion. "My aunt was a real sweetheart. Ask anybody who knew her. I can't imagine what he's talking about. Regardless, I'm not going to open the door again. I'm not even dressed."

There was a strange silence coming from the other end of the conversation.

"Tripp? Are you still there?"

"Yeah, I'm here, but let me get this straight. You answered the door without getting dressed? No wonder the guy wants to get in. You're lucky he isn't trying to crawl through an open window."

What was he talking about now? She replayed their conversation in her head and groaned. "I'm not naked, you big jerk. I'm wearing ratty pajamas. I also have a bad case of bed head and haven't brushed my teeth yet. What's more, I'd kill for a cup of coffee right now."

"If that's the case, the man must really be determined to get that interview." Tripp's laughter rang out bright and clear. "Tell you what. I'll see what I can do to run him off. I'll even bring over a thermos of coffee, provided you have some of those cinnamon-covered cookies to go with it."

"You really think you can make him leave?"

"He might be determined, but I'm a lot bigger. Believe it or not, I can be pretty darn intimidating when I want to be."

She believed it, but she didn't think the reporter would be easily deterred, even by Tripp in total badass mode. Crossing her fingers she was wrong, she said, "Give me fifteen minutes to make myself presentable, and you can have all the cookies you can eat."

"It's a deal."

It was closer to twenty minutes before she made it back downstairs, but at least the pounding had stopped. The smell of fresh coffee wafted through the air. Bless the man, Tripp had evidently made good on his promise. It didn't surprise her to find him sitting at her kitchen table. She'd given him his own key so he could let himself in whenever he had chores to do inside the house. Unfortunately, he wasn't alone. Chief Logan was standing at the kitchen window, once again staring out into the backyard.

Both men turned to face her as soon as she appeared in the doorway. At least Tripp looked apologetic. "Gage pulled in just about the time I was about to physically toss your reporter friend out in the street just to see how high he'd bounce. As it turns out, he's pretty gutsy for such a scrawny guy."

Gage couldn't quite hide his smile. "Yeah, Reilly can be a real pain at times. He likes to act like he works for one of the big city papers rather than a small town weekly. Big stories like the death of Dolly Cayhill don't come around very often, not that I'm complaining."

Abby put her shaky hands to work pouring herself a cup of coffee. After taking that heavenly first sip, she filled a plate with cookies and set it down in front of Tripp. "So Reilly was right about it being Mrs. Cayhill who was . . . back there."

Gage sat down at the table and reached for a cookie to go with his coffee. "Yeah, he was. We were pretty sure that was the case from the beginning. It was her purse that we found with the body, but we didn't want to say anything until the coroner verified her identity and the cause of death. That was blunt force trauma to the back of her head, by the way. Her next of kin was notified late last night, a niece who lives over in eastern Washington. They weren't particularly close, but Dolly named her as the executrix of her will."

Zeke strolled into the room, most likely in response to her opening the cookie jar. Since it was identical to the one that held his treats, he was probably hoping she'd share some of the doggy cookies she'd made in the dark hours of the night. She dug out a handful and carried them over to the table to dole them out to him one at a time.

"I don't know the etiquette of a situation like this. Should I send the niece flowers or a condolence card or something?"

Tripp only shrugged, but Gage looked grim as he shook his head. "Under the circumstances, I wouldn't."

The bite of cookie she'd just eaten stuck in her throat. She washed it down with a big gulp of coffee before asking, "Exactly what circumstances would those be?"

Not that she really wanted to know. Not with the reporter throwing around words like "archrival" and her aunt's name in the same sentence.

Gage leaned back in his chair. "Did your aunt ever talk about Mrs. Cayhill to you?"

"Not that I remember. I have heard her name before, most recently when Glenda Unger and two other ladies were here several days ago. We were working on plans for the quilting guild's garage sale, and I wasn't sure if I wanted to have it here. Jean Benson, or maybe it was Louise Allan, wondered if they couldn't hold it at Mrs. Cayhill's house. They both were surprised to realize that they hadn't heard from her recently. Evidently, she was a snowbird who normally came back to Snowberry Creek about this time every year."

He pulled out his notebook and made a few notes. "Did they say when they'd last talked to her?"

"Nothing specific."

"I'll have a talk with all three of them. I'm trying to narrow down the time frame when Dolly was last seen in town." He reached for another cookie. "You might as well hear the rest of what I've found out so far. With Reilly poking around, it's all bound to come out sooner rather than later."

Clearly the news wasn't going to be good. Tripp started to stand up. "Maybe I should get going since you two have important stuff to talk about."

She started to protest, wanting him there when Gage unloaded the rest of the bad news, but that wasn't fair to Tripp. It was bad enough that he'd been the one to find the body. He didn't need to hear all the sordid details or get even more tangled up in her problems. "If you want more cookies, grab the red container out of the freezer on your way out. Zeke and I stayed up baking last night, and I made way more than I can use."

Gage had a different opinion on the subject of Tripp leaving. "You should listen to this, too. The small town gossip hotline is probably already in full swing, and you're both sure to hear all kinds of crazy rumors floating around. I'd rather you hear the facts from me."

Tripp had already gotten his cookie supply out of the freezer. He sat back down clutching it in a tight grip as if he was afraid Gage was going to try to take it from him. "I'm listening."

"We've been talking to Dolly's closest friends. Ladies from her church and a few neighbors." He paused to give Abby a sympathetic look before continuing. "They all said pretty much the same thing you did. Dolly leaves town after Christmas and doesn't come back until spring. She never learned to use a computer or how to text, so she doesn't stay in touch like most folks would these days. They also said she was having trouble with arthritis in her hands, so she didn't write letters or even Christmas cards much anymore. When no one heard from her, they all figured that was why."

Then he flipped through a few pages in his notebook. Abby wondered where he was headed with all of this. Nothing he'd said so far would account for his grim demeanor or why he thought Tripp should stick around. Finally, he looked up again. "I knew your aunt slightly, mainly from some of the committees she served on, and I'd met Mrs. Cayhill a time or two along the way. I can't say that I really knew either of them very well. What I do know is that both of them were born and raised right here in Snowberry Creek. They went all the way through school together. Sometimes that kind of proximity ends up meaning people become lifelong friends."

He twirled his pen through his fingers like a baton, the only sign that he was finding this discussion difficult. "The other option is that they become rivals, which is evidently what happened in this case. The two of them competed in everything imaginable—academics, spelling bees, and even for things like Miss Snowberry Creek in the Fourth of July parade. A few people mentioned them vying for the same handsome beau."

His stern mouth softened just a bit when he added, "The ladies' description of the guy, by the way, not mine. Evidently Sybil won that particular contest, because she ended up married to him."

Abby smiled for the first time all day. "My aunt always

talked about Uncle Isaac as if he were Paul Newman and Cary Grant all rolled into one."

Not that Gage probably cared about any of that. He started tapping his pen on the table. "Then I spoke to a couple of women from the quilting guild, and that's when things got interesting."

One look at the renewed grim expression Gage was now sporting made it clear that something being "interesting" was a bad, bad thing in his world. "Several of the ladies said that late last year both Sybil and Dolly were lobbying to head up the guild for this year. They'd each been president the same number of times in the past, and this would've put one of them ahead again."

He shook his head. "Hard to believe the politics involved in a group like a quilting guild, but evidently that's the way it was between them. Your aunt hosted something called a high tea at her house, hoping to garner votes. In turn, Dolly had everyone in the group over to her house for a buffet luncheon."

When he paused to sip his coffee, she asked, "Is there a problem with that?"

"Yeah, everyone had a wonderful time at your aunt's tea, but the ladies who ate Dolly's famous crab dip at her luncheon got food poisoning. Your aunt was one of the few who didn't eat any and so didn't get sick. When Dolly recovered, she accused your aunt of sabotaging the dip in order to get elected. She even stated full out that Sybil had been trying to kill her and her supporters because she was afraid of what losing the election would do to her status here in town. Their argument, which took place on December twenty-third, was very loud and very public in the narthex of their church. One of my deputies attended the same service and thought he might have to intervene. Eventually, the two of them finally separated and walked off in a huff."

The image of her aunt screaming in church wouldn't quite come into focus. "You're kidding, right?"

Evidently, Abby wasn't the only one struggling to take what Gage was telling them as seriously as he was. Tripp leaned forward, elbows on the table and his lips twitching as if he was trying hard not to laugh. "Seriously, Gage, are you actually saying that Abby's aunt is your prime suspect because of some bad crab dip?"

"No, that's not what I'm saying. Not exactly, anyway. What I am saying is that Mrs. Cayhill accused your aunt of some pretty terrible things in front of all their friends. Normally, I wouldn't give a care about an argument between two old ladies, but I can't ignore this one."

His ice-blue gaze met Abby's head on, sending a chill straight through her. "The problem is, that argument with your aunt is the last time anyone can remember seeing Dolly, alive or dead, until you two found her buried here in Sybil's backyard."

Abby leapt to her feet, determined to defend her aunt's honor, although she had no idea how to do that. "I'm sorry, Chief Logan, but I want you to leave. I won't let you sit there and insult my aunt's memory by hinting she might have committed murder."

Tripp rose to his feet beside her and put his hand on her shoulder. "Abby, this isn't Gage's fault. He's doing his job, and all he can do is play the fact cards that he's been dealt."

Then he pegged his friend with a hard look. "It's still early in your investigation, right?"

When Gage nodded, Tripp let his hand drop away from her shoulder but made no move to step away from her side. "Let the man do his job. I know those things were tough to hear, but at least you're forewarned what people might be saying."

She swallowed hard, trying to get a few words past the

huge lump of worry and anger that threatened to choke her. "I'm sorry, Gage. Tripp's right, and I do appreciate your letting me know what's being said. I understand that you didn't know my aunt very well, but she simply wasn't capable of anything like this. Ask anyone. Heck, the mayor just gave me a plaque last week honoring all the work Aunt Sybil did for this town."

Tripp gave her a sympathetic look. "Not to mention the fact that the woman didn't weigh more than a hundred and ten pounds. She wasn't strong enough to haul dead bodies around."

Gage grimaced. "That's true enough, Tripp, but a couple of people have gone out of their way to point out that you live right next to where the body was buried. Since you don't fit the usual profile of the students Sybil typically rented the place to, they wondered if you might have had something to do with Mrs. Cayhill's death, or at least the cover-up afterward."

Tripp took the news far better than Abby, who found herself sputtering, "What? Are they crazy? He wouldn't—"

Gage cut off her protest. "I agree. He wouldn't, and I set them straight on that score. I pointed out that I'd served with Tripp and made it extremely clear that I had personally vouched for him when he moved to town." He glanced at his friend. "I stand by that recommendation. If anyone has questions, tell them to come find me."

By that point, Gage's hands were curled in tight fists. Clearly he hadn't appreciated anyone questioning his friend's honor. He finally took a deep breath as if trying to control his temper before speaking again. "Listen, it's very likely that you weren't even living here when the woman was killed, but we won't know that for sure until we can narrow down the time frame involved."

"Thanks for the vote of confidence." Tripp picked up his

cookie container. "Now, if you two don't need me anymore, I have a test to study for. Thanks for the cookies, Abby."

On the way out, he stopped to pat Zeke on the head. "And if that reporter comes back, let me know. I might have a hand grenade or two tucked away that I could lob in his direction."

He was gone before Abby could decide whether or not he was serious. Probably not, considering Gage didn't seem all that worried.

"I know your investigation is complicated by the fact that my aunt isn't here for you to interview." She drew herself up to her full height, which meant she was still more than half a foot shorter than the police chief. "But just be aware, I will do everything I can to clear her name, no matter what it takes."

Gage stuck his notebook back in his uniform pocket and picked up his hat. She followed him out onto the back porch, where he stopped to say, "Abby, I know you're upset and have every right to be. But remember this— investigating this murder is my job, not yours. Like Tripp said, I'm just getting started. We're waiting for the autopsy report and results from forensics. There are a lot of people I still need to interview. If I have questions for you, I'll get in touch."

She bit back the urge to argue. Just because he liked issuing orders didn't mean she had to follow them. "Fine, but I'll say this one more time. My aunt wouldn't have murdered anyone, not even her archrival. It wasn't in her to do such a thing."

She didn't know where Gage's thoughts took him at that moment, but it clearly wasn't a happy place. "You'd be surprised what people are capable of when they're feeling cornered. I would also point out that by your own admission, except for that one time twenty years ago, your visits with your aunt have been few and far between. Think about how well you really knew her."

Then he walked away, leaving her staring at his back and hating the little bit of doubt about her aunt's innocence that had suddenly stirred to life.

Chapter Five

Abby's day had started off bad and hadn't gotten any better as the hours passed by. The freezer was already overflowing with the cookies and treats that she'd baked during the night. The laundry was done, and she'd already vacuumed the entire house, top to bottom. She supposed she could dust or wash windows, but why punish herself anymore for that one little moment of doubt? Besides, she was pretty sure Aunt Sybil would've forgiven her even if Abby couldn't quite forgive herself.

After pouring a tall glass of iced tea, she grabbed a handful of oatmeal cookies and wandered out to sit on the back porch. She angled herself so that she was facing away from the blackberry patch, which still had yards and yards of crime scene tape looped around its perimeter. Even if she'd been able to forget the events of the past two days, the garish yellow streamers were there to remind her.

The sound of a car door closing drew her attention to the front of the house. Who could that be? As tired as she was, it was tempting to stay sitting right where she was and leave it up to the unexpected visitor to find her, or, better yet, not. But what if it was that awful reporter again? Tripp wasn't home to lob those promised hand grenades in her defense. Not that she thought he really had any. Probably not, anyway.

It was time to see who it was, just in case she needed to hightail it inside and barricade herself behind locked doors. She set her cookies up on the railing in the futile hope that Zeke would leave them alone and crept around to the front yard while huddling close to the overgrown rhododendrons along the side of the house. When she spotted a head of brassy red hair, she breathed a sigh of relief. It had to be Glenda. Hopefully she was alone.

She stepped around the corner just as the older woman knocked on the front door. Abby hurried around to the steps to catch her friend's attention. "Hey, Glenda, I'm down here."

The woman jumped as if Abby had hit her with a Taser. "Abby! Don't sneak up on an old woman like that."

"Sorry, I guess I was sneaking, but I really didn't mean to startle you. I was sitting on the back porch when I heard someone pull up out front. A local reporter came banging on my door earlier today, and it took both Tripp and Gage Logan to run him off. I was afraid he'd come slithering back."

Glenda slowly made her way back down the steps. "I heard the awful news about Dolly and wanted to see if you were all right. I tried twice to stop by yesterday, but with so many policemen wandering all over the place, I couldn't even park."

The two of them made their way around to the back of the house. Abby kept to a slow pace, knowing that Glenda wasn't always steady on her feet, especially on rough ground. When they rounded the last corner, her friend gasped and froze midstep. She stared at the tangled web of crime scene tape, a look of horror on her face. "Is that where they found Dolly? Back there in that tangle of blackberries?"

What had she been thinking bringing Glenda back

there? Aunt Sybil and Dolly Cayhill had had issues with
each other over the years, but it didn't follow that Glenda
had felt the same way about the woman. After all, she'd also
grown up in Snowberry Creek. She undoubtedly had known
Dolly for decades. Although Abby had been feeling a bit
claustrophobic in the house, it wasn't good manners to
force a guest to stare at the scene of a crime.

"Why don't we go inside so I can fix us a cup of tea?"

Glenda immediately turned her back on the stark reminder of what had happened in the yard and started up the
steps. "Actually, something cold sounds better if it's not too
much trouble."

"I've got iced tea, ice water, and a couple of kinds of
pop. We can sit in the living room where it's more comfortable and relax for a while."

There was also the added benefit that they couldn't
see the backyard from there. Out of sight, out of mind, at
least for a few minutes. Still, she needed to ask someone
about what had happened between Sybil and Dolly. If
Glenda didn't know the answers, she might know someone
who did.

When they were comfortably ensconced in the matching
easy chairs that flanked the bay window in the living room,
Abby struggled to frame the questions she'd been pondering since her earlier conversation with Gage. Meanwhile,
the warm sunlight streaming in felt good against her skin.
It was probably her imagination, but Abby had felt cold
ever since she'd first realized what had been lurking under
that half-rotted piece of plywood in the back corner of the
yard. And if she was horrified by the discovery, how much
worse was it for Tripp when he'd actually seen the body?

"Are you all right, Abby?"

She hadn't realized she was crying until she saw the

tissue that Glenda was holding out to her. A couple of quick dabs took care of the problem. "Sorry about that. It's been a tough twenty-four hours."

"Well, I'd say that's an understatement. I'm so sorry you got caught up in this mess."

The sympathy in her elderly friend's voice proved to be Abby's undoing, and the tears began to fall in earnest. "I'm sorry. I don't even know why I'm crying. It's not like I even knew the woman, and it was poor Tripp who actually uncovered the body. All I really saw was my aunt's quilt."

Glenda settled back into the chair. "I'm sure it was terrible for Tripp, but that doesn't mean it wasn't traumatic for you as well. Anyone would be upset to learn that the perpetrator in a homicide case had used her backyard as a dumping ground."

Perpetrator? Dumping ground? Where had she picked up those terms? Probably from watching television.

As if guessing the direction Abby's thoughts had gone, Glenda smiled just a little. "My late husband loved reading those true crime books. I never understood his fascination with such things. We'd be lying there in bed, and he'd share some gruesome detail with me just when I was ready to turn out the lights and go to sleep. I can't tell you how many times I asked him not to do that because it gave me nightmares."

Now her eyes looked a bit misty, too. "I never thought I'd miss that, but I do. Howard has been gone for nearly five years now, and I still keep the last book he was reading on the bedside table. It might be silly, but somehow it makes me feel closer to him."

"I think it's sweet, Glenda. It's nice to hear about two people staying happily married for so long."

She'd hoped to grow old with Chad. Now Abby couldn't

look at him without wondering what she'd ever seen in the man. Maybe that was her anger over his betrayal talking, but on the few occasions their paths had crossed since the divorce, he'd seemed like a stranger to her. No, that wasn't right. It was more like talking to someone she'd gone to high school with. They shared a few common memories, but they no longer had an important role to play in each other's lives. Sometimes she was almost as disappointed in herself as she was in him. They'd been so focused on creating a successful business that they'd lost sight of what was really important. They were supposed to build a life together, not just a healthy bank account.

Too late now.

She and Glenda sat in peaceful silence for a few minutes. Finally, the other woman sighed heavily and set her empty glass aside. "While I did come by to make sure you were okay, I also needed to warn you that you may hear some things about your aunt and Dolly." She turned to stare out at the front yard. "Unpleasant things."

It was obvious Glenda was uncomfortable broaching the subject. To ease the way, Abby said, "You mean about the crab dip and the fight the two of them had in the narthex at church?"

Glenda jerked her head back around to look directly at Abby, her knobby hands clenched in fists. "Who had the gall to come gossiping to you about that? I want to give them a piece of my mind."

"I appreciate the offer, but there's no need." Abby reached over to pat her friend on the arm. "It was Gage Logan. He stopped by this morning to let me know how the investigation is progressing. Seems he's been getting an earful from some folks, but he didn't mention any specific names. He figured I should be warned about what was being said."

Glenda's flash of temper faded a bit. "That was nice of him. I'm glad you heard about it from someone who would give you the straight story without taking sides. Unfortunately, that isn't true of some other people I could name, especially with emotions running a bit hot right now. A lot of us took it hard when we lost your aunt. And then to find out about what happened to poor Dolly . . . well, it's a lot to take in."

"I can imagine."

Which was only the simple truth. Her own divorce, followed so closely by Sybil's death, had left Abby reeling. Losing two friends so close together had to be just as hard for Glenda and the other ladies in their tightly knit group.

"Gage said he didn't actually know either of them very well. I know he's trying to be fair, but all he could tell me was what he'd heard from other people."

"I can only imagine what all he heard. People do love a good scandal." Glenda sighed and paused. "You see, both Sybil and Dolly have . . . *had* . . . their supporters here in town. I'm not saying they couldn't work together if the occasion called for it, but usually they did better if someone else was actually in charge. Even though Snowberry Creek isn't all that big of a town, there are enough organizations and committees around to keep all of us busy and involved. It was only when Sybil and Dolly were thrown into direct competition that sometimes there were problems. I guess you could say that it was like having two queen bees trying to rule one hive."

Now that was one heck of an image, but it painted a clear picture of what Glenda was trying to tell her. Obviously Sybil and Dolly both had strong personalities and leadership qualities. The problem was that Snowberry Creek was a small town. With a population of fewer than two thousand people, it was probably difficult for the two women to avoid each other. Having said that, they had clearly managed to coexist for over eighty years. It was hard to imagine that some bad crab dip would've resulted in murder.

No, that's not what happened. She was convinced of it. "I have to say that Aunt Sybil taught me everything I ever knew about good old-fashioned etiquette. I can't picture her getting into a screaming match in public, much less at church."

Glenda actually laughed a little. "Sybil got along with almost everyone she ever met, Dolly being the main exception to that. It took a lot to get your aunt all riled up, but you could only push her so far before she'd dig in her heels. Before that incident at the church, I would never have expected her to make such a spectacle of herself. Dolly either, for that matter. She was always about keeping up appearances."

"If we assume that Aunt Sybil wasn't the culprit, did they ever figure out what really went wrong with the crab dip?"

"Not that I know of. It's not like the police were called or any kind of investigation done. Everyone felt fine at the actual luncheon. It wasn't until hours later that people started getting sick. From what I heard, the dip was such a hit that there wasn't any left over."

Interesting. "So what made Dolly think it was the crab dip that made everyone sick?"

"Since not everyone got sick, there was a lot of discussion about who had eaten what. The ladies who hadn't eaten the crab dip were the only ones who didn't get deathly ill at the end of the day."

"So my aunt wasn't the only one who didn't eat the dip?"

Glenda murmured a series of names under her breath, counting them off on her fingers. When she ran out of names, she said, "No, there were at least six women at the luncheon who didn't get sick."

"So why assume that it was Sybil who was at fault?"

"I'm not actually sure who put that bug in Dolly's ear. Maybe she thought of it all on her own, but I've always had the impression that it was someone else's idea. I can ask around if you think I should."

Abby suspected that Gage wouldn't appreciate her encouraging Glenda to get involved in the investigation. Besides, since someone had already told him about the incident, he was probably already asking these same questions. The only problem was that he would be unlikely to share his findings with her.

"No, you don't need to do that. It would only upset Dolly's friends and bring back bad memories for some others."

"I'm sorry I couldn't be more help, Abby. I know you're anxious to clear Sybil's name, not that she's officially been accused of anything."

For the second time, Abby's eyes burned, but she wasn't going to give in to tears again. She'd learned the hard way that they wouldn't fix a darn thing—not a broken heart or a wreck of a marriage, not to mention the reputation of a woman who wasn't there to defend herself.

Only a determined effort to get at the truth would do that. Gage had promised to find out what really happened, but Abby wasn't going to trust her aunt's beloved memory to a man she barely knew. She'd wallowed long enough in her own grief and sense of loss. It was time to throw her shoulders back and take charge of the situation.

"You've been plenty of help, Glenda. Not just now, but in helping me to get my bearings here in Snowberry Creek. I couldn't have done it without you smoothing the way."

"It's little enough to have done, my dear. We've all been

through a lot lately. If I haven't said so before, it has been gratifying to all of us who were friends of Sybil's to see the work you and your young man have been doing to restore your aunt's landscaping. She would love knowing the care you're taking with her gardens."

Abby was pretty sure Tripp wouldn't appreciate being referred to as her young man. "Tripp has definitely done the brunt of the work on the yard, but that's part of the rental agreement he had with Aunt Sybil. I will say he's been a great tenant."

That wicked twinkle that showed up in Glenda's eyes every time she caught sight of Tripp was back. Abby didn't have to look to know that the man in question was hard at work in the front yard. She took a peek anyway. What was it about that man and going shirtless, anyway? Didn't he know that some old ladies had heart trouble? A few younger ones were evidently prone to having a few flutters, too, although that had more to do with hormones than age.

Time for a distraction.

"I don't mean to put you on the spot, but I don't know who else I can ask this. First, I'm not questioning the fact that my aunt and Dolly had their issues over the years. I also don't mean to speak ill of the dead, but I have to wonder if there was anyone else that Dolly had problems with that I should know about. If you'd rather not say, that's fine. I don't want to put you in an uncomfortable position."

Glenda slowly dragged her gaze away from the front window. If she'd seemed at all reluctant to speak, Abby would have to let her off the hook. She was about to do that when the other woman drew a long, slow breath.

"Dolly did a lot of good things for this community over the years, but she wasn't always an easy person to please. She set high standards for her own behavior and expected everyone else to live up to them as well. When they failed, which most people do on occasion, she could be difficult to deal with and rather unforgiving. She also wasn't above using her money and her clout to get her way."

Abby had had her own experiences with the so-called movers and shakers using their money and influence in various ways. To give the people credit, most of them did a lot of good for their communities, supporting a wide variety of causes. The problem came when they used their money as an inducement to get their way, even if it wasn't exactly what other people wanted.

"Can you give me an example?"

Up until that point, Glenda had been looking straight at Abby, but now her gaze slid to the side, and not so she could sneak another peek at Tripp. "I'll have to think about it, Abby. If I come up with any names, I'll be sure to let you know."

Then she was up and heading for the door, purse in hand. Abby caught up with her within a few steps. "I'm sorry, Glenda. I shouldn't have put you on the spot like that. Please don't give the matter another thought."

Her friend looked so relieved that Abby felt even more terrible. "Do you, Jean, and Louise still plan to come over tomorrow to finalize the details for the garage sale? I'll understand if you want to meet somewhere else until the police take down that awful tape in the backyard."

"If you're sure you want us, we'll be here. I think we'll all feel better if things get back to normal."

Abby smiled even if it felt a little forced. "Of course I want you. The three of you always brighten my day."

Although maybe she should warn Tripp that his fan club would be coming, in case he wanted to make himself scarce. It would be interesting to see if one of them showed up with a dessert or even an entrée for him. It had happened before. The last time he'd glared at her for smirking when

Jean handed him a pan of tuna casserole. After the ladies had left, he'd offered to share it with her, but she'd given it a pass.

As she and Glenda walked outside, she thought of one more thing. "I meant to tell you that I got sidetracked on clearing out space in the garage. I can work on that today, so I should have it ready to start taking donations by the weekend."

"Are you sure you still want to host the garage sale? You know, with everything that's happened?"

"I'm sure."

Besides, the more people she had a chance to talk to, the more likely it was that she'd learn who in Snowberry Creek had failed to live up to Dolly Cayhill's exacting standards, and maybe who had wanted her dead.

Chapter Six

All right, encouraging people to drop off anything and everything they wanted to get rid of for the garage sale hadn't been Abby's brightest idea. Maybe she should've put together some guidelines or set some standards for everyone to follow. Right now, she felt like she was hip deep in junk, with remarkably few hidden gems buried in the pile. If she had to guess, less than half of the items scattered around the garage were likely to sell. But then, what did she know? She'd never been involved in a garage sale of any kind, so her opinion on what would or wouldn't sell was admittedly a bit suspect.

She sighed and went back to work, trying to bring some sense of order to the chaos. As she bent down to pull a handful of paperbacks out of a box of old magazines, a bottle of water appeared in front of her face.

Tripp waited until she took it out of his hand before stepping back out of her way. "You looked like you could use a cold one."

Bless the man. A beer might have been better, but she'd take what she could get. When she opened the bottle, she was tempted to pour it over her head, but that would be tacky. Instead, she took a long drink and then screwed the lid back on before setting it aside. "Thanks. That helped."

He looked around the garage and let out a low whistle. "I noticed a lot of people coming and going, but I had no idea you'd turned the garage into the new city dump."

His assessment wasn't far off the mark. "Glenda assures me that the garage sale earns quite a bit of money for the quilting guild every year. I don't see how, though, if this is the kind of stuff they sell. I wouldn't give you ten bucks for the whole mess."

Tripp picked up a chunk of metal and studied it for a few seconds before shaking his head and setting it back down. Her best guess was that it was some kind of car part. Judging by Tripp's expression, he wasn't sure what it was either. "Let me know if you need any heavy lifting done."

He started for the door and then stopped to root through a box of old action figures. A big grin spread over his face as he pulled out several and arranged them in a neat row. "I haven't seen these since I was a kid. I had a whole set."

She wound her way between the boxes to see what had him so excited. It was a bunch of plastic soldiers, all built along the same lines as Tripp himself with only minor differences in hair color and weaponry. "If you want those, I can set them aside until Glenda has a chance to price them."

His face flushed a little as he quickly shoved them back into the box. "No, I don't need a bunch of toys. Like I said, I just hadn't seen any since I was a kid."

"Okay, but let me know if you change your mind."

But even if he didn't, she might just buy them for him anyway. Time to change the subject. She pointed to a box that blocked half the doorway and then toward the make-shift table she'd made with two sawhorses and a sheet of plywood. "While you're here, would you mind lifting that up onto the table? It's too heavy for me."

"Sure thing."

Even Tripp strained a bit to pick it up, his impressive set of arm muscles flexing nicely underneath the soft cotton of his T-shirt. Not that she noticed or anything. Nope, not her. He set it down and backed away. "What the heck is in there? It feels like rocks."

"No idea."

She stripped off the packing tape and peeked inside. "It's a set of dishes. They look old, but they're in good shape. Maybe an antiques dealer will be interested in them."

Rather than unpack them now, she closed the box up again and wrote "dishes" on the top. Tripp moved it off the table and set it back down on the floor near several other cartons that held other dishes as well as pots and pans. Without waiting to be asked, he set two more unopened boxes up on the table for her. One held more books, but the other one was far more interesting. It was filled with quilt squares. The pattern was a pinwheel of vivid, jewel-toned colors.

She spread several out on the table, rearranging them until they looked right to her. Lovely. "Someone put a lot of work into this project. I wonder why they never stitched these all together. There's enough of them to make at least a nice afghan-sized quilt, and it wouldn't take much to finish it. Who knows, maybe Glenda or one of the others will even recognize the work."

Tripp picked up one of the squares and turned it over to study the stitches on the back. "They can do that?"

"Sometimes. Not everyone who quilts is part of the guild, but they all tend to frequent the same fabric stores and share pattern books."

That got her to thinking about another quilt, the one that

had been used as a shroud for Dolly Cayhill. She'd been trying to concentrate on other things the past few days, but the woman's death was never far from her mind.

Tripp tapped her on the shoulder, dragging her back to the matter at hand. "What are you thinking about so hard?"

Maybe it wouldn't hurt to bounce a few ideas off him. "I can't help but wonder how someone got their hands on one of Aunt Sybil's quilts. Not only that, why that specific one? She always had several scattered around the house and not just on the beds. It's expensive to heat a house that size, so she kept some handy to use as lap blankets if her visitors felt chilly. I used to love curling up under one in the bay window with a good book and a mug of hot chocolate."

Tripp turned his full attention to her. "You're thinking that if one of her quilts went missing, she would've noticed, especially one that was special to her. But since she'd already promised it to you, it seems unlikely she would have left it lying around for other people to use."

Was he saying what she thought he was? That Sybil was the only one who had easy access to the quilt? Well, she'd set him straight on that subject right now.

"My aunt loved being involved in all kinds of groups here in town. She had people in and out of the house all the time. Even if she did pack that quilt away for me, someone else could've found it. With all the boxes of stuff in the attic and the bedroom up on the third floor, it's possible she might not have even realized it was gone. She would have no reason to go looking for it unless I was due for a visit."

His answering grunt was noncommittal, which stirred her temper to life.

"My aunt was not a murderer, Tripp."

Another grunt, this one more like a sigh. "I never said she was, Abby."

She reached for her water, more for something to do

with her hands other than tear her hair out in frustration. "I'm sorry. I just can't seem to think about anything else. My mind keeps spinning in circles until I'm going crazy. I've got to figure out what happened."

Tripp was already shaking his head. "No, you don't. That's Gage's job, and you need to stay out of his way while he does it."

It was her turn to look disgusted. "The last time I talked to him, it sounded as if his entire investigation consisted of listening to a bunch of old gossip. How is that going to prove anything one way or another?"

"As I recall, he also told you that he was waiting for the autopsy report and to see what the forensics showed. Just because you haven't heard anything doesn't mean he isn't working the case."

Darn it, she knew that. "But what if he doesn't learn anything from those things? It would be easier for him to place the blame on Aunt Sybil and close the case. Her reputation would be ruined, and the real murderer will go free."

By this point, Tripp's voice had a lot of gravel in it. "Gage is not the kind of man who takes the easy way out. He won't stop searching for the truth until he finds it."

She wanted to believe that; she really did.

"I can tell you think a lot of Gage, but how well do you really know him?"

"We served together for a while." Tripp stared into the distance, his eyes looking a bit haunted, his mouth set in a harsh line. "The details about the circumstances don't matter now. Just know that it was the kind of situation that shows a man's real character. I trusted Gage Logan with my life then. I still do. Your aunt's reputation is in good hands."

Then he walked away, leaving her staring at his broad back and wishing she hadn't managed to stir up what had to be some pretty ugly memories for him. It was tempting to run after him . . . and do what? Somehow, she doubted he'd appreciate either her sympathy or a hug.

Feeling as if she were failing not only her aunt but her tenant, she went back to sorting junk. Come tomorrow, though, she'd check in with Gage. If he didn't have any answers for her, then she'd start hunting for them herself.

The birds were just starting to chirp outside Abby's bedroom window when she finally gave up on sleep and sat up on the side of her bed. Zeke briefly lifted his head and blinked at her in the dim morning light but made no effort to get up. Who could blame him? She'd crawl back under the blankets herself if she hadn't been tossing and turning for the past hour.

She ran a brush through her hair and put on some sweats before heading downstairs to the kitchen. The coffeemaker wasn't programed to turn on for another two hours, so she flipped the switch and watched as the ambrosia known as dark roast began dripping down into the carafe. She'd heard somewhere that the first cupful was several times stronger than the last one to trickle into the pot. Normally, she'd wait until it finished brewing before filling her mug, but not this morning.

She took the steaming cup of coffee, a blueberry muffin, and a notepad out onto the back porch, hoping to enjoy the peace and quiet of the early morning. It was chilly enough that she dashed back inside to grab one of the lap quilts she'd mentioned to Tripp just yesterday. Before she made it back outside, Zeke came stalking into the kitchen.

"Sorry I woke you up so early, boy."

To make it up to him, she quickly filled his bowl with kibble and gave him fresh water. She left the door propped open in case he decided to join her out on the porch instead of going back to bed. It wasn't long before he was stretched out beside her chair, the quiet rumble of his snores playing in counterpoint to the birds' early morning songs.

She'd just finished the last bite of her muffin when the sound of pounding feet coming her way drew her attention. Tripp rounded the corner on his way back to his place. He slowed at the bottom of the steps to jog in place.

He gave her a surprised look. "Wow, you're up early."

Well, duh. The sun was just beginning to light up the mountain ridge to the east.

She gave him a bleary-eyed glare. "Do you always run at this ungodly hour?"

He grinned. "Yep. Five miles every day. You should join me sometime."

She rolled her eyes. That was so not happening, especially since she hated spending a lot of time around morning people. They were too energetic, not to mention all smug and superior, like being able to smile before dawn somehow made them special. She waved her hand toward the door behind her. "There's fresh coffee and more muffins on the counter. I'm not up to playing hostess this early, but feel free to help yourself."

"Thanks, I think I'll take you up on that. Want a refill on your coffee?"

Nice of him to offer. She handed him her mug. "Sure."

As he passed by, she spotted a rolled-up newspaper in his other hand. "Hey, is that this week's edition?"

He glanced at the paper as if surprised he even had it. "I found it lying under a bush out by the sidewalk and figured it was last week's. I'll just recycle it."

Bless him. He was trying to protect her from what people were saying. She could only imagine what kind of lurid headlines Reilly Molitor had come up with to describe the events of the past week. When she held out her hand, Tripp reluctantly surrendered the paper.

Before letting go of it completely, though, he said, "Just so you know, the offer to find out how high that reporter would bounce off the pavement still stands."

"Good to know."

She waited until he disappeared inside the house before unrolling the paper. Even then, she averted her eyes for a few seconds, which left her looking out toward the crime scene tape and blackberries. They served as a stark reminder that this wasn't about her delicate sensibilities. No, this was about a woman whose life was stolen from her, a woman who deserved justice.

The headline wasn't as bad as she'd feared, simply stating the fact that a local woman had been murdered. The opening paragraph identified the victim as Dolly Cayhill and said she'd been missing for several months before her body was found. Okay, no surprises there. Her main worry was that Reilly might have given out Abby's specific address. She quickly skimmed the rest of the article, her frustration growing with each paragraph.

He'd danced all around the subject without actually stating her house number. Instead, Reilly had identified the location as the backyard of a large Victorian house on the third block of Tenth Street. He might as well have put a sign in her front yard. Not only that, he'd said that he'd attempted to interview the current owner of the property, but she'd refused to comment on the subject. Abby supposed that was better than reporting she'd slammed the door in his face, but he still managed to make it sound as if she'd had something to hide.

Tripp was back. "How bad is it?"

"Not as bad as it could be, I suppose. He didn't give out our actual address, but he did name the street and what block we live on. I'm guessing we might get another flurry of gawkers."

He set her coffee down within easy reach before settling down on the steps with his own cup and a plate containing three muffins. When Zeke perked up enough to give the plate a hopeful look, Tripp laughed and pulled a couple of doggy treats out of his pocket. The dog woofed his gratitude before gulping them down. It didn't take Tripp much longer to finish off his own breakfast.

"Thanks, that hit the spot."

"Good. Just leave your dishes. I'll take them back inside when I go."

"Okay." He reached over to pet Zeke one last time and then stood up. "And about any gawkers, I'm guessing there's not much you can do if they stay out on the street or even the sidewalk. However, if any of them bother you, let Gage know. He promised to have his deputies run off anyone who makes a pest of themselves."

"I will. I plan to call him anyway to see when I can get rid of all that lovely tape. Once that comes down, there won't be anything left for people to look at."

"I'll be in and out today, but let me know if you need help with that."

Not for the first time, it hit her how supportive Tripp had been about this whole mess. The poor guy hadn't signed on to live at ground zero of a murder investigation. Crossing her fingers that he wouldn't take her up on what she was about to offer, she asked, "I should've asked this before now, but do you want out of your lease? I mean, if all of this is interfering with your studies."

He didn't even hesitate. "Nope, I'm good. On the other hand, if Jean shows up here with another of her tuna casseroles anytime soon, we might revisit the subject. My mother used to make it for us for dinner pretty often, but it never tasted like Jean's. I don't know what that woman's secret ingredient is, but she really should leave it out."

For the first time all morning, Abby laughed. "I'll talk to her. At the very least, I'll take it off your hands as soon as she leaves. Maybe Zeke would like it."

Tripp put his hand over his heart and staggered back a step. "Tell me you wouldn't do that to him. I'm pretty sure the animal rights people would be upset, not to mention a certain reporter who would jump all over a story like that."

"You're right. No tuna casserole for man or beast."

"Glad to hear it. Before I go, is there anything new on my chore list?"

"Not that I can think of. By the way, Glenda said all of Sybil's friends are really pleased to see how good the yard is looking. I promised to pass along their compliments on a job well done."

He didn't seem to know how to react. Finally, he went into full retreat, walking away after mumbling, "Thanks, I guess."

Then he was gone, once again leaving her confused and staring at his back. That man had more moods than anyone else she knew. Chasing after him to apologize for saying he was doing a good job didn't make any sense, so she turned her attention back to the newspaper article. She read it again, this time more carefully, mining it for specific details and taking notes along the way. Gradually, she developed a bare bones starting point for when Dolly was most likely killed.

She'd been really hoping someone had seen her after Aunt Sybil had died, but no such luck. The reporter hadn't been able to locate anyone who had spoken to her more than a day or two after the two women had argued at church the day before Christmas Eve. That meant she hadn't been seen since right after Christmas. That could be significant, or it could just be that she'd been busy packing for her annual trip to the Sunbelt. Had she actually made plans to go? Another question for Gage.

Abby always functioned better when she made lists and kept important events marked on the calendar. After walking away from her job, she'd let that habit slide. Since her divorce and then moving to Snowberry Creek, she'd been content to let one day drift into the next. It was time to get her life organized again, especially now that she was taking on some of Aunt Sybil's committee responsibilities.

Flipping to a clean page on the notepad, she began writing down questions she wanted to ask about Dolly Cayhill and even a few about her aunt. It didn't take long to fill the page. Even if she didn't get answers to all of them, she had a feeling that what she did learn would give direction to any additional lines of inquiry she might discover. If Dolly was on the abrasive side, there had to be other people out there who might have had grudges against the woman. Once Abby learned who they were, she'd figure out what she needed to ask them.

At the top of the list, she wanted to know if her aunt and Dolly had had any further contact after their fight. Even if they hadn't, had Sybil told any of her close friends how she felt about the encounter? Since Sybil had been elected to head up the quilting guild for the current year, how did Dolly's supporters feel about that? Did they resent Abby stepping in to serve out her aunt's term of office? It was hard to guess, but everyone she'd met so far had been really supportive and seemed appreciative of her efforts.

So did that mean Dolly's supporters had left the group? Those would all be good questions for Glenda, Jean, or even Louise.

Who else had had problems with Dolly? Were the problems long-standing ones or had some new ones cropped up shortly before she disappeared? Gage might be a good source of information on that subject, but she wasn't sure how much he'd be willing to share with her.

But there was one question that really stood out to Abby: what could a woman like Dolly have done that was so heinous someone would have killed her over it? That was an idea Abby couldn't even get her head around. Chad had cheated on her, and then tried to steal the business they'd built together by denigrating Abby's contributions to their joint effort. He destroyed their marriage and stomped on her self-esteem in the process.

But even when the wounds were fresh and things were at their worst between the two of them, she hadn't wished him dead. Bruised and battered, maybe. Seeing him flat broke and on the verge of living on the street wouldn't have upset her too much either. But dead? No, her anger and hurt had never reached that level.

But someone had been that angry with Dolly Cayhill, someone who committed a vicious act of violence and then hid the evidence. For months now, the killer had gone on with his or her life, most likely hiding in plain sight among the people of Snowberry Creek. Just knowing that the picturesque town was home to a cold-blooded murderer was enough to send a shiver of fear sliding across Abby's skin.

She stared in frustration at her long list of unanswered questions. Finally, she realized that she did know one thing for sure. Until someone hunted down the killer and dragged him out of the shadows where he was hiding, no one was really safe.

And although defending her aunt's reputation was important to her, finding justice for Dolly Cayhill was right up at the top of Abby's list, too.

Chapter Seven

Abby drove up and down Main Street a few times trying to spot Gage Logan's car. Earlier, she'd dropped in at the municipal building that housed the mayor's office, the police department, and the town's library. She'd used registering for a library card as her main excuse for being there, but also she'd stopped by Mayor McKay's office to finally set up an appointment with her assistant to go over the duties and expectations for the chair of the Committee on Senior Affairs. On her way out, doing her best to act casual, she'd asked the desk sergeant in the police department if Gage was around.

After informing her that he was out covering a patrol shift for one of the other officers whose wife had gone into labor, the sergeant had asked if he could take a message. He also said if it was urgent, he could call Gage and let him know she was looking for him. Abby had immediately backed away, saying she'd catch up with the police chief when he wasn't quite so busy.

Frustrated and disappointed over her lack of progress in her self-appointed mission to get answers, she continued to cruise through town, promising herself she'd make one more lap and then go home. Or better yet, she'd stop in at Something's Brewing and see what marvels Bridey Kyser had created that morning. Bridey, who owned the coffee-shop-slash-bakery, was a true genius when it came to baked goods of all kinds. Lately, she'd been featuring a different flavor of brownies every week.

Abby managed to snag a parking spot half a block away, which she hoped meant her luck was changing. The coffee shop had become the hub of social activity in town, and parking spots anywhere close were often scarce. Stepping inside the shop, she was instantly engulfed in the intoxicating aromas of cinnamon, yeast, coffee, and an intriguing hint of chocolate. Her mouth was watering before she reached the counter. For once, the shop was empty except for one group of older women sitting at a table in the back corner.

As soon as they spotted Abby, they leaned in closer and started whispering while shooting hostile looks in her direction. She was surprised how much their actions hurt her feelings, but she wasn't about to let it show. It was tempting to stick her tongue out or hold up her hand and wiggle her fingers in greeting. Better yet, she could pull another chair up to their table and join the conversation.

Instead, she took the high road and simply pretended the old gossips didn't exist. A few seconds later, they gathered up their things and stalked out. One went so far as to sniff in disapproval as she passed by. Abby had no idea who they were and didn't care to find out.

Bridey had just walked up to take Abby's order. "Huh, what's up with them?"

"I'm not actually sure. I've never met any of them before that I can remember." She glanced out the front window to make sure they weren't still out there glaring at her. "My best guess is that they were friends of Dolly Cayhill. I've been warned that a few people think my aunt had something to do with her death and that Tripp helped her."

Bridey looked genuinely shocked. "Seriously? That's just crazy. I don't believe that for a minute, and I can't understand why anyone else would."

Abby shrugged. "Me either, but I'm afraid the whispers and rumors will continue until Chief Logan finds the real culprit."

"I'm so sorry to hear that. Ever since I heard what happened, I've been hoping you'd stop by. I've been worried about you, but I didn't want to intrude."

Ignoring the burn of tears, Abby managed a wobbly smile. "This whole experience has been pretty awful, but I'm doing all right. Okay, that's a lie, but I'm doing my best to hang in there."

"I'm glad to hear it. I just can't imagine stumbling across something like that." Bridey shivered and rubbed her hands up and down her arms as if chilled. "I hear it was your tenant who actually . . . well, you know."

"It was. Poor Tripp handled it all so well, while I was a complete mess."

"Well, who wouldn't be?" Bridey's smile was sympathetic. "Besides Tripp, that is. He's tough enough to handle it. Now, on to a happier subject. What can I get you?"

Abby studied the goodies behind the glass. "One . . . no, two of those brownies and a chai tea sounds good."

Bridey rang up her order. "I was about to take a break. Mind if I join you?"

Her undemanding company would be welcome. "That would be great."

Abby took her tea and brownies over to a table in the back, out of sight of the bank of windows across the front of the shop. Intellectually, she knew it was unlikely that a crowd would gather outside just to stare at her. Emotionally, she didn't want to risk it. It was a relief when Bridey joined her.

"Whew, it feels good to sit down. I have about twenty minutes before the high school lets out, and the afternoon rush begins. Until then, my assistant can handle anyone else who comes in."

She studied Abby over the rim of her coffee cup. "I'm guessing you didn't come in just for the brownies."

There was no use in denying it. "Not exactly, although I do love everything you bake. I was just wondering if you knew Dorothy Cayhill at all. If so, I just thought you might be able to give me your perspective on her."

Bridey looked as if she'd bitten into a lemon. "I only met the woman a few times, so I can't claim to have really known her well at all. And to be truthful, I tried to avoid her as much as possible. She came in a time or two with that bunch who just left. I swear, she would look around my shop as if she wanted to put on white gloves and test my counters for dust."

Abby looked at all the gleaming wood and spotless glass and shook her head. "She wouldn't have found any."

"Thank you for that. I do try." Bridey's smile faded. "But back to Dolly and her friends. While my customers are entitled to their privacy, sometimes I can't help but overhear their conversations, especially during quiet moments like this." She paused to sip her drink. "I also don't like to speak ill of anyone, but those ladies sure don't hesitate to do so. I'm not sure anyone in this town lives up to their standards."

Abby hesitated before trying to nudge Bridey into sharing some details. It probably wasn't fair to ask her to rat out some of her customers. Still, how was she supposed to figure out who else had had it in for Dolly if she didn't ask questions?

Maybe a little nudge wouldn't hurt. "I'd heard that about Dolly myself. That kind of attitude is bound to have rubbed some people the wrong way."

"I'm sure it did. While I won't repeat any gossip I happened to overhear, I do know about one case where Dolly really stirred up a hornet's nest. I saw some of the fallout myself."

"What happened?"

Bridey studied her over the rim of her coffee cup for a few seconds before answering. "I'm guessing you've always lived in or near a big city. Am I right about that?"

Abby nodded as she broke off another bite of her brownie. "Yep. I grew up in Seattle, although I spent time in the Portland area, too. That's where my father and his second wife live. My ex and I lived east of Lake Washington until the divorce."

Bridey smiled. "In some ways, life in a small town isn't all that different than anywhere else, but we do tend to know a lot more about each other's lives. When something good happens, we all find out about it and celebrate. Unfortunately, the opposite is also true. It's hard to keep secrets in a town this size. When someone screws up, everybody knows. Stories that wouldn't rate even a hint of a mention in a major newspaper end up being banner headlines here in town."

"I've already had a taste of that myself. Reilly Molitor came knocking on my door the day after we found the body. He wanted to interview me about finding my aunt's archrival buried in the backyard. That's actually how he described Dolly. Anyway, I slammed the door in his face and hid." To lighten the moment, she added, "In my defense, I was still in my pajamas and rocking some serious bed head."

Bridey's eyebrows shot up, her eyes open wide. "And you didn't want to have your picture plastered on the front page of the *Clarion*?"

"Not so much."

Bridey grinned. "I don't blame you, although I'm surprised he gave up so easily."

"Actually, he didn't. Luckily for me, Tripp and Gage Logan were able to convince him to leave." The memory made Abby smile. "Tripp said he was tempted to toss Reilly out on the street to see how high he'd bounce."

"Good for him. But back to the story. We have a fair number of veterans living in and around Snowberry Creek, so it was considered a very big deal when JB Burton Jr., captain of the high school football team and a top student, was accepted by one of the military academies. Two of his friends had also enlisted and are scheduled to report for duty right after they graduate this spring. Anyway, JB and his buddies decided to celebrate. There was beer involved, but there was no indication that JB did any drinking at all. He's always been a sensible kid, and this was his first brush with trouble."

She stared down at the table. "The young idiots might have gotten by with it if they hadn't parked their car, with the stereo cranked up, behind Dolly Cayhill's place. When she told them she'd called the police, they hopped in the car and took off. Unfortunately, one of the tires blew out and sent the car tearing across a corner of Dolly's yard, taking out some of her prize roses in the process. Again, the damage was not intentional, but no one could convince her of that."

Abby could already guess where this story was heading, but she let Bridey tell it at her own pace.

"It was a first offense for all of the boys, which Gage and the judge took into consideration. The judge came down hard on the two boys who had been drinking and ordered them to take a course on the effects of drugs and alcohol. They all got community service rather than being officially charged."

"That sounds reasonable."

"That's what we all thought, but Dolly was furious. She told the judge and Gage if they didn't bring actual charges, she would write the academy herself and tell them about the low caliber of cadet they would be getting."

"Could that have really kept him from getting into the academy?"

"There's no way to know. Regardless, JB's father didn't take the threat well at all. He confronted her right outside my shop. It was a really ugly scene, and Gage had to intervene."

"Did the boy lose his appointment?"

"Not that I've heard of, which is a relief. It would have been a darn shame for one stupid mistake to cost him everything he'd worked so hard for. Besides, if JB doesn't go to the academy, he might not be able to go to college at all, at least not full time. His younger sister had some serious medical problems last year. She's fine now, but the family finances took a big hit. His parents wouldn't be able to send him without some serious financial aid."

It was easy to see why the boy's father would have gone ballistic when his son's future was threatened by a vindictive old woman. "When did all of this happen?"

Bridey counted off several months on her fingers. "It would have been right around Thanksgiving, because I remember the front windows were decorated with fall leaves and turkeys."

That fit the timeline Abby had been putting together. Clearly Mr. Burton had a good reason to be upset with Dolly, and a far more compelling one than her aunt's. Not that she believed for one instant that her aunt had stooped to tainting crab dip and making her friends sick just to win votes. By comparison, Dolly had presented a clear threat to the man's son and the plans he had for his future. If she'd carried out her threat to contact the academy, it could've cost the boy dearly.

Abby realized she'd lapsed into an uncomfortably long silence. "Sorry, I didn't mean to drift off like that. I just can't help but wonder what really happened to Dolly. Even if she wasn't the nicest person, she didn't deserve what happened to her."

"No, she didn't."

Bridey glanced up at the clock. "Oops, I'd better get back to work. The hordes will come pouring through the door any second, not that I'm complaining. Those high school kids contribute more than you'd think to my monthly income."

Bridey gathered up their empty cups and plates as she prepared to go back to work. Abby followed her over to the counter. "I think I'll take a tall latte for the road and two of the lemon bars. Tripp has a sweet tooth, and I owe him for offering to send Reilly bouncing down the street." Although she would have probably bought him a treat anyway. Besides, if she didn't happen to see him, she loved lemon bars herself.

Before getting into her car, she looked up and down the street one last time in case she spotted Gage. No dice. It was time to give up and go home. At least Bridey had given her a lot to think about. If Gage had known about the fight between JB's father and Dolly Cayhill, how come he hadn't mentioned it to her?

Either he knew something about the situation that she didn't, or he was playing his cards close to his chest. He sure hadn't hesitated to tell her about the crab dip fiasco, but maybe that was because that confrontation had involved Aunt Sybil directly.

Or since he'd already helped protect the boy and his friends from the possible consequences of their actions, maybe he was doing so again. She mulled that idea over as she drove the short distance back to the house, and finally rejected it. Gage struck her as a man who believed in second chances where they were warranted, but she couldn't see him allowing someone to skate on a major crime, especially a violent one.

She also knew Gage had been genuinely shocked by the goats' gruesome discovery, which meant he had no idea Dolly had been missing, much less murdered. That left *him* off the hook, but not the Burtons. At the moment, they were at the top of her suspect list. Well, actually, right now they were the only ones on it. She refused to include Aunt Sybil's name, but there had to be other names that should be listed. She just hadn't discovered them yet. Her gut feeling was that other people had tangled with Dolly at some point.

As she pulled into her driveway, she sat and pondered her next move. Maybe she should contact Gage and ask him if he'd talked to the Burtons about Dolly's death. No, he wouldn't appreciate what he'd consider interference in his investigation, especially when all she had to offer was secondhand gossip. There was no way she'd drag Bridey's name into this. Besides, it wouldn't be right to further risk messing up the boy's future plans if he and his father were innocent. Aunt Sybil wouldn't have wanted Abby to tarnish someone else's reputation to save hers.

That left only one path forward: one way or another, she needed to talk to JB or his father herself.

Chapter Eight

Abby studied the ragtag stacks of boxes piled all over the garage. She'd already made several trips up to the third floor to carry down the items she'd designated for the sale. Progress was being made, but she had at least two more trips ahead of her before the day was over. She'd picked up Glenda to come help her with pricing, but there was no way she was going to ask her elderly friend to do any heavy lifting. In fact, she was actually more worried about how the group would handle everything that needed to be done on the two days of the upcoming garage sale. It would be less than tactful to ask how they had managed in the past.

Maybe she'd approach the subject from a different direction. "I'm thinking we could use some hired muscle both early Friday and Saturday mornings to get everything set up." Not that she actually believed it for a minute, but she hastened to add, "I know we could do it all ourselves, but I'm guessing timing is everything. We wouldn't want potential customers to miss out on all this great stuff because we didn't get it set out in time."

Glenda looked up from the table full of books and magazines that she was organizing. "Do you think we could ask Tripp?"

It was hard to miss the hopeful note in her voice, but there was no way Abby was going to ask the man to waste his weekend doing grunt work for the quilting guild. He'd already voluntarily pitched in and helped her lift the heavier boxes, when Glenda and the other ladies weren't standing around watching his muscles flex. It was bad enough that Abby herself hadn't been able to keep her eyes off him while he moved things around. She'd done her best to avoid being caught, but she suspected he'd noticed anyway. Maybe all those years he'd spent in the army had given him an uncanny knack for sensing when he was being watched.

Dragging her attention back to Glenda, she said, "Actually, I was wondering if there might be some teenage boys who wouldn't mind earning some extra cash by helping us set everything out, and then coming back at five when we close down for the day. What do you think?"

When Glenda hesitated, Abby added, "I'd pay them myself since it was my idea. I wouldn't expect the guild to foot the bill for their services. Since you and Jean are providing lunch for everyone who is working at the sale, this could be my contribution."

The older woman immediately looked more enthusiastic. No doubt she was worried about anything that might adversely affect the net profits from the sale. The proceeds from the garage sale went to buy materials for the charitable projects the guild members were involved in. She knew they made a bunch of lap quilts to donate to nursing homes. Aunt Sybil had also mentioned making baby blankets and small quilts for the fire and police departments to hand out to children when they responded to emergency calls.

Glenda finally nodded. "I say we go for it. Did you have someone in mind?"

"No, I don't personally know any of the local kids, but

I'm guessing Bridey might be able to suggest some names since her coffee shop is where the high school kids like to hang out after class is done for the day. Better yet, I'm pretty sure Gage Logan could point us in the right direction since he has a daughter about the right age."

And with any luck, JB Burton's name would come up, affording Abby the chance to meet the boy and decide for herself if he might have been involved in Dolly's disappearance. It was a bit underhanded, but it was true they could use the help. If he wasn't interested in participating, she'd just find another way to cross paths with either him or his father.

She checked the time. "I'll talk to Gage first. Otherwise, I can ask Bridey. She told me the other day that she has a brief lull right before the kids come pouring in. Maybe she can give my number to anyone who might be interested."

"Sounds like a plan. For now, I've sorted all the books. What should I do next?"

Abby had been trying to steer Glenda toward jobs that she could do sitting down. "Yeah, here's a couple things." She dug out the box of quilt pieces. "Someone donated these, and I was wondering if you recognized the work."

Glenda studied them. "Not for sure, but it looks like a pattern that two members were working on together. Unfortunately, Betsy lost her husband a few months back and moved out of state to live to be closer to her kids. I'm guessing Kate lost interest in the project. If it's all right with you, I'd like to set these aside for Jean to look at. She might enjoy making some kids' quilts out of them."

"What a great idea. Otherwise, how about organizing the jewelry? I've put everything I've found so far in that carton over there. I ran across a bunch of small boxes that Aunt Sybil had stored up in the attic and thought we could showcase some of the nicer items in them. I also brought down a couple of jewelry trees she had on her dresser so we can better display a lot of the necklaces and bracelets."

She set the bag full of little boxes on the table within easy reach of where Glenda was sitting, along with all the jewelry that had been donated. Most of it was inexpensive, but there were also some really nice pieces in the mix.

Glenda dug right in. "In the past, we've never worried this much about how everything was laid out, but doing all of this organizing will definitely make it easier for people to find what they're looking for. I'm betting we'll have a record year for sales."

She gave Abby a sly look. "You know, for someone who has never done a garage sale before, you sure have a knack for it. If we do as well as I am thinking we will, you'd better hope word doesn't get out. We're not the only group in town that earns a big chunk of their annual budget with a garage sale. I know for a fact that the high school marching band is holding one next month to help pay for the big trip they're planning to take next fall."

That was a terrifying idea. Was that what her life would be like here in Snowberry Creek? Organizing one fund-raiser after another? The thought left her more than a little queasy. Shoving that scary idea into the darkest recesses of her mind to deal with later, she looked around the garage for something else to do. Nothing called out for her attention. Rather than stand around watching Glenda sort the earrings, she decided to fetch the last few boxes from upstairs.

"I'll be back in a few minutes. I have a few more things laid out to donate to the sale. When I'm done, would you like to go get some lunch?"

Glenda's face lit up. "I'd love a burger and fries at the Creek Café. I know I shouldn't, but I can always have a salad for dinner tonight to offset all those delicious calories Frannie packs into her cooking. I might even go for broke and have a piece of pie, too."

Abby laughed. "I'll try to remain strong, but we both know I'll succumb to temptation, too. It will take me about fifteen minutes to haul down the last few boxes. Will that give you enough time to finish what you're doing?"

"Sure thing."

Half an hour later, the two of them walked into the Creek Café. All the booths were taken, but a familiar figure was sitting by himself in the far corner. It was tempting to head back there to see if Tripp would mind sharing, but she hesitated. He had a book open on the table, which probably meant he was studying.

Glenda spotted him, too, but Abby managed to block her headlong charge in his direction. "I don't think we should bother him. It looks like he's studying."

The crowded room was understandably noisy, but somehow Tripp heard her anyway. At least she assumed he had, because his head jerked up, and his gaze instantly zeroed in on her. He glanced around the room, sighed, and waved them forward. Glenda was off like a shot. By the time she reached the booth, Tripp had closed his book and pasted a smile on his face, but it only lasted long enough for him to greet Glenda. His look was a bit more frosty when Abby slid into the booth.

"Sorry, Tripp. If you need to study, we can wait until another booth opens up."

He closed the book and shoved it aside. "No, it's okay. I have to leave for class soon. Another few minutes of cramming for my test wouldn't help all that much."

Glenda seemed content to leave the talking up to Abby and Tripp while she perused the menu.

"What class is the test in?"

"Freshman American History." He leaned back and stretched his arms across the back of his seat. "I've taken a number of college courses over the years, but I'm still having to fill in a few gaps in the general education classes."

It was a shame he seemed a bit embarrassed by that admission. "I suspect you had more important things to do than freshman level history classes."

His gaze shifted to stare out of the window beside him. "Seemed so at the time."

She glanced over to see what had caught his attention, but there was nothing out there on Main Street that would account for the hard edge to his expression. A second later, he shook it off and smiled at Glenda. "So, what are you ladies going to have today?"

"A good question. Are you ready to order, or should I come back?"

Abby jumped. She'd been so intent on Tripp that she hadn't noticed the waitress's approach. "No, I'm ready. I'll have a BLT, a side Caesar salad, and chocolate cream pie."

Glenda set her menu aside. "I'll have a burger, fries, and a piece of that peach pie."

The waitress picked up Tripp's empty plate. "Can I get you anything else, or do you want me to bring your check?"

Tripp shook his head. "I was trying to be good, but I can't resist Frannie's pie. I'll have a slice of the apple warmed up, with a scoop of vanilla ice cream on the side. I'll need the check, too, because I have to leave in a few minutes."

"I'll put a rush on the pie for you."

While they waited, Abby tried to think of a safe topic of discussion. Before she came up with anything, Tripp went on point and raised his hand in greeting. His smile was more genuine this time. That had her twisting in her seat to see who had caught his attention. Gage Logan was already headed in their direction, stopping along the way to greet a few of the other diners.

Tripp slid over against the far side of his seat to make room for the police chief. Considering the size of the two men, it was a tight fit.

"I hope you guys don't mind me joining you. Frannie is doing a brisk business today."

Abby had been wanting to talk to him for a few days now, but this wasn't the time or place to interrogate him about the case. It was, however, the perfect time to ask him about any teenage boys who might want to earn a few bucks.

"Actually, I was going to call you later, Gage."

His friendly expression was quickly replaced by his official lawman one. He dropped his voice to just above a whisper. "I can't discuss the status of the investigation, Abby."

She hastened to reassure him. "No, this is something else entirely. The quilting guild is having its annual garage sale this Friday and Saturday at my house. Since you have a daughter in high school, I thought you might know some burly boys who would like to earn a few extra dollars helping us set up early in the morning and then coming back later to help us tear it all down again."

The brief flash of tension in Gage's shoulders drained away. "Actually, I can think of several. How many and how much?"

She did some quick calculations in her head. "Three or four should be enough. Fifteen dollars an hour each. Does that seem fair?"

He pulled out his spiral notebook and jotted down a

few notes. "Should be. I'll call them this evening. If they're interested, I'll give them your number so you can fill them in on the details."

"Thanks. That will be a big help."

Glenda joined the conversation. "I was just telling Abby this morning that I'm betting this will be our best sale ever. She's done such a great job with organizing everything, even the advertising. I also warned her that other groups are going to come knocking on her door once they hear about it."

Abby fought the urge to elbow her friend in the ribs, to remind her that the last thing Abby wanted was to get tangled up in any more projects around town. "Really, it's been a group effort. I would have been lost without everyone's help."

Never one to take a hint, Glenda snorted. "Nonsense, my dear. I'm just amazed at how you've managed to pull it all together despite everything that's happened. I just wish someone would take down that awful yellow tape in your yard. It hurts my heart every time I have to look at it."

Okay, that was something else Abby had been meaning to ask Gage as soon she managed to catch up with him. Too late now.

He offered the older woman a sympathetic smile. "I know it's upsetting, Mrs. Unger. The good news is that I'm pretty sure we're done back there. I'll check in with the lab one last time as soon as I get back to the office. Unless they object, I'll stop by on my way home tonight and tear it down. That is, if it's okay with you, Abby."

She would be so glad to see the constant reminder of Dolly's death gone. "That would be great."

Tripp intervened. "I'm guessing you've got better things to do, Gage. Text me if it's okay to tear it down, and I'll do it after I get out of class. No use in you going out of your way when I'm already there."

"If you're sure."

Abby wanted to kick her overly helpful tenant. He meant well, but he'd just blown the perfect chance for her to talk to Gage alone. From the slight smirk on Tripp's face, the big jerk knew exactly what she'd been planning to do.

The waitress arrived with an armload of plates, including a piece of peach pie for Gage. Evidently, he'd given her his order on the way to their booth. He and Tripp quickly devoured their desserts and left together, while she and Glenda dawdled over their meal, neither one in a hurry to get back to the garage.

Glenda toyed with her napkin, folding it into odd shapes. "I probably shouldn't have put Chief Logan on the spot like that about the crime scene tape, but it really does bother me. I don't know how you can stand having to look at it all this time."

Abby patted her on the arm. "I had planned to talk to Gage about it myself. I don't like looking at it either. I didn't actually know the woman, but you and the others did. I understand why it would bother you so much. I'm sure Gage does, too. Besides, we don't need to draw attention to that area of the yard while the sale is going on."

As they talked, she noticed how tired Glenda looked. She had a feeling the woman would deny it, but it was time for her to call it a day. "Would it be okay if we got our desserts to go? I don't want to leave Zeke alone any longer than I have to. If you don't mind, I'll drop you off at your place on the way."

"Don't you need my help finishing up the sorting?"

Abby hurried to reassure her friend. "There isn't much

left to do, and I can handle it by myself after I take my furry roommate for his afternoon walk."

"If you're sure, I have a few things I need to do at home myself, starting with a long nap and then maybe I'll do some quilting."

"That sounds like a good plan," Abby said as she flagged down their waitress to settle their bill and get their pie boxed up to go. "Are you working on something special?"

Glenda followed her up to the register near the door. "I'm trying to duplicate a quilt that I made for a niece who is getting married next month. I'd hoped to have it done in time, but I'm having trouble finding some of the same fabrics. Time is getting so short now, I'd settle for something that just comes close. I hate that, though, because the original was just perfect. I keep hoping the first one will turn up, but so far it hasn't."

That seemed odd. How could she have lost an entire quilt, especially one that was obviously special to her? Was she getting forgetful? Not that Abby was about to ask her that particular question.

Instead, she offered a possible solution to her problem. "You're welcome to look through Aunt Sybil's fabric stash to see if she has what you're looking for. Feel free to take anything that might work."

Glenda brightened right up. "That would be great. I'd really appreciate it. And when you decide to work on a project of your own, you'd be welcome to raid my stash in return."

"I'll keep that in mind. Aunt Sybil has a couple of quilts in progress that I want to finish first, before I try my hand at creating something new."

They'd reached the car. "Do you want to stop by the house and see what you find up there? While you do that,

I'll take Zeke for a quick walk and then run you home when you're done."

"That's perfect."

Two hours later, Abby waited for Zeke to follow her out of the garage before closing the door.

She used the hem of her T-shirt to wipe the sweat off her face. "I don't know about you, dog, but I'm done for the day. The only things on my agenda for the evening are a shower, an easy dinner, and a good book."

Zeke shoved his head under her hand, demanding some attention. Or maybe he was reminding her that she wasn't the only one looking forward to dinner. She knelt down on one knee to put herself at his eye level. "Don't worry, I won't forget your kibble, big guy."

He gave her face a quick lick before she could dodge it, his huge tongue leaving a thick layer of slobber on her cheek. One more reason she needed that shower.

"Come on, let's head inside."

Before she'd gone two steps, Tripp walked out onto his porch. Zeke immediately abandoned her for his other favorite person. She followed after him at a slower pace.

"How was your test?"

He sat down on the steps and let Zeke sprawl across his lap. "Not as bad as it could've been. Most of it was multiple choice, but there were a couple of nasty essay questions just to keep things interesting. The professor said he'd post the grades by the end of the week."

"I'm sure you did great."

His mouth kicked up in a quick grin. "When I was in high school, my mom made it clear that a C was never an acceptable grade. She tells me that still holds true."

"Afraid you'll get grounded?"

He laughed a little as he rubbed Zeke's ears. "She didn't quite go that far, but you never know with her."

"I'm sure she's proud of you and everything you've accomplished."

His smile faded. "She never wanted me to enlist, much less spend twenty years in the army. It was her dream that I'd go to college."

Abby could understand why his mother wouldn't have wanted her son to put himself at risk in combat. She'd seen the dark shadows in Tripp's eyes often enough to know his time in the service had had a profound effect on him. "Is that why you decided to go back to school? To make her happy?"

"Not entirely, but she was thrilled to find out that's what I was doing. Like I told you, I've been taking classes for a while now, but it would've taken me forever to get a degree taking one or two courses at a time. By going full time, I should finish up in a couple of years."

"What are you majoring in?"

He gently shoved Zeke off his legs and stood up. "Listen, I just came out to tell you that Gage said I can tear down the tape. I'll take care of it this evening."

The abrupt change in topics left her momentarily speechless and floundering on how to respond. Clearly she'd overstepped her bounds by asking about his major. Rather than ask what made that particular topic taboo, she settled for nodding as she called Zeke back to her side.

"Come on, Zeke. It's dinner time."

The dog immediately made a beeline from Tripp's porch toward the house. She followed in his wake, calling back over her shoulder. "Thanks for taking care of the tape. Let me know if you need any help."

The sound of Tripp's door closing was his only response.

Chapter Nine

Abby wondered if it was a crime to kill an alarm clock. After all, it wasn't the poor thing's fault that she'd set it to go off at the crack of dawn. She slapped the snooze button a little harder than necessary, but the clock would live to buzz another day. Rolling over on her back, she did her best to pry her eyes open to greet the day.

"Screw you, Day."

Okay, again, it wasn't Friday's fault that she had to be up and moving while the sky was still dark. She had to make a quick run to Bridey's shop to pick up the pastries and coffee she'd ordered for the volunteers who were due to arrive by six-thirty at the latest. What else did she need to do besides drag herself out of bed and into the shower? Feed Zeke, get the cash boxes out of the attic where she'd hidden them, and set the garage sale signs out on the porch. She didn't want to put them out on the street until after the sale was set up and ready to go.

Rather than wait for the buzzer to go off again, she turned off the alarm and rolled out of bed. A quick shower helped chase the cobwebs out of her head, and she dressed for comfort rather than to impress. Slipping on her tennis shoes, she headed downstairs, trying not to resent the fact that Zeke had taken her place on the bed as soon as she'd left it.

As she pulled out of the driveway, her headlights illuminated Tripp already heading out for his morning run. She slowed to keep pace with him and rolled down the window.

"I'm headed to Bridey's shop to get goodies for the hired help. I'm not expecting you to pitch in today, but you've already earned your fair share. Any preference on what I should set aside for you?"

"A couple of her muffins would be great. The peach ones are my current favorite, but they're all good. See you back at the house."

When he veered off at the next corner and picked up speed, she yelled, "Show off!"

He turned back around and ran backwards for several steps, a big grin on his face. She gunned the engine and continued on her mission. Maybe she really should think about running with him sometime, but she'd have to build up some stamina first. It shouldn't take her more than a year, five at the most, to be able to keep up with him.

Yeah, right. Like that was ever going to happen.

Luckily, everything was all packed up and ready to go when Abby got to the coffee shop. Since she'd already paid for the order, Bridey had told her to drive around to the back to pick it up. When she drove past the shop on her way to the alley that ran behind the shop, she was glad they'd made those arrangements. The line was already out the door and growing longer by the second.

As soon as she pulled up, Seth Kyser, Bridey's husband, opened the door and smiled at her. "I'll carry it all out for you."

She hustled around to open the trunk of her car before he arrived with three large boxes of goodies.

"I'll go back for the coffee." Seth was back in a jiffy.

After surrendering the large cardboard containers, he held up a small bag. "This has the creamers, sugars, and sweeteners. I also stuck in a big pile of napkins. Bridey's pastries are delicious, but they can be messy."

"Thanks." She took the bag and added it to the rest of the stash in the trunk. "I saw the line out front. Is it always that crazy at this ungodly hour?"

"Yep, pretty much. It's a good thing we're both morning people. As soon as we get your stuff loaded, I'll go help her out. She and her assistant do a great job waiting on everyone, but they let me pretend I'm useful and not just in their way. Good luck with your garage sale."

"We'll need it. It's not like I know what I'm doing." She closed the trunk and walked back around to the driver's side door. "Thank Bridey again for everything. I know everyone will be thrilled to get their hands on this stuff."

Back at the house, she noticed Tripp's lights were on. He must have survived his morning run. She circled behind the house to park on the grass near the back porch. She'd already set up a pair of folding tables to hold the food. She made quick work of covering them with tablecloths and then arranged the beverages at one end and the boxes full of pastries on the other. Besides Bridey's coffee, she'd bought orange juice and bottled water. In between, she set out paper plates, napkins, and cups along with plastic forks and spoons.

She used tongs to pick out two of the muffins for Tripp and then added a small tart that she thought he might like. After covering them with a napkin, she took them inside and hid them in the cabinet over the stove.

The sound of footsteps caught her attention. She put her hands on her hips and pretended an aggravation she really didn't feel. "It's about time you dragged your lazy backside out of bed."

Zeke padded across the room to stare at his still-empty food bowl. He looked in her direction, his disappointment all too clear.

"Fine, I'll feed you, but then you're on greeter duty."

His tail made a halfhearted effort to wag. Clearly, he wasn't going to get overly excited about anything until he had his morning kibble, so she dutifully filled his bowl. "I'll leave the door open, so you can come out whenever you're ready."

As she stepped outside, she ran into a solid wall that hadn't been there a few minutes before. Tripp caught her arms to keep her from bouncing back into the door. "Sorry. Didn't mean to startle you."

"That's okay. I should be paying more attention, but my mind's going a hundred miles an hour trying to figure out if I've forgotten anything."

She took another step back. "One thing I didn't forget, though, was to set a couple of the muffins aside for you. They're inside in the cabinet over the stove. Help yourself to some coffee, too, if you want."

"Sounds good."

Zeke poked his head out the door and then greeted Tripp with considerably more enthusiasm than he had her. It was hard not to be jealous over how happy the two males were to see each other.

"What are you doing with Zeke today? I'll be home most of the day, so he can hang out with me if he wants."

Another hard hit of envy washed over her. Not only was the dog going to spend time with Tripp, neither of them was going to have to deal with all the hassles she was going to have to face today.

"That's fine. Now, I'd better get back to work."

He stepped aside to let her pass and then disappeared into the house, her four-footed traitor of a pet hot on his heels.

When she headed toward the garage to start opening up, she spotted someone standing in the shadows in the far corner of the backyard. At any other time, it might have scared her, but she was expecting the three high school boys she'd hired to show up any minute now. There was one in particular she was looking forward to meeting. Even so, she was glad Tripp was within screaming distance if she was wrong about who was lurking near the blackberry brambles.

She slowly made her approach. "Hi, can I help you?"

The guy started as if her voice had surprised him. Then he stepped out of the shadows into the dim light cast by the porch lights. He was tall and a little on the lanky side, as if he hadn't quite filled out to fit his frame. His hair was some shade of brown, his face open and friendly. "Are you Abby? I'm JB Burton. We spoke on the phone."

Holding out her hand, she closed the distance between them. "Hi, JB. I'm so glad you could make it. Did you come alone?"

He nodded. "My friends should be here soon. They live on the opposite side of town from where I do, so my dad dropped me off on his way to work. We'll leave for school from here."

After shaking her hand, he glanced back over his shoulder toward the corner where he'd been standing. What thoughts were going through his head right then? Was he recalling the moment he or his father had buried Dolly under that piece of plywood? It was hard to imagine this polite young man having done something so horrible, but killers came in all shapes and sizes.

JB cleared his throat. "Is that where you found her? Mrs. Cayhill, I mean."

"Yes, it is."

Thank goodness Tripp had made good on his promise to

remove the tape last night. Somehow, she sensed seeing the vivid reminder would have been hard for JB to handle.

His shoulders hunched in the early morning chill. "I knew her."

When he didn't say anything else, Abby kept the conversation going. "I never met Mrs. Cayhill, but I haven't lived here very long. I just moved to Snowberry Creek a few weeks ago when my aunt passed away."

He turned his back on the blackberries. "I know a lot of people said some bad things about her, but she wasn't always like that. Not once you got to know her."

Interesting. How well had he gotten to know the woman?

"I know she had good friends here in town. Several of the ladies who will be here to help with our garage sale knew her quite well. They've taken her death hard."

JB shuffled his feet and stuck his hands in his hip pockets. "I heard rumors about your aunt and Mrs. Cayhill. You know, that they'd had a big argument at church."

Where was he going with this? He'd better not be trying to blame Aunt Sybil for Dolly's death. Before she could say anything, he kept talking.

"It's hard even to imagine the two of them yelling at each other in public. But even if they did have a fight, it would have never come to blows." He offered her a small grin. "I don't know about your aunt, but Mrs. Cayhill would have never stooped to physical violence. Such things were beneath her dignity."

He said those last three words in a quivery, high pitched voice as if quoting something she'd said to him directly. He also seemed more amused by the woman's comment than he should've been, especially if she'd actually threatened his appointment to one of the military academies.

"She and my father got in a huge fight over the night

my friends and I messed up her yard. I've never seen Dad that mad."

Gossiping with a teenager wasn't something Abby should be doing, but she needed every bit of information she could glean from their conversation. "What happened then?"

"To quote my dad, 'Chief Logan negotiated a cease fire and left it up to the three of us to settle the problem.'" JB glanced back at the blackberries again. "She said she would stop insisting all of us get charged if I showed her I was worthy to go to West Point. Her husband served, and she wanted to make sure they hadn't lowered their standards to the point they would accept a juvenile delinquent. I offered to do chores for her, eight hours a week for a month."

He rolled his shoulders. "I did a lot of heavy lifting for her, moving things around in her attic, hauling trash to the dump, hanging some pictures, and other stuff. None of it was hard, mostly the kind of thing she couldn't do for herself. Sometimes she'd bake cookies, and we would end up looking at old photo albums. Some of the stories she told were pretty interesting."

"Sounds like a fair deal for both of you. I bet she enjoyed having the company."

"Maybe." His smile had faded. "Even if she'd been as mean as some people thought, Mrs. C didn't deserve to die like that."

"No, she didn't."

Was he thinking of anyone specific who might have had it in for Dolly? Unfortunately, the sound of a car pulling into the driveway ended their conversation. At least she'd learned enough to know that she should cross both JB and his father off her list of suspects. She was glad for their sakes, especially JB's, even if it left her with no one else to blame. Obviously, she'd have to do more digging, but not right now. She had a garage sale to get through.

Two more boys came strolling up the driveway.

She pointed toward the back porch. "While I open up the garage and turn the lights on, you and your friends can help yourself to some drinks and the pastries I bought at Something's Brewing this morning. Make it quick, though. We really need to get started if we're going to get everything out and arranged before the onrushing hordes arrive."

He waved to his buddies. "We'll be back in a second."

Good to his word, they appeared at the front of the garage in an amazingly short time. They must have shoved the muffins down their throats to have finished eating them that fast. At least they'd had the good sense to grab some water to wash them down.

It didn't take the boys long to haul out the folding tables that Louise had borrowed from her church and set them up in the driveway. Next, they carried out the boxes containing all the donated items and put them on the ground in front of the tables, where her next group of volunteers could unload them.

While the boys worked, she set up the smaller tables where the customers could check out and pay. She made sure both stations had bags for purchases, some tissue paper to wrap the more fragile items, and a cash box. That done, she paused to look around. So far, so good. Hopefully the rest of the day would go as smoothly.

JB set the last box on the table. "Is there anything else we can do for you?"

"If you don't mind staying a little longer, you could start setting everything out on the tables. Don't worry about trying to organize it. The ladies will take care of that as soon as they get here."

"No problem."

She'd promised the three boys a minimum of three hours pay for each day, even if the set up and tear down took less time than that. It looked like they were determined to earn it. She'd have to thank Gage for recommending them to her. They had nearly everything unloaded and the boxes stacked neatly in the back of the garage before the first of the quilting guild members arrived at seven-thirty.

Tripp joined her at the side of the driveway. "I thought Zeke and I would walk over to the park and hang out for a while if that's okay. Do you want me to put your signs out on the way?"

"That would be great. I'd like one at the front of the driveway, one at the corner in each direction, and the last one out on Main Street. If that's too many to carry, I can ask JB or one of the other boys to help."

He gave her one of *those* looks, the kind where he thought maybe she was insulting his manhood or something. "I can handle four signs, Abby. It's not like they're all that heavy."

Before she could apologize, he was gone. Darn, that man was touchy, but there wasn't anything she could do about it now.

Two cars pulled up in front of the house, the first one Glenda's. Abby buried her aggravation with her temperamental tenant and her disappointment over losing her prime suspects, and hurried to help her elderly friends maneuver their way up to the garage. Most of them got around just fine, but others needed a little help now and then.

At least they were all pleased when they saw how much work had already been done. Louise put her hands on her hips and looked around. "Abby, I'm amazed at all you've accomplished. You must have been up for hours to get this much done already."

"I didn't have to get up that early."

Okay, that was a lie. Since her divorce, she'd gotten out of practice getting up before sunrise. "Besides, I had a lot of help. JB and his friends have been working really hard since they got here."

She smiled at the boys. "Help yourself to more goodies if you'd like, but otherwise you're done for this morning. We officially close each day at four-thirty, but I'm not sure how hard and fast that timing is. Why don't you aim for getting back here at five. I'm hoping we'll have sold enough that we won't have nearly this much to lug back into the garage."

JB nodded. "We'll be back."

After they were gone, Abby turned her attention back to her friends. "I know we need to finish getting organized, but there are breakfast pastries, juice, water, and coffee around on the back porch. Help yourselves whenever you need a bit of a pick-me-up."

The rest of the morning passed by in a blur. People came and went, sometimes in bunches, at other times only one or two would be poking around. The ladies traded off covering the checkout tables while the others prowled around filling in the gaps left when things were sold. So far, the hottest items seemed to be jewelry and tools, although a fair number of the books were gone, too. Abby had been surprised when the mushroom-covered canisters had been snatched up by one of the very first customers. There was no accounting for taste.

Around noon, things slowed to the point that Glenda and Jean set out the sandwiches and salads they'd brought for lunch. Once everyone had filled a plate, they returned to their chairs around the tables in the driveway. Abby let the conversation swirl around her, not really paying much attention until she heard Dolly Cayhill's name mentioned. She immediately tuned into what was being said.

Rebecca Hagerty was saying, "I guess that new development will go forward now that Dolly's gone. She'd be so disappointed to see that happen."

Louise nodded. "She would be, but I told her all the time that she couldn't stop progress. Eventually, we all knew Frank Jeffries would finally convince the zoning commission to let him build on that lot. Besides, it's his property. Maybe he should be able to do what he wants with it."

"What property is that?"

The two women turned their attention to Abby. "The old Embrey place," Louise said. "It's a big parcel of land that backed up to Dolly's yard. Frank Jeffries bought it a couple of years ago. She was happy at the time, thinking he'd fix up the old farm house. Instead, he and some investors decided to tear it down and subdivide the parcel to build a bunch of smaller houses."

Rebecca picked up where Louise stopped off. "She did everything she could to block the development from going forward, saying that old house was a historical site and should be preserved."

Gerri, a member of the group who Abby didn't know all that well, snorted. "Old doesn't mean always mean valuable. If you ask me, Dolly just doesn't want a neighborhood of young families with kids backing up on her place. She won't like the noise."

"Gerri!" Louise gave the far corner of the backyard a pointed look, reminding her friend that Dolly was beyond caring about such things now.

In response, Gerri drew a sharp breath. "Sorry, everyone. I forget sometimes that she's gone. I didn't mean to be disrespectful."

Jean played peacemaker. "We're all struggling with what

happened, Gerri. I think we should find something else to talk about."

Louise immediately pointed toward a quilt that was prominently displayed on a rack by the front of the garage. "We've sold a lot of chances for the quilt. More than we did last year, I think."

Abby filed away the comments about Frank Jeffries. He might have had good reason to want Dolly gone if her interference in his plans had caused him financial difficulties. Meanwhile, she studied the quilt they were raffling off. It was a star pattern, although she didn't know the specific name for the design. Rather than being quilted, the corners of the squares had been knotted with embroidery thread in dark blue to match the binding. She loved the hodgepodge of colors that would warm any room it was displayed in. "Who made it?"

Glenda smiled. "We all worked on it. Each of us picked out the fabric and colors for at least two of the squares. Once the top was all sewn together, we got together to tie it. It's a project we all look forward to every year."

One of the other women sighed. "It was supposed to be the cover for our calendar."

It was impossible to miss the air of disappointment that swept through the group. Abby glanced at Glenda and asked, "What calendar is that?"

"We were going to do a calendar to sell as another fundraiser for the group. It was Sybil's idea, actually. I think she was inspired by that movie that came out several years ago about the women who wanted to buy a couch for the hospital. The idea was to feature a different special quilt for each month, and then the cover would be the quilt we all worked on. We thought we'd offer it to sell through the mail, at church, and anywhere else we could think of."

Jean patted her friend on the arm. "It was a good idea. I think we should try to do it again sometime."

Louise didn't look happy about that idea. "Not after what it cost so many of us. I'm still just heartbroken over how it all turned out."

Abby was about to ask what happened to derail the project when two large vans pulled up in front of the house and eight people piled out of each one. She tossed her empty plate in the trash. "Looks like we're back in business, ladies."

Later, though, she would ask Glenda, or maybe Jean, about the calendar project. It was obvious that something had gone horribly wrong. Whatever it was, it had had a profound effect on the group. As she took her spot at the checkout table, Abby remembered Glenda was having to duplicate that quilt for her niece's wedding. It would be interesting to learn if the two things connected, but now wasn't the time to ask.

The new arrivals were already starting to line up to pay for their purchases and Abby mustered up a smile. "Here, let me put those in a bag for you. That's eight paperback books at fifty cents apiece, so four dollars total."

As she accepted the handful of quarters and dimes, she couldn't help but quietly laugh to herself. A year ago, she'd spent her days balancing the company's books and dealing with five- and six-digit numbers without batting an eye. Today, she got excited if a sale broke the five-dollar mark. The funny thing was how much she was enjoying herself.

Who woulda thunk it?

Chapter Ten

"Come on, boy. We need to keep moving."

Zeke resisted Abby's best efforts to pull him away from the tree trunk that had caught his attention as they walked past. She had no idea what messages other dogs had left on it when they'd stopped to lift their legs, but evidently it made for fascinating reading. So far, her furry companion had circled the tree three times, sniffing each and every inch of the bark and dragging her along behind him in the process.

Finally, he snorted loudly and then proceeded to leave his own message, an incredibly lengthy missive considering he'd already left similar notes on several other bushes and trees along the way. When he was satisfied with his efforts, he shook himself head to tail before resuming their walk. She smiled at an older couple who went single file to give her and Zeke room to pass.

Most adults instinctively gave Zeke a wide berth. If she didn't know what a sweetheart he was, she might have been just as leery of a dog of his size, too. The truth was, the only real threat the bighearted fellow presented to the world was his ability to produce an excessive amount of drool, which often left behind an icky trail of mastiff goo wherever he went.

So gross, not dangerous.

Children, on the other hand, loved the big guy. More than a few thought he was a pony rather than a dog. Every time they went for a walk, she had to ward off one or two munchkins who demanded a chance to go for a ride. Zeke would've probably tolerated the indignity of it all, but for his sake she refused all such requests. Hugs and back scratches, though, were always welcome.

She gave Zeke's leash a firm tug, telling him that they were going left instead of their usual right. He gave the vine maple tree on the other corner a longing look but didn't fight her as they turned the other way. Normally, Zeke liked to move along pretty briskly between his favorite places to stop and sniff around, but today she was glad he was content to go at a slower pace. They'd gotten a late start on their walk because both of them had slept in that morning. She'd been exhausted by the time the garage sale had ended the previous evening and everything that was left had been packed up to be dealt with later.

While she and the boys had done most of the grunt work outside, Glenda and the other ladies had pitched in to clean up her kitchen and divide up the leftover food to go home with whoever wanted some. When that was done, they'd stood by and watched while she and Louise counted all the money. That had taken longer than she'd expected because so much of it was in coins and small bills. Still, Glenda had been right on target with her prediction. The net proceeds after expenses exceeded their prior best sale by nearly three hundred dollars.

That would make a lot of small quilts.

With the sale over, Abby was now free to concentrate on other things—like taking a peek at the property that Frank

Jeffries wanted to develop. On the way, she also planned to walk by Dolly Cayhill's house, although she wasn't sure why. Curiosity, mostly. Seeing where Dolly had lived might help her get a better handle on what the woman had been like when she'd been alive.

She kept Zeke moving along at slightly faster clip while keeping an eye on the addresses of the houses they passed. As it turned out, she needn't have worried about the house numbers at all. If she'd been asked to pick out the one place on the entire street that looked most like what Dolly Cayhill would've lived in, it would've been the immense house on the corner.

All-brick homes weren't all that common in the area, so that alone made it stand out from the crowd. The stately, two-story house stood proudly on top of a slight rise, allowing it to look down at all of the neighboring houses. Abby didn't know a lot about architecture, but she was willing to bet the grand old dame had been built well over a hundred years ago. It didn't take much imagination to see it as the centerpiece of some rich family's sprawling estate. She wondered if it had been in the Cayhill family for generations.

Although the yard was large by today's standards, the imposing size of the house still made it look crowded. In part, that was due to the ornate landscaping, which was still being well maintained despite the death of its owner. It would be interesting to know if the niece planned to keep the place, or if she would put it on the market.

That thought brought Abby to an abrupt halt as she pondered the possibilities. Considering how she herself had just inherited a house and all of its furnishings, it should've occurred to her long before now that someone stood to profit from Dolly's unexpected death. Gage had said the niece was the next of kin, but the woman and Dolly hadn't been all that close. With that being the case, who stood to inherit? The house alone had to be worth a serious chunk of change.

Something else to think about. Right now, she had one more place she wanted to check out. The property that Mr. Jeffries owned supposedly backed up to Dolly's yard. Abby nudged Zeke into moving on, turning at the next corner to circle around to the next street. Again, it wasn't hard to pick out the old farmhouse that the ladies in the quilting guild had mentioned. She paused to study it from a distance and wasn't all that impressed. While it might have been as old as Dolly's house, it had never possessed the same elegant grace.

At one time, it had probably been white with cheery green trim. Now the peeling paint had streaks of mold that matched the faded shutters in color. Could an architect or an historian look at all that damage and still see something worth saving? Maybe it still had good bones like they said on those TV shows where they flipped houses. But considering the way the peak of the roof sagged in the middle, she seriously doubted it.

Zeke sighed heavily and sat down beside her on the edge of the gravel driveway that led up to the house. When he leaned into her leg, she patted his head. "We'll get moving again in a second. Give me a minute to look around, and I'll give you an extra treat when we get home for being so patient."

His tail did a slow sweep through the dirt and gravel in acceptance of her offer. Before setting off cross-country to look at the house up close, she did a slow three-sixty turn to see if anyone was paying any attention to her. Most of the nearby houses were separated from this one by six-foot tall cedar fences. Even if the homeowners were out in their backyards, they wouldn't be able to see what she was doing.

The view from the remaining two sides was blocked by a stand of trees.

Okay, then. No reason not to do some snooping. She headed straight for the house, which looked worse the closer she got to it. The old wooden porch was missing several boards, so she had to really watch her step to get near the windows. Shading the sides of her face with her hands, she pressed her nose against the cracked glass and looked inside. The interior looked every bit as bad as the outside. Trash was scattered on the floor, the ceiling light fixture dangled from a single wire, and there were mildew stains on the walls. It would take more than a superficial face-lift to make this place livable.

She jumped back when something scurried across the floor inside. "Rats!"

Literally. Shuddering, she backed away and headed straight toward the road, her curiosity satisfied. Maybe Dolly Cayhill had felt some connection to the Embrey family that made the place special to her. Regardless, there was no way that crumbling mess of a house was worth saving.

When she got home, she'd do some snooping online to see if she could find anything that would explain why Dolly had tried to block the development. Maybe Gerri had been right about her motivations being purely selfish and simply not wanting a bunch of young families moving into the neighborhood.

Before she reached the street, a big pickup pulled into the driveway. The driver climbed out and headed straight for her. He appeared to be in his early fifties. Although not as tall as Tripp or Gage Logan, he still carried quite a bit of muscle on his frame. He looked like a man who'd earned his living with his hands, making it quite likely she was looking at Frank Jeffries. Whoever he was, he didn't look happy to see her and was frowning big time as he watched her walk toward him.

"Excuse me, but can I help you? Was there something you needed?"

He sounded more exasperated than angry, but how much had he seen? Abby crossed her fingers that he'd turned the corner after she'd stepped off the porch. "No, I . . . we were just walking by when my dog spotted something running through the grass. He took off after it before I could stop him."

The man didn't call her on the lie, which was a relief. "That's some dog you've got there."

Patting her companion on the head, she said, "Zeke's a real sweetheart. I should've had a tighter hold on his leash, but he's usually better behaved than that. I'm not sure what it was that he spotted."

"Probably an opossum, but it could've been a rat, too. The old place is infested with them."

She didn't have to fake the shudder of distaste. "In that case, I'm glad he didn't manage to catch whatever he was chasing. Next time we walk this way, I'll be sure to keep him on the other side of the street."

He looked past her at the house and land, shading his face with his hand. "That's a good idea. Like I said, the place is infested with rats and other vermin, and the house itself is an accident waiting to happen. I'm hoping to clear this whole plot out soon, which should eliminate any pest problems."

"What are you going to do with it?"

He sighed, his expression grim. "I've been hoping to build six new homes on it. Still will if city hall would stop screwing around and issue the permits I need to get started. Every day they delay costs me money, and my investors are getting twitchy enough to maybe pull out of the deal. I still don't know why the planning commission listened to that interfering old biddy."

His frustration came across loud and clear, but then he apologized. "Sorry about that. I didn't mean to take my frustration out on you. It's my problem, not yours."

He hadn't mentioned Dolly by name, but it was clear she was the one who'd thrown a wrench in the works for him. Abby wasn't sure how to respond, but settled for simply saying, "I'm sorry, too."

He gave her an odd look. "For what? You're not the one who blocked my building permits."

She shrugged and then smiled. "It was the only thing I could think of to say. My aunt always said, 'when in doubt in a social situation, you can never go wrong with an apology.'"

"Sounds like something my grandmother would've said." Mr. Jeffries took off his baseball cap and ran his fingers through his hair. "Well, I need to get back to work. Enjoy the rest of your walk."

"Thanks, we will."

Zeke had stretched out in the grass, but he lumbered back up to his feet when she tugged on his leash. The two of them set off back the way they'd come. She didn't want to appear anxious to get away from Mr. Jeffries, but it seemed prudent to put some distance between them as quickly as possible. At least he hadn't asked who she was, nor had he identified himself, which was just dandy with her.

She didn't know if he'd recognize her name from the newspaper reports about Dolly Cayhill's murder, but it was safer to err on the side of caution. If she'd met him under other circumstances, she wouldn't have thought him threatening, and he wasn't the kind of man who stood out in a crowd. But just because he was ordinary didn't mean he wasn't capable of violence if cornered.

Clearly Dolly's actions had caused him problems, but

Abby had no idea if they were a minor inconvenience or much, much worse. Something else to think about when she got home.

Maybe she hadn't really learned anything concrete about Mr. Jeffries or anyone else who might have benefited financially from Dolly's death, but at least she had some new avenues to explore.

Feeling more energized than she had all day, she didn't rush Zeke at all when he stopped to check out some extra trees on their way home.

"So how did the garage sale go?"

Abby closed the lid on the box of odds and ends she'd just finished packing. "Really well, actually. Glenda and the other ladies were thrilled with how much we made. I guess we set a new record."

Tripp wandered into the garage with her to poke around the items she still had to box up. He seemed more curious than actually interested in anything he was looking at, so she filled another box, this time with books and magazines. After setting it over in the corner with the others, she looked around to see what she wanted to work on next. Then something caught her eye. There was that one thing she needed to take care of before she chickened out altogether.

"That small box under the table there is yours."

Tripp glanced at it and then shook his head. "I didn't leave anything in here."

She wished she knew how he would react to her buying him a present. To say the man was unpredictable was putting it mildly. There was only one way to find out. "You didn't leave it here. It's something I bought for you at the garage sale."

He moved marginally closer to the box, staring at it as if he thought the whole thing would explode. "Really?"

When he nudged it with the toe of his shoe, she glared at him in exasperation. You'd think no one had ever surprised him with a gift. "Really, Tripp. Would you open it already? I promise what's in there won't bite, and my feelings won't be hurt if you don't like what I got you." Okay, that last part was a lie, but she wasn't going to admit that to him.

He finally picked the box up and carried it over to her makeshift table. It might have been smarter to look away, not wanting to see his reaction. Instead, she held her breath and watched as he lifted the flaps on the box and leaned in closer to look inside.

A slow smile spread across his face, briefly softening the sharp edges that were his more usual expression. He reached in and pulled out one of the action figure soldiers that had reminded him of the ones he'd played with when he was a kid. Although he'd said he hadn't wanted them, she hadn't been able to resist buying them for him.

One by one, he set them all out on the table before finally glancing in her direction. "I told you I didn't want them."

"Well, I didn't believe you. If I'm wrong about that, you can put them back in the box and set it over there with the ones I'm taking to the thrift shop donation center."

He studied them for a long time before speaking again. "That would be rude, considering you went to all the trouble to buy them for me."

That might be as close to thanks as she was going to get from him, but that was okay. The fact that he took such care putting them back into the box spoke volumes.

"You and Zeke were gone a long time on your walk today."

"We went a different route." Which was all she wanted to say on the matter.

"Someplace interesting?"

Leave it to Tripp to keep poking and prodding. It wasn't as if he always answered when she asked him questions. Was he simply making conversation or had she done something to rouse his suspicions? She'd confess to wanting to see Dolly's house, but she wouldn't say a word about the farmhouse or meeting Frank Jeffries. After all, Tripp hadn't been around when the man's name had come up in the conversation.

Or had he? Now that she thought about it, she and the other ladies been sitting out on the driveway eating their lunch when they were talking about Dolly and the problems she'd caused the man. Tripp hadn't been in the immediate vicinity, but that didn't mean anything. The man had some serious stealth skills despite his size.

She tossed a handful of old screwdrivers into a box with more force than necessary. "If you must know, Glenda and a couple of the other women in the quilting guild had mentioned Dolly Cayhill's house, and I wanted to see it for myself."

Tripp tucked his boxful of soldiers under his arm. "And I suppose while you were in the neighborhood, you also decided to look at the property she'd tried to block from being developed."

Well, rats, so he had overheard their conversation. "Yes, I did. Again, I was just curious."

Not for the first time, Tripp tried to intimidate her with his superior height. Glaring down at her, he snapped, "And if you'd run into the contractor? How do you think that would've gone?"

She stood her ground, determined not to let him get the best of her. "For your information, it went just fine. Frank Jeffries doesn't know my name, and he had no idea that I knew who he was. He happened to pull up while Zeke and I were . . ."

When she didn't continue, Tripp stepped closer. "Were what?"

"Okay, fine. I wanted to look at the farmhouse that Dolly had tried to have declared a historical site, which would've prevented Mr. Jeffries from building new houses on that land."

The memory of the rat skittering across the floor still had the power to creep her out. "I can't imagine that dump was worth saving. The roof is caving in, the porch is half-rotted away, and it's infested with rats inside." Not the smartest thing she could've said. The only way she would've seen that last bit was if she was actually standing on those rotted boards.

"So, not only were you on the man's property, you were walking around on a porch that could have collapsed."

Not a question, but she nodded anyway.

"Seriously, Abby, how many times do you have to be reminded that this is a murder case? Someone out there killed that old woman and tossed her body in a hole to rot. Do you have some kind of death wish?"

Fury came off Tripp in waves, the power of it sending her staggering back a couple of steps. "No, of course not. I'm not suicidal."

"Well, you couldn't prove it by me. It's either that, or you've suddenly lost all common sense."

Enough was enough. There was no winning this argument with him, and they both knew it. "I'm done with this for the day."

And by that, she meant both working in the garage and dealing with Tripp's overprotective nature. When he didn't immediately give her some space, she gave him a small shove. When that didn't work, she did it again, this time with a little more force. He stepped aside after a brief hesitation, letting her know without words that it had been his choice.

He followed her outside, a silent but angry shadow on her heels. They both watched the garage door close as if it was the most fascinating thing they'd ever seen. When it finally hit bottom, she stalked away.

"Enjoy your evening." Not that she really meant it.

"I will. And thanks for the toys. It was thoughtful of you."

Oddly enough, she believed he meant that, which made her marginally less mad at him.

But then he just had to add, "I'm meeting Gage to play pool later. Maybe I should let him know what you've been up to."

She spun back to give him a piece of her mind, but he'd already disappeared into his house.

"Snitch."

As she walked away, she was almost sure she heard him say, "Sticks and stones."

Chapter Eleven

Abby had already circled the parking lot at city hall three times looking for a place to park. As soon as she saw a car start to back out in the next row over, she gunned the engine to zip around the end of the aisle. Luck was with her because the driver backed out in the opposite direction, thereby blocking the car approaching from behind him. As a result, Abby managed to whip into the spot before the other driver had a chance. The elderly man drove on past shaking his head. She would've felt worse about commandeering the parking place, but she was already late for her appointment with the mayor's assistant.

After grabbing her purse and the small tablet she'd brought in case she needed to take notes, she hustled into the building. She paused inside the door to catch her breath before crossing the foyer to the part of the building that housed the city administrative offices. As soon as she walked in, she wished she hadn't. Everyone in the room stood frozen in place as Frank Jeffries slammed his clipboard down on the counter and shouted at the poor woman standing in front of him.

"No, for the final time, I don't have an appointment! Regardless, I want to talk to the mayor, and I want to talk to her now. I've had it up to here—" he paused to slash at his forehead with the side of his hand "—with all the excuses and runarounds I've been getting, not just from this office, but the planning commission and that historical bunch, too. Every day they delay costs me money. The mayor makes all this noise about supporting small businesses. But from where I stand, she's not doing a single thing to keep mine from going under."

Maybe a discreet retreat was in order. Before she made it back to the door, the mayor herself walked out of her office to join the conversation. The night Abby had met her, Rosalyn McKay had been both warm and friendly. Right now, she looked as if she could take on an angry bear without hesitation.

"Mr. Jeffries, please lower your voice. People here are trying to work."

To Abby's surprise, the man immediately shut up, but none of the tension in his stance softened in the least. Meanwhile, the mayor glanced around the room and gave the other city employees a pointed look, which immediately set everyone around her back in motion. Evidently satisfied that her employees had gotten the message, she gently nudged the other woman at the counter aside, so that she was the one facing Mr. Jeffries directly.

"Connie, I believe Ms. McCree is here to see you. Why don't you take her into the conference room while I see what I can do to help Mr. Jeffries with his problem?"

Then the mayor opened the gate that separated the small lobby from the desks, her smile to the angry man only slightly warmer now. "Please come in. I have another appointment in about fifteen minutes, but we can talk until then."

After they were gone, Connie drew a deep breath and let it out slowly. "Sorry about that, Ms. McCree. Some days don't always go the way we plan. Come on back, and we'll go over the information I've put together for you about the Committee on Senior Affairs. Would you like some coffee before we get started?"

"I'd love some, and please call me Abby."

The other woman picked up a file folder from her desk before leading the way down a short hall to a door on the far end. "Go on in and make yourself comfortable. Feel free to glance through the file while I get the coffee. Cream or sugar?"

"Black is fine."

"Great, I'll be right back."

Abby took a seat at one end of the large table that nearly filled the room. She flipped through the depressingly thick stack of papers inside the file folder. It was a relief to see that most of it appeared to be informational in nature, the kind of brochures that were meant to familiarize a person with the services already available in town.

Although she did her best to concentrate on the matter at hand, it was nearly impossible to ignore the sound of Mr. Jeffries's still-angry voice coming through the wall that divided the conference room from the mayor's personal office.

There was a momentary lull in the noise just as Connie walked back in with two mugs of coffee. She handed one to Abby and then winced when the racket immediately resumed.

"Abby, I apologize again for . . . well, for the noise. He's a local contractor. I've known him for years, and he's not normally like that."

The temptation to do a little discreet snooping was irresistible. "I met him briefly just recently, and he seemed really nice. My dog had gotten away from me to chase some varmint in the long grass around an abandoned farmhouse. Mr. Jeffries happened to pull up just after I captured Zeke and was heading back down to the street. While we talked, he mentioned having some problems with getting the permits he needed to develop that property. I think he said he wants to build some new homes on it."

Connie nodded as she stirred her coffee. "He was all set to send in the bulldozers when one of the neighbors protested and everything got complicated. His is a fairly small operation, so a setback like this could prove disastrous for him. He wasn't at all happy when I tried to explain that everything still has to go through proper channels, even if the person who originated the complaint is no longer living."

Abby debated how much she should admit to knowing about the situation. Finally, she said, "You're talking about Dolly Cayhill."

"Oh, did you know—" Connie choked back whatever she'd been about to say. "I'm sorry, Abby. I wasn't thinking. You were the one who found her."

"Well, it was really my tenant, Tripp Blackston, but I was there."

"Regardless, that must have been so awful for both of you."

The sound of a door slamming and the ensuing silence made it clear that the discussion between the mayor and Mr. Jeffries had ended. All things considered, Abby figured it hadn't gone particularly well for him. Unfortunately, his abrupt departure seemed to remind Connie that the two of them were there to discuss Senior Affairs, not gossip.

She reached for the folder and said, "Shall we get started?"

Thirty minutes later Abby walked out of city hall into the bright sunshine. Thanks to Connie's efficiency, she now knew a whole lot more about the issues seniors faced in

Snowberry Creek than she had going in. Now she had to figure out what to do with all that newfound knowledge. The next committee meeting wasn't for another three weeks, so she'd think about it later.

Right now, all she wanted to do was go home, fix a cold drink, and doze out on the back porch. That wasn't going to happen, though. She had just enough time to stop at the store for a few things and then have lunch before the executive board of the quilting guild was due to show up on her doorstep. She'd meant to warn Tripp they were coming. He'd mentioned yesterday evening that he planned to mow the yard that afternoon.

Somehow she'd forgotten to tell him, and now he'd have to put up with them standing at her front window and giggling amongst themselves as he pushed the mower back and forth.

She was sure her lapse of memory was due to having so many other things on her mind. It had nothing to do with the fact he'd threatened to snitch to Gage that she was still trying to figure out who'd killed Dolly.

Maybe she'd warn him when she got back home. Maybe not. It all depended on her mood when she got there.

The store was surprisingly crowded for the middle of the day, so she grabbed the few things she really needed and headed toward the checkout. Along the way, she ran into a familiar figure. Almost literally, as Frank Jeffries stepped out of a cross aisle to stand in front of her cart.

She was pretty sure she squeaked at his sudden appearance. "Mr. Jeffries, you startled me."

He didn't apologize. "I must say, you really get around, Ms. McCree. This is the third time our paths have crossed in a very short time. First, out at my property, then at the mayor's office, and now here. Tell me, is that deliberate on your part?"

"No, of course not. I had an appointment with Connie, the mayor's assistant, and I was out of milk. Nothing diabolic about either of those things."

He crossed his arms over his broad chest. "Maybe not. But looking back, I'm guessing snooping around the farmhouse wasn't an accident. Does your sudden curiosity have something to do with Dolly Cayhill's death? You failed to mention you were the one who dug up her body in your aunt's backyard."

Even if she'd tried to lie, the embarrassed flush creeping up her cheeks would have given her away. It didn't help that the other shoppers in their immediate area had stopped to stare, and weren't at all shy about eavesdropping on their conversation.

"If you'll excuse me, Mr. Jeffries. I need to be going."

When she tried to steer her cart around him, he sidestepped to block her escape. "You know, it's bad enough that I'm going broke while everybody else takes their grand old time getting anything done. To make matters worse, the police chief decides to pay me a visit to find out how mad I was about that old woman throwing a wrench in the works."

He leaned in closer. "The bottom line is that I don't need you poking your nose into my business, too. Stay away from me, Abby McCree, and stay away from my property."

Then he walked away without giving her a chance to respond. That was okay. She wasn't sure if she could've come up with anything coherent to say. Several of the people who'd stopped to stare moved on down the aisles, but a few still remained motionless. Didn't they have anything better to do? She picked up a can of green beans and studied the label as if it were the most fascinating reading she'd ever done. After dropping it into her cart, she started forward again, doing her best to ignore the whispered fragments of conversation behind her back.

"Is she the one who found . . ."

"Her dead aunt is the chief suspect . . ."

"That poor woman, thrown in a hole like she was a piece of trash."

"What's this town coming to?"

"What kind of person would do such a thing?"

For a relatively small grocery store, it took forever to reach the end of the aisle. She kept her head down and continued forward, wishing her eyes weren't so blurry. She blinked to clear them. When that didn't work, she dug through her purse to find a tissue to dab at her eyes. She opened them again only to realize that once again, a large man had blocked her way. Her heart did a stutter step. Hadn't Frank Jeffries yelled at her enough for one day?

"Abby, are you okay?"

Thank God, it was Tripp, not Jeffries. Her pulse slowed and breathing became easy again. "I will be when I get out of here."

He came around to her end of the cart and used his fingertip to wipe away a stray tear on her cheek. "What the heck happened now?"

It was tempting to lean in closer to his touch, but now wasn't the time or the place. Taking a still-shaky breath, she tightened her grip on the cart. "Can we not talk about this right now?" Then she realized he'd set an empty handbasket down on the ground. "Really, Tripp, it can wait until you've finished your shopping. I'm okay now."

Clearly, he doubted that, but he stepped out of her way. "I'll stick close until you've checked out."

While she appreciated his concern, she'd already drawn enough attention from the other shoppers for one day. At least the gossips had all scattered when he arrived. Even so, having Tripp tailing after her and glaring at anyone who got close wouldn't help the situation. It took considerable effort to ease up her white-knuckled grip on the cart handle and offer up a small smile. "Seriously, Tripp, I'm on my way out. I'll be fine."

Mainly because she'd just seen Frank Jeffries walk out the front door of the store. Just in case, though, she'd keep a wary eye on him while she paid for her groceries, to make sure he actually left the parking lot.

Tripp turned to see what had caught her attention, but Jeffries was already out of sight. "Okay, but two things before you go."

"Which are?"

He held up his forefinger. "One, I won't be long. I just need milk and bread."

A second finger joined that one. "And two, you *will* tell me who made you cry."

Then he walked away, once again leaving her staring at his broad back. That had become a habit with him, one she didn't much appreciate. It was tempting to call him on it, but for now it was better to opt for discretion. There would be plenty of time to fight it out with him when he got home.

And for the record, there was no way she was going to warn Tripp that his fan club would be on hand to watch him mow the lawn. With that happy thought, she headed for the checkout line.

Abby wasn't sure if she was relieved or disappointed that Tripp had managed to finish mowing the front yard before her fellow board members arrived. She knew how the ladies felt about it, though. All three of them had found a surprising number of excuses to venture into her kitchen, which offered a clear view of where he was working in the backyard.

"I'm going to get another glass of water. Does anyone else need anything?"

Abby's conscience belatedly kicked in, and she decided to get the water herself. She started to reach for Louise's empty glass, but then changed her mind. "Let me get it for you. In fact, I'll fill a pitcher with ice water since you all seem to be extra thirsty today."

The three women couldn't quite hide their disappointment, but too bad. Tripp wasn't performing for their entertainment. Or hers, either, but that didn't keep her from peeking out the window to see how he was progressing on the yard. Another few laps and he'd be done. Hopefully, the pitcher of water would last long enough to afford him some privacy.

She'd managed to avoid the talk he wanted to have when he got home from the store, claiming that the imminent arrival of her guests prevented her from having time. He'd settled for a postponement, not a cancellation. It wasn't likely to be a fun conversation anyway, but his being ogled again by the quilting guild wouldn't help the situation.

On the way out of the kitchen, Abby grabbed the rest of the cookies off the counter to replenish the plate on the dining room table where they were working. She wasn't particularly hungry for any herself, but it might eliminate another possible excuse for the ladies to wander back in that direction.

After topping off everyone's glass, she sat back down at the head of the table. "So, where were we? Glenda, I think you were up next. Can you tell us where we are on the budget for the next year?"

She suspected the group wasn't used to following a set agenda for their meetings, but she was doing her best to hold them to it. There would be plenty of time for idle conversation afterward if they had other things they wanted to talk about.

Glenda dutifully reviewed her notes with them. "The extra money from the garage sale will help make up the shortfall on our projected budget."

She looked up from the page she was studying. "We should still have enough to purchase the necessary supplies for the small quilts we wanted to make, but we won't be able to increase the number over last year's production. While some of us are in a position to make up the difference from our own fabric stashes, that isn't true for some of our members."

Jean fiddled with her pencil, making Abby wonder if she was one of the quilters who did so on a shoestring budget, not that she was about to pry into the woman's finances. On the other hand, why was there a significant shortage in the projected budget? Their membership had remained more or less stable, with enough new members to offset the few who had left the group, so the amount taken in from dues wouldn't account for it.

She'd read through the minutes from past board meetings when she'd agreed to take over Aunt Sybil's term in office, but they weren't all that helpful. Some months, there hadn't been any minutes at all. In others, the notes were little more than the date and who had attended. The regular group meetings where they got together to tie the lap quilts or pick out fabrics to start new ones were more social gatherings than organized meetings. No one ever took attendance or wrote up minutes.

It wouldn't do to say something that might be taken as a criticism. After all, the members of the guild could run their affairs any way they wanted to. After shuffling through a stack of papers that wouldn't contribute anything useful to the conversation, Abby set them back down.

"With everything that's happened, I'm not quite up to speed on what the budget was expected to be, and I apologize for that. Other than dues and the garage sale, was there another source of funding that I'm not aware of?"

Glenda, Jean, and Louise all exchanged looks, maybe deciding whose tale it was to tell. It wasn't a surprise when Glenda sighed and then began speaking.

"Some of this might be hard for you to hear, Abby, and I apologize for that."

Glenda paused as if waiting for some kind of response from her, but Abby didn't know what to say. For one thing, she couldn't possibly imagine what might upset her about the guild's finances. She'd only been part of the group for a short time. Reaching for a cookie she really didn't want, she smiled at the older woman. "Don't worry about it, Glenda. I'll be fine."

Crossing her fingers that was true, she took a healthy bite of the oatmeal cookie and settled back to listen.

"I think we talked about it a little at the garage sale. Do you remember that movie a few years back about the women in England who put together a calendar to raise money to buy a comfortable sofa for the hospital?"

Jean broke in to say, "Theirs was pretty racy."

Glenda rolled her eyes. "Yes, Jean, it was. We all thought so, but it was for a good cause."

"That didn't change the fact it was scandalous."

"Am I telling this story, or are you?"

Jean hunched her shoulders at the rebuke. "Sorry, I was trying to help."

Abby fought to be patient while they worked out their problems. At the same time, she was struggling very hard not to picture what the various members of the guild would look like while posing for "racy" photos, good cause or not. It was all she could do not to shudder at the pictures her overactive imagination was producing.

After giving Jean one last quelling look, Glenda

launched back into her story. "We really wanted to do more for the community, you see. There are so many good uses for the kinds of quilts we make to give away. Even though the patterns are simple ones, the bright colors are cheery. I know we've told you that nursing homes use them for lap quilts, and the police and fire department like to give them to children along with a stuffed animal when something bad happens."

"I can see how much that would mean to folks."

"We all pay dues, of course, and we considered raising the amount. However, that might have meant some members wouldn't have been able to renew. We didn't want to do that to them, and we know a few would walk away before they'd let someone else pay for them. The garage sale provides the bulk of our income, but this is the first really successful sale we've had in years. That left us floundering for what other fundraiser we could do that some other group in town wasn't already doing."

With fewer than two thousand living there, it was easy to see how that could be a problem in a community the size of Snowberry Creek. From what Abby could tell, there were a lot of local groups all vying for the same pot of money—church groups, the schools, the quilting guild, not to mention all the other national charities.

"Anyway, back to the movie. We had a girls' night last fall with pizza, ice cream, and all kinds of goodies."

Louise broke in for the first time. "Do you really think Abby cares what we had to eat that night?"

Glenda looked as if she'd like to argue the point, but she got right back on track. "We were amazed how successful those ladies were with their calendar, and Sybil asked why we couldn't do something similar." She quickly glanced at the other two older women, maybe to forestall any more interruptions. "Nothing like what they did, of course. But maybe a calendar that featured our most special quilts. The only downside was that there would only be thirteen slots available. One for the cover and then one for each month. Jean came up with the idea that to make sure the entire guild was represented, the cover would be the quilt that we all worked on. You saw it when we sold chances for it at the garage sale. At that time, we all thought that was clever thinking on Jean's part, because it would let all of our members participate."

Abby smiled at Jean to acknowledge her genius suggestion. Meanwhile, Glenda paused for a sip of water. Evidently, telling a saga was thirsty work.

"Sybil agreed to do some investigating to see how much it would cost to have a calendar designed and printed. We knew we'd also need a professional photographer to do the pictures. There was no use in doing the project if we weren't going to do it right. All of that would cost money, but there wasn't any extra in the budget to cover any additional expenses. In the end, we decided that the first twelve people who paid a set fee would have their quilts included in the calendar."

Again, smart thinking. The more well-to-do members could provide the initial outlay of money, but the cover would make everyone feel included. It would be interesting to know who all had stepped up to buy a page on the calendar. From what had already been said, Abby was willing to bet that her aunt, Glenda, and Louise had ponied up. Was Dolly Cayhill another member of that select group? Not that it mattered at this point.

"As it turned out, Julie Tolbert, one of our newer members, had studied photography in college. Although she hadn't done any professional work in recent years, she had a few things published in magazines and such when she was younger. She offered to bring her camera to our next meeting and take a few sample pictures so we could see the quality of her work."

When Glenda drifted to a stop again, Louise jumped in to pick up the thread of the story. "The photos she took of one of my quilts with her digital camera were lovely. I even framed them to hang in my sewing room. They were that good."

She paused to dig her cell phone out of the depths of her purse. After bringing up the pictures in question, she passed the phone around so everyone could admire the JPEGs of the shots. Even with the small size of the screen, it was easy to see that there had been a lot of thought put into the lighting and how the quilt was draped to show the pattern at its best advantage.

Handing the phone back, Abby said, "These pictures are great. She's clearly a talented photographer, but don't forget she also had great subject matter to work with. I love the colors in your quilt."

Louise beamed with pride. "Thanks. I designed that pattern. It was some of my best work, if I do say so myself."

Louise's smile didn't last long, as if that last comment had taken the wind out of her sails for some reason. In fact, all three women looked pretty glum. "So, why did the guild decide not to go forward with the project?"

There was another long exchange of looks between the other three ladies before Glenda finally answered. "It wasn't our decision, not exactly anyway. Julie moved away unexpectedly."

So why not hire another photographer? Of course, maybe there hadn't been time to find one and still get the calendar designed and printed in time. But judging by everyone's grim expression, the reason was something far worse.

"What happened?"

Glenda picked up her budget paperwork and shoved it back into a file folder. "We all trusted Julie, you see. She might have been a recent addition to our group, but several of our members knew her through church. When she asked if we'd bring the quilts to her house to photograph, we didn't hesitate. Sybil and I picked up all twelve of the quilts that were supposed to be in the calendar. We asked everyone to wrap their quilts in some way so we couldn't see them. That way, no one but Julie would know what the quilts looked like for sure until she was ready to share the pictures with the whole group. We were still working on the cover quilt, but Julie said that was all right. She could do that one last to give us the extra time to finish it."

The slight tremble in Glenda's hand made it clear that they'd finally reached the dark moment in the story. "She'd said it would only take a few days to take all the shots. That sounded reasonable to us, but we did tell her to take longer if she needed it."

Louise interrupted. "I don't mean to contradict you, Glenda, but what she actually said was that she only *had* a few days to take all the shots. Something about Troy being due back home soon, and they were thinking about taking a short trip. I think she intended to take all the pictures and return the quilts before they left." Then she glanced at Abby. "He's one of those long-haul truck drivers. You know, the kind who is gone for days at a time."

Glenda frowned and then slowly nodded. "I don't re-member it quite that way, but you may be right. Dolly and I were busy making a list of possible sponsors for the cal-endar as well as possible retail spots where we could sell it." She frowned. "Regardless, we didn't think anything of it when three weeks went by without us hearing from her. But when she didn't come to our next monthly meeting, I tried calling her. It went straight to voicemail, so I left a message. I know Sybil tried again a few days later. Dolly was concerned, too."

Jean reached for another cookie. "It was right about then that I heard from a mutual friend that Julie had run off with another man, leaving that nice husband of hers. They'd been married for over twenty years, and Troy had no idea she was so unhappy. The poor man was devastated, and I don't blame him. I can't even imagine walking out on my husband like that. You'd think if they'd been together that long, their marriage would've been rock solid."

Not necessarily, but Abby wasn't going to argue the point. Considering her recent experience with her own ex, she might not be the most impartial judge of what constituted a rock-solid marriage these days. "So what happened to the quilts?"

Jean sighed. "No one knows."

Louise studied the photos of her quilt one last time and then shoved her phone back into her purse. "We asked Troy, but he didn't know anything about them. Julie had never mentioned the quilts or our project to him, and they weren't anywhere in the house. All we can figure is that Julie took them with her."

That didn't make any sense. Why would a woman making a quick getaway waste time packing up twelve quilts. If nothing else, they'd be bulky and take up a lot of room in a car. "But why would she do that?"

For the first time, there was a hint of temper in Glenda's eyes. "In the right shop, they would sell for a lot of money. Each one was special for some reason, and it's left several of us scrambling to replace them."

Abby cringed as she realized which quilt Glenda had lost. "That's why you're having to replicate the one you made for your niece."

A nod was her only answer.

"I'm so sorry. Has anyone heard from Julie since all of this happened? If she had friends here in town, you'd think she would've been in contact with someone."

Louise sighed. "Not that we've heard. I see Troy once in a while. He lives near me, and sometimes he's out working in the yard when I take my walk in the morning. From what I've heard, he keeps hoping she'll come to her senses and return home. I feel bad pestering him about her, though. He just seems so sad whenever her name gets mentioned, and none of this is his fault."

"He's so good to help his neighbors, and he's always the first one to volunteer for projects at his church. I know people have tried to help him out since this happened." Jean paused to look around at the other ladies. "Do you think I should take him another one of my tuna casseroles?"

Abby ignored the memory of Tripp's thoughts on that particular dish and said, "I'm sure he'd appreciate knowing that you're thinking of him."

While Jean beamed in response, Glenda frowned. "That's got me to thinking, Abby. I don't suppose you'd be willing to approach Troy one more time about the quilts?"

Before Abby could say that she didn't want to do that, Glenda kept talking. "I know he's already said he doesn't know anything about them several times, but that was weeks and weeks ago. Maybe he's finally heard from Julie by now or at least has found out where she is."

Louise took the ball and ran with it. "What a great idea, Glenda. Even if he doesn't want to talk to her, we could contact her ourselves. Abby, if you mentioned that you'd only recently found out about the calendar project, surely he'd understand why you're bringing it up again."

She so didn't want to do that, but what would it hurt? If it meant possibly getting back even a few of the quilts, it would be worth a few minutes of her time. She could always pass by his house on the pretext of walking Zeke.

"Fine. No promises, but I'll try."

"That's all anyone can do." Then Glenda glanced at the grandfather clock in the corner. "Would you look at the time? We should help Abby clean up and then head out. I have a couple of stops to make on the way home."

All three women were up and moving before Abby could protest. "Just leave everything. I can take care of it after you're gone."

Too late. They grabbed everything and headed right for the kitchen. Maybe they were hoping for one last peek at Tripp. She doubted they were going to have much luck, considering the lawnmower had shut off some time ago. Still, who was she to crush their hopes?

As they filed out of the house, making sure that Jean made it down the steps safely with her walker, Abby continued to ponder the mystery of the lost quilts. Had they reported the theft, which is what it was, to the authorities? It was a shame if they hadn't, because maybe the police could have tracked down Julie Tolbert and gotten at least some of them back.

She had to wonder which one had Aunt Sybil had decided to feature in the calendar. There was no way to know, since the ladies had decided to keep their choices secret even from each other. But if she could somehow prove it was the one she and Sybil had made together, that someone else had had it . . . well, that would be something else that maybe Gage would find interesting.

Chapter Twelve

Waiting for Tripp to show up on her doorstep to have the dreaded talk about Frank Jeffries felt a lot like the one time in middle school when she'd been sent to detention after class. She'd gotten into a debate with one of her teachers regarding the Vietnam War, and the old witch didn't much like it when Abby had proved her wrong on several points.

Looking back, she'd no doubt embarrassed the woman in front of the other students, but that didn't excuse the woman from retaliating by kicking her out of class with no warning. She'd never been in trouble before, and the sense of dread while she waited to speak to the vice principal had left her almost physically ill.

To make matters worse, her mother had been called to come pick up Abby afterward. Considering her mom had to take off work, it had been a really long ride home. Nothing like being a captive audience in the car with a pissed-off parent to make for an unpleasant drive. She'd ended up having to write an apology to the teacher, not that she'd meant a single word in the entire note. All things considered, she still hated that woman.

Today's situation wasn't quite the same. Regardless, she was willing to bet that Tripp wasn't going to believe the confrontation at the grocery store hadn't been her fault any more than her mother had believed Abby had been the innocent one that day in school.

Well, she wasn't going to cower inside the house. Picking up her book, she grabbed a soft drink out of the fridge and headed outside to enjoy the warm afternoon sun. For one long moment, she thought about dragging her favorite chair down off the porch and around to the front of the house. If Tripp was determined to yell at her, he might be less likely to do so where anyone driving by could see him being a big bully.

However, that was cowardly on her part. If he wanted to yell, so be it. She'd done nothing wrong or particularly stupid this time. She'd make her position on the subject perfectly clear to him and then get on with her day. Her plans made, she settled back in the chair and opened the book to the last page she'd read. Fifteen minutes later and thoroughly disgusted, she closed the book and tossed it on the floor at her feet. Thank goodness there wasn't going to be a pop quiz on what she'd just read because she would've failed that test. It was impossible to concentrate on words on a page when her mind insisted on going in so many other directions.

At least the sound of a nearby door opening and closing gave her something else to focus on. A few seconds later, Tripp rounded the corner headed straight for her. Zeke, who'd been dozing in the shade under a nearby tree, immediately perked right up and headed straight for his buddy. Tripp paused to give the furry traitor a head-to-toe scratching that had the dog's tail going a million miles an hour.

Zeke gave himself a thorough shake before heading up onto the porch with Tripp, who took the other chair without waiting for an invitation. Zeke stopped at the top of the steps to look first at her and then at his friend, maybe sensing all was not well between his two favorite people. Rather than pick sides, he erred on the side of caution and immediately retreated to his spot in the shade.

The corner of Tripp's mouth quirked up in a hint of a grin. "Smart dog."

She couldn't argue with that assessment. It was tempting to join Zeke down there in the grass, but she suspected Tripp wouldn't be far behind. Instead of launching right into whatever lecture he'd prepared since they'd last crossed paths, he popped the top on the beer he'd brought with him and took a long drink.

The suspense was killing her. The vice principal at her middle school had nothing on Tripp when it came to making her squirm. She wasn't going to make it easy on him, though. To give herself something else to do besides fidget, she reached for her book. He wouldn't know that she wasn't really paying attention to the story as she skimmed the pages.

She'd only gotten as far as the second paragraph when he finally spoke. "Okay, tell me what was going on at the store today."

Taking her time, she pretended to finish the page before carefully closing the book and setting it aside. "I did the same thing everyone else did. I bought groceries."

If looks could kill, she'd be splattered all over the backyard right now. For some reason, that improved her mood considerably.

"You'd been crying, Abby." He turned to look right at her. "Explain. What. Happened."

Although his voice remained calm and quiet, each of those last three words had enough edge in them to cut glass.

"Fine. You already know that Zeke and I walked past Dolly Cayhill's house and then stopped to take a look at the farmhouse that she wanted declared a historical building to prevent it from being bulldozed. We were already on our way off the property when Frank Jeffries pulled up. At no point did I tell him who I was or why I was there. I let him think that I'd chased Zeke down after he'd gotten away from me to chase some varmint."

In fact, Tripp had planned to snitch to Gage Logan about that. She wasn't going to ask if he'd carried out that particular threat in case he'd actually forgotten about it.

"Well, this morning I had an appointment at city hall with Connie Pohler, the mayor's executive assistant. She was supposed to go over my duties as the new head of the Committee on Senior Affairs here in Snowberry Creek."

A big grin flashed across Tripp's face. "So how did you get roped into that?"

She let some of her own grumpy feelings on the subject show. "If you must know, I was volunteered. It seems Glenda and her buddies told the mayor that since I'd stepped up to take Aunt Sybil's position on the quilting guild's board for the rest of her term, I'd be happy to fill in on this committee, too. The only reason I went to the city council meeting was to accept the plaque the city wanted to present to me honoring Sybil's service to Snowberry Creek over the years. As it turned out, I accepted a whole lot more than that."

His smile faded a just a bit. "You could've turned them down."

As if it had been that easy. "Do you think I didn't try? I pointed out that there were a lot of people who already knew a lot more about the subject than I do, but that didn't fly. The good news is that they have someone else set to take over in the fall when he's recuperated from hip replacement surgery, so my tenure is only for the short term."

He took another drink of his beer, murmuring something

that sounded like "sucker." She couldn't argue with his assessment of the situation, so she didn't bother trying.

"Anyway, when I walked into city hall, Mr. Jeffries was already there, yelling at Connie and anyone else who'd listen to him. I guess he thought that once it was learned that Dolly was dead, his problems with getting permits and stuff would simply go away. The delays are costing him money and making his investors twitchy. Eventually, Mayor McKay came out and invited him into her office. I have no idea what she told him, but from the sound of their voices, it wasn't a happy conversation."

"And how did you end up in the middle of it?"

"I didn't. I hung back, out of the way. He was awfully angry, but he made no threatening moves toward anyone as far as I know. If he had, I'm sure the mayor would have notified the police. Considering their headquarters is on the other side of the lobby, they'd have gotten there in a hurry."

She let the events play out in her head. "When the mayor came out, she told Connie to take me down the hall to the conference room so we could go over the material about the committee. Unfortunately, she called me by name, and he must have connected the dots at some point. In a town this size, it's only to be expected that folks would find out the body was found in my backyard, even if they sort of kept my address out of the papers."

"So he tore into you at city hall?"

"No, he was already gone when I got out of my meeting with Connie. I went straight from the meeting to the store."

Her temper flared hot and bright. "How the heck was I supposed to know the big jerk needed groceries, too? He stood right there in the middle of the store, blocking my way, and accused me of following him. I'm not sure he believed me when I denied it. Anyway, he was practically yelling by that point, announcing to everybody within hearing that I was the one who'd dug up Dolly's body in my aunt's backyard. If there was anyone in the store who didn't already know that, they did by the time he got done railing at me."

No longer able to sit still, she lurched up out of her chair to pace the few steps across the porch and back, nearly falling over Tripp's big feet in the process. "Mr. Jeffries was so upset, and he probably had every right to be, not that any of it was my fault. From what he said, Gage had been by to talk to him about the murder, wanting to know just how mad he'd been at Dolly for interfering with his planned development."

Tripp joined her by the railing. Unlike Frank Jeffries, his big presence was comforting rather than scary. "Did he threaten you?"

The deep growl in Tripp's voice brought Zeke to his feet. The dog was now at full attention and standing guard.

"No, not really. He crowded me a bit, but that was all. I was mostly embarrassed by the amount of attention we were getting. He told me to stay away from him and his property." She managed a small smile. "For what it's worth, I had already made the decision to avoid him in the future. And I meant what I said, running into him twice today was purely accidental."

After a second, Tripp nodded. "I believe you. I would point out that if you'd stayed away from his land in the first place none of this would've happened."

"Thanks, Mr. Hindsight-Is-Twenty-Twenty. I would've never figured that out for myself."

"I had a great lecture all planned, but I think you've learned your lesson."

She crossed her arms over her chest and widened her stance. A girl had to use every weapon in her arsenal to stand up against an oversized, overprotective male. "Don't push it, Tripp. At the risk of sounding like a five-year-old, you're not the boss of me."

He mirrored her stance, pulling it off with far greater success than she had thanks to his superior height. "I want your word that you won't go poking that cute nose of yours into Gage's investigation again. It's already gotten you into enough trouble."

"Again, not my boss. Besides, I don't think Frank Jeffries did it."

Tripp tipped his head to one side to stare down at her. "And what brought you to that conclusion, Sherlock?"

She wasn't even sure when she'd decided that, but it felt right. "There's no way that crappy farmhouse would have ended up on the historical register. I doubt it was ever a showcase, and right now it's on the verge of collapsing in on itself. It was only a matter of time before he would've gotten his permits. It might have taken longer than he liked, but it wouldn't have been worth killing over. Well, unless his investors did pull their funding, but he made it sound as if that hadn't happened yet."

And as long as they didn't, that left her with no viable suspect. "There has to be someone else, someone with a more compelling reason to have wanted her dead. Did Gage mention who stands to inherit Dolly's house? Is it the niece?"

Tripp threw up his hands. "Give it a rest, Abby! For the last time, it's not your job to figure out who killed that old woman, and every question you ask brings you that much closer to being in the crosshairs of a killer. Do you really think he or she would hesitate to kill again? Even if the first time was an accident, which I don't believe for a minute, feeling cornered will only make it more likely the killer will strike out again. I don't want to find you wrapped up in a quilt and buried in a hole someplace."

Now there was an image guaranteed to give her night-mares. She didn't want that either. It was time to shift gears.

"Just tell me this much. You played pool with Gage last night. Did it sound like he'd made any real progress on the case?"

"We played pool and drank beer, Abby, at a concrete bunker of a bar out in the boonies with some other former soldiers. Maybe things are different on a girls' night out, but we were having fun giving each other grief and blowing off steam. The last thing any of us wanted to do was talk about killing people. That's the kind of thing we would prefer to keep in the past."

That last comment made it clear she'd once again brought back some bad memories for him. Rather than apologize, she changed subjects. "I'm going to order pizza for dinner tonight. Want to split an extra-large?"

The abrupt change in topics had him staring at her and looking a little confused. Then he asked the all-important, manly question. "That depends. Will it be a proper pizza loaded down with meat?"

She laughed. "What's the matter, soldier boy? Afraid of a few veggies?"

His sneer was perfection. "No, but I like my veggies in a bowl and smothered in bleu cheese dressing, not getting in the way of pepperoni and sausage."

"Fine, pepperoni and sausage and two side salads will be my contribution to dinner. You take care of drinks and dessert, which can be store bought as long as it's packed with sugary goodness . . . and chocolate."

The shadows that had darkened his eyes when he men-tioned killing people were gone now. "Got it. Meet you out here at about six?"

"It's a deal."

Chapter Thirteen

Today was the one day Abby would have preferred Zeke to take his good old time wandering down the sidewalk. But instead of stopping to visit each of his favorite bushes and trees along the way, for some mysterious reason he had decided that it was time to take up power walking.

Tugging on his leash only proved marginally effective at slowing him down. "Darn it, Zeke, I'm in no hurry to get where we're headed."

He just woofed and kept chugging right on down the street, leaving her no choice but to keep up with him as best she could. She'd put off trying to talk to Troy Tolbert for two days, in the futile hope that the ladies would forget they'd even brought it up. She should've known better. Glenda had called last night to see if she'd had any success in her assigned mission. Her friend had pretended to believe that Abby had been busy with other things, but her disappointment had still come across the phone line loud and clear.

In a last ditch effort to avoid having to bother the poor man, she'd done some online searches to see if she could track down Julie Tolbert through various types of social media. Although there was nothing on Twitter or several other outlets, she did find the woman's Facebook page. That was the good news. The bad news was that the page didn't appear to have been updated since Julie had posted a couple of pictures taken at a church service on Christmas Eve. That wasn't particularly helpful and neither was the fact that if Julie had posted anything else, it was all private. Unfortunately, that left Abby no choice but to make good on her promise to talk to Troy Tolbert about his wife.

Her plan was to approach him after wandering past Dolly Cayhill's house again, to see if there was any sign of activity. She still hadn't figured out who had actually inherited the place. Glenda hadn't heard, and Abby hadn't spoken to either Jean or Louise since their board meeting. After scoping out Dolly's house, she'd circle around the block in the opposite direction of Frank Jeffries's land. No way would she risk running into him again, and her chosen route would take her right past Troy's house. Since he was a long haul trucker, chances were good he wouldn't be home anyway, but at least she'd be able to tell Glenda that she'd tried.

"Darn it, slow down, Zeke. Please."

This time he finally listened. He abruptly sat down in the shade of a vine maple, offering up a doggy grin as if particularly proud of himself. She patted his head as she pulled his collapsible water bowl out of her pack and filled it with bottled water. He cheerfully lapped it up, storing a fair portion of the water in his jowls, no doubt planning to drool on her at the first opportunity.

She finished off the rest of the bottle herself while they both caught their breath. It was the perfect spot to linger for a while. From where they stood, she had a clear view of Dolly's house, which was a hive of activity right now. There were four elderly ladies standing on the front porch listening intently to whatever a younger woman was telling them.

Their body language indicated the conversation wasn't a happy one. From the sharp way the young woman's hands were waving in the air, she wasn't in the best of moods, either.

It was hard to tell from a distance, but two of the older women looked familiar. She was pretty sure they were the ones who'd given her the cold shoulder that day at Bridey's coffee shop. Nice to know she wasn't the only one who didn't much care for their attitude. There was no way to know what was really going on, but it appeared that the younger woman was guarding the door into Dolly's house, while the older women seemed just as determined to come inside.

Well, they might have had her outnumbered, but she eventually managed to drive them off. Abby would give anything to know what she'd said to them, because they clearly took exception to it. Right now, they were filing down off the porch, righteous indignation clear in each step they took. It was probably rude to laugh, but she couldn't help herself.

The sound must have carried the rest of the way down the block. All four of them immediately turned in her direction like a pack of hunting dogs going on point. Great, now they were headed straight for her. Deciding it would be cowardly to run, she planted her feet and stood her ground.

Well, actually, she stood behind Zeke.

It didn't take long for the gaggle of women to reach her. It was tempting to fire the opening salvo, something both sassy and rude, but these women were Aunt Sybil's contemporaries. She wouldn't have approved of Abby going on the attack unless provoked.

Three of the women formed up in a shoulder-to-shoulder line behind the fourth, marking her as their leader. She glared first at Abby and then at Zeke. He normally greeted newcomers with a wag of the tail and a friendly doggy smile, but not this time. Maybe he sensed their hostility and didn't know what to make of it. When he shifted slightly to face them more directly, all four backed up a step.

The leader glared at Abby. "If that . . . that beast makes one aggressive move toward us, I will call Animal Control."

All right, then. That's how it was going to be.

"Zeke has never met a person he didn't like." She curled her lip just a little and gave the four women a withering look. "Until now. If you'll excuse us, ladies, we have places to be."

She gave Zeke's leash a tug, ready to move on, the situation no longer amusing in the least. The women, though, had other ideas. Evidently their encounter with the woman at Dolly's house had left them fired up and with no target for their temper other than Abby.

"You, young lady, are just as rude and arrogant as your aunt was."

Enough was enough. Abby drew herself up to her full height, shoulders back, and stared down at her diminutive opponent. "My aunt was a lady, first, last, and always. She was only ever rude to those who deserved it. That's obviously more than I can say about the four of you."

They gasped in chorus. Had they really thought she'd stand there and cower?

"Now, we'll be on our way."

Before Abby could go two steps, the woman upped the ante. "Bad manners obviously run in your family. It's bad enough that Sybil did her best to poison us just to get herself elected as head of the quilting guild."

Seriously? They were still spouting that line of crap? "My aunt would not have poisoned anyone. It was just some bad crab dip, for Pete's sake. Who knows what happened? Maybe Mrs. Cayhill used tainted mayonnaise."

"That's ridiculous. That was Dolly's prize recipe. She took pride in it and wouldn't have embarrassed herself by using substandard ingredients."

Speaking of embarrassing. Never in a million years would she have expected to be standing on a public street arguing about the quality of someone's crab dip ingredients. It was past time to be moving on.

"Come on, boy, let's go."

The women retreated to a safe distance as soon as Zeke moved. They waited until Abby's back was turned to fire one more shot.

"We all know what really happened to your *dear* Aunt Sybil."

She shouldn't respond. She really shouldn't, not if she was going to be smart about this. Evidently, she wasn't feeling all that bright right now because she whirled back around. "And what is that?"

"Let's just say that everyone thinks Sybil died of a heart attack, but it was really guilt over what she did to Dolly that killed her. And until the truth comes out, we will be keeping pressure on the police to admit that there is only one logical culprit in our friend's death—your aunt. Everyone else loved Dolly."

The old woman poked her finger toward Abby. "And Gage Logan might think he can protect that thug Tripp Blackston, but the truth will come out. When it does, he will pay for his part in Dolly's death. We will also make sure the city council knows about Gage's dereliction of his duty. Even if that doesn't result in criminal charges against him, too, I'm sure he'll have a hard time finding another job in law enforcement."

There was so much wrong with the woman's assessment of the facts. For starters, not everyone loved Dolly Cayhill, and Aunt Sybil had been an avowed pacifist. Besides, Sybil

wouldn't have been dumb enough to hide the body in her
own backyard. She also wouldn't have used her own quilt
as a shroud, especially the one she'd promised to Abby.

"You're wrong about my aunt and even more wrong
about Tripp. For your information, he spent twenty years
serving our country. Like Gage, he's a hero who deserves
your respect, not your stupid, vicious, and small-minded
suspicions."

There was so much more she wanted to say, to rail
against the injustice of their attack, not only on her aunt,
but Tripp as well. However, the lump of grief and anger in
her throat choked off her ability to talk. She also hated—
HATED—that once again she was reduced to tears in
public. At least Zeke knew what to do. He licked Abby's
hand and then started walking, dragging her along in his
wake. She stumbled along after him, glad that at least one
of them had enough sense to get away from such awful
women. Once they'd gone a few steps, she used the hem of
her shirt to wipe away the evidence of how much they'd
upset her.

They'd almost reached the far end of the block when the
sound of a car slowly approaching from behind them had
her hurrying her steps. There was no way she wanted to go
a second round with Dolly's fan club. Keeping her eyes
straight ahead, she urged Zeke to pick up speed. Whoever
was driving the car wasn't giving up. It sped up just enough
to get in front of them and stopped.

As soon as she recognized Gage Logan, her first reaction was relief. Her second was a mild rush of panic. No
way did she want him to see she'd been crying, but luck
definitely wasn't on her side today. He'd already parked and
was climbing out of the squad car to head right for her.

"Abby, are you all right?"

She figured her smile was more crazy than convincing,

but she gave it her best shot. "I'm fine, Gage. Zeke and I are just making our rounds."

She would've kept on walking, but Gage blocked her way. What was it with men planting their big feet in front of her this week? And traitor that he was, Zeke parked his backside on the sidewalk and waited to be petted. Gage took off his hat and ran his fingers through his hair. After shooting a frustrated look back in the direction she'd come, he asked, "Tell me, what did those women say to upset you?"

Then, without waiting for her response, he pointed toward Dolly Cayhill's house. "Allison Samuels, that's Mrs. Cayhill's niece, called me about them. Evidently, they showed up on her doorstep making a bunch of crazy demands. She ordered them off the property, but she was afraid they wouldn't stay gone."

They both looked back toward the women, who were just now getting into a car. "By the way, they gave me an earful about you and your vicious dog."

Luckily he was smiling when he said that last part or else she would've gone charging back down the street to tear into them but good. Instead, she patted Zeke on the head and slipped him a couple of treats.

"He was a perfect gentleman the whole time. If anyone was vicious in that discussion, it was them." Petting Zeke helped to hide her shaky hands. "They've convinced themselves that Aunt Sybil killed their friend and then died out of guilt. If that wasn't bad enough, they think you're covering up for Tripp. They still think he was Aunt Sybil's accomplice in all of this."

Gage looked thoroughly disgusted. "I know. I'm afraid nothing will change their minds until the actual culprit is behind bars."

If only it were that easy. "And the truth is that maybe not

even then, Gage. They are so angry. It's not bad enough that they tell everyone who'll listen that Aunt Sybil tried to poison the entire quilting guild. No, she has to be a cold-blooded murderer, too."

"I'm sorry, Abby. I'll talk to them again."

"Don't bother on my account. They've lost a friend in a horrible fashion, which is making them lash out because they're hurting."

Regardless, her anger over their attack only strengthened her resolve to make sure the truth over Dolly's death came out. She owed that much to both Aunt Sybil and Tripp.

They both watched as the women slowly drove past, all four of them glaring at both Gage and Abby. He shook his head as they turned the corner and drove out of sight. "Look, I can give you a ride home if you and Zeke want one."

She actually considered accepting his offer, but she'd already come this far. She'd continue past Troy Tolbert's house and then head back home. Otherwise, she'd have to walk this way again tomorrow, perhaps risking running into those women again if they did come back to bother Dolly's niece a second time. "No, we're fine, but thanks anyway."

"Okay, if you're sure. If they come after you again, though, let me know. I will put a stop to their interference in my case, even if it means I have to haul them off to jail. Maybe spending a night in a cell will give them a much-needed attitude adjustment."

Okay, that was a hoot, and she didn't bother trying to hide her laughter. "Can you imagine how they'd react to that? And I bet Reilly Molitor would have a heyday with that story."

Gage's answering grin was evil. "Yeah, he probably would. Can you imagine the shock of seeing their mugshots plastered on the front page of the *Clarion*? Their reputations would be ruined."

"Or it just might cement their reputations among their friends. Martyrs for the cause, you know. Any chance they'd have to wear one of those orange jumpsuits for the photo shoot? I'm pretty sure that's not a good color for any of them."

"Abby, now you're just being mean." He settled his hat back on his head. "But I like the way you think."

As he headed around the front end of his cruiser and opened the door, she considered asking him a question or two while she had the chance. Either he'd answer, or he wouldn't.

"Have you cleared Frank Jeffries of any involvement in Dolly's death?"

Okay, just that quickly the good-humored lawman was gone. "I thought I'd made it clear that I don't appreciate anyone poking their nose into my investigation. Not those ladies, and not you. What were you doing talking to him, anyway?"

"We crossed paths at city hall the other day. He said you'd been talking to him."

Which was more, or really less, than the truth.

Police chiefs must have a sixth sense when it came to interrogations. Gage slammed his car door shut and marched back over to the sidewalk. "And the subject of Mrs. Cayhill's murder just happened to come up in the conversation?"

So Tripp hadn't carried through on his threat to snitch to Gage about her confrontation with the contractor, not that it mattered now. She was well and truly busted.

"Zeke and I were out walking the other day, and we came down this same street so I could see where Dolly lived. I was just curious. Anyway, some of the ladies in the quilting guild happened to mention how upset Frank Jeffries was when she threw a roadblock in his plans to tear down an old farmhouse and build on the land. Since I was already in the neighborhood, I might have wandered onto his property to look around."

Gage looked at her as if she'd just sprouted a second head. "Might have, or did?"

"Okay, fine, I did. So I went up on the porch to see if the place really was worth saving, or if she'd interfered because she didn't want to look at a bunch of lesser homes over her back fence. I was just leaving when Mr. Jeffries pulled up. We didn't exchange names, so he didn't learn who I was. That didn't happen until he heard the mayor call me by name at city hall."

Might as well tell him all of it. "When he ran into me afterward at the grocery store, he was still upset from his discussion with the mayor. Evidently, he's worried that the delay in getting his permits is making some of his funding for the project a little shaky. I was just a handy target for his temper. He told me that you'd been out to talk to him about his problems with Dolly. And then Mr. Jeffries told me to stay away from him and his property, which I have, and I will."

It was nothing but the truth, but Gage didn't look convinced. With that suspicious nature of his, no wonder he and Tripp were such good friends. "If you've already seen Mrs. Cayhill's house and promised to stay away from Frank's place, why are you walking through this area? It's not like you don't have an entire town full of other streets to choose from."

Seriously, the man was like a dog with a bone, although that might be an insult to Zeke and his brethren. "Because Glenda, Louise, and Jean asked me to drop by and check on a member of our quilting guild to see how she's doing. Her house is on the next block over."

Again, that was the truth even if she'd glossed over the details a bit. It wasn't as if Gage had any vested interest in what happened to a bunch of quilts. It was a relief when he once again relaxed and headed back to get into his car.

Before climbing inside, he stopped to give her one last long look. "I repeat, if those ladies give you any more grief, I want to hear about it. That's the same thing I told Mrs. Samuels, too. No matter what they think, the law says she has every right to dispose of the estate as she sees fit."

"So they have issues with whatever she has planned to do?"

"They seriously want her to turn that house into some kind of museum or some such idiocy. Actually, it sounded more like it would be the Dolly Cayhill Shrine." Then he winced. "Sorry, that was unprofessional. Please forget I said anything."

She winked at him and cupped her ear. "What? Did you say something? I didn't quite catch that."

He grinned and did a drumroll with his hands on the roof of the car. "Take care, Abby. Tell Tripp I want a rematch soon. I ended up buying four rounds the other night."

She waved one last time as he drove off.

"Zeke, you've been most patient. Let's swing by Troy's house, verify he's off on a road trip, and then head home. I'm ready to be done with this day."

Her furry friend woofed his agreement and charged off down the sidewalk.

They'd only gone a short distance down the street when she heard someone running in her direction. With everything that had happened, she hurried her steps even as she glanced back to check out the woman coming up behind her at a fast clip. Even though she'd only seen her from a distance, Abby immediately recognized her as Dolly's niece.

"Excuse me, but Chief Logan just told me that you're Abby McCree."

Not at all sure she wanted to admit it, Abby nodded
anyway. She couldn't very well call Gage a liar.

After taking a few seconds to catch her breath, the
woman said, "My name is Allison Samuels. I believe you
knew my aunt, Dolly Cayhill."

Still feeling her way into this conversation, Abby shook
her head. "No, actually I never had the pleasure of meeting her."

Not while she was alive anyway.

Allison snorted. "I'm not sure it would've been a pleasure. To say Aunt Dolly could be difficult is putting it
mildly. All rigid good manners and God help you if you
didn't live up to her standards. I never quite managed to do
that and gave up trying years ago."

Before Abby could decide on a safe response to that
comment, Allison continued talking. "Would you mind
coming back to the house for a few minutes? I promise I
won't keep you long. You're on my list of people I need to
talk to, but I'd rather not hang out here on the sidewalk in
case those lovely ladies decide to cruise by again."

"Sure, why not?" Especially considering Abby had
questions for Allison, too, not to mention she'd love to get
a peek inside Dolly's house. "Unless you mind Zeke coming
inside, too. I don't want to leave him alone."

"He's a good-looking dog." Allision immediately held
her hand out to let Zeke sniff it. She smiled when he gave
it a sloppy lick. "Having him come with us won't be a problem. My aunt wouldn't have approved and neither would
her friends, but it's my place now."

As they walked the short distance back to the house,
Abby studied her companion. Allison looked to be a few
years older than Abby was, maybe just a year or two past
forty. There was an air of no-nonsense about the woman.
She had on a plain white T-shirt with jeans and wore her

dark blond hair pulled back in a ponytail. With no makeup and the simple gold studs in her ears, she wouldn't have stood out in any crowd.

She opened the front door and stood back to let Abby and Zeke walk inside and then ushered them into the living room. "Have a seat. Like I said, I won't take much of your time, but I've been wanting to talk to you."

Abby couldn't imagine why, but it was too late now. Bracing herself for the worst, she waited until she was seated on the couch before asking, "What can I do for you?"

Allison perched on the edge of an uncomfortable-looking chair. "First, I wanted to say I'm sorry that bunch of old hens tore into you after I ran them off. They had no right to take their anger out on you."

"That wasn't your fault."

"Maybe not, but I still feel bad about it." Allison shrugged. "Anyway, Gage stopped by to make sure I was all right just after you escaped their evil clutches."

"And were you okay?"

"For the most part, yeah." She leaned back in her chair and sighed. "All of this has been a major upheaval in my life. My aunt and I weren't really close, and the last thing I expected was to be named the executrix in her will. You would've thought she might have had the courtesy to ask me first, but that was Aunt Dolly for you." Her expression turned more serious. "I'm guessing her death has been hard on you, too. That whole mess must have been awful."

What could Abby say to that? She settled on the truth. "It was really horrible. No one expects to have something like that happen or knows how to deal with it when it does."

Allison pinched the bridge of her nose as if fighting a headache. "I know the police are doing everything they can to figure out who did it. But to be honest, I'm not holding out much hope. From what I've been told, Gage Logan has a solid reputation in police circles, but they always say the longer a murder goes unsolved, the less chance they'll find out who did it. According to what they told me, she'd already been dead for several months when you found her. Again, it's just a real shame you got sucked into this mess."

"It wasn't your fault, much less Dolly's."

That was true on both counts.

Allison's concern seemed sincere, though, spurring Abby to ask a few questions of her own. "Has it been hard for you to deal with everything? Have those ladies been bothering you a lot?"

"Yes, on both counts. I had to take a personal leave from my job to deal with everything involved in settling the estate. I work in the office at one of the big apple orchards over in eastern Washington. They promised to hold my job for me as long as they can."

"That's good. I know from personal experience that settling an estate can get complicated, especially if not everyone is happy with the terms of the will or trust."

Which was true. Aunt Sybil's late husband had two cousins who thought the house should have stayed in their family. Fortunately, the attorney who had set up the trust had made darn sure it was rock solid. In an effort to appease them, Abby had made arrangements to ship them, at her own expense, the pieces of furniture that Sybil had wanted them to have. Only one of them had been gracious enough to send a thank-you note.

Allison sighed and shrugged. "I'm doing the best I can to take care of things, but it's complicated. You could've knocked me over with a feather when I learned she'd left the house and almost everything in it to me. Like I said, we weren't close. However, I was her last blood relative, and pedigree was everything to Dolly."

She fell silent for a second. "Anyway, there are a few

items that she left to other people, which is why those awful women have been camped out on my front porch. They're afraid I'll ignore Dolly's wishes and sell off the items she promised them, which isn't true. Like I told them, I've already packed those items and set them aside until the lawyer gives me the okay to hand them over. There were also a few organizations that she wanted to receive specific amounts of money."

She met Abby's gaze head on. "Which is where you come in. I understand that you're the current head of the quilting guild that Aunt Dolly belonged to."

"I am."

"Well, for starters, Aunt Dolly bequeathed her fabric collection to the guild members to divide up however seems fair to the group. She also wanted to make a cash donation to support their charity projects."

Abby almost choked when Allison went on to name a five-figure amount. It took some effort to clear her throat enough to breathe again. "Really? Wow, the ladies will be thrilled. That will fund their projects for years to come. Are you sure about the amount? That seems like an awful lot of money."

"Aunt Dolly could afford it. And to be honest, the guild is just one of several groups in town that she mentioned in her will. There's a whole list of stuff I'm supposed to give to specific people, and some of it seems pretty odd."

"Like what?"

"Dolly wanted some kid in town to have her late husband's medals from his time in the army during World War II. She left him some money, too. Something about a college fund."

That made sense. "I'm guessing you're talking about JB Burton. Dolly got to know him awhile back when he did some work around the house for her. They ended up friends of a sort. He's an honor student who earned an appointment to West Point."

Allison smiled. "Hearing that makes me glad she decided to help him. She also named your aunt in the will, so that particular item would have ended up coming to you. At least that's what the lawyer said."

From everything Abby had heard about the rocky relationship between Dolly and her aunt, she couldn't imagine why the woman would've left Sybil anything at all. Curiosity more than anything else had her asking, "What on earth did she leave Sybil?"

"It was one of her quilts. Unfortunately, I haven't been able to find it anywhere in the house. Aunt Dolly was one of those disgustingly organized people. She made a notebook for me to use to identify the items listed in her will. Along with the contact information for the recipient, she wrote a detailed description of the item, where it came from, where it was in the house, and even included a color photograph. I'm still going through things, but the quilt isn't with the rest of her collection."

And there they were back to the missing quilts. "I think I know what might have happened to it." Abby quickly explained the situation to Allison. "It doesn't seem likely that we'll ever know what happened to all of the quilts, which is a real shame."

Maybe it was time to change the subject. She glanced around the room and into the adjoining dining room. "Looks like you've got a lot of stuff to go through. It's quite a job, isn't it?"

Allison nodded. "Yeah, I figure it's going to take me months to sort through it all. I know Aunt Dolly was really proud of this place, but her taste in decorating and mine are nothing alike. I haven't decided if I'm going to keep the house or sell it. It seems silly to rattle around in a big place like this all by myself. On the other hand, it is paid for."

"Yeah, I've had similar thoughts on the house my aunt left me. I've been slowly working my way through everything one room at a time. It's amazing how much worthless stuff people hang on to for no good reason."

That had Allison laughing. "Amen, sister. While you're here, would you like to get the grand tour?"

"I'd love it."

About forty-five minutes later, Abby said good-bye as she and Zeke resumed their walk. Along the way, it occurred to her that the unplanned encounter with the heir to Dolly's estate had eliminated another viable suspect in the woman's murder. Considering how much she'd liked Allison, she should've been relieved. Instead, she was frustrated big time. She'd done everything she could think of to figure out who would've benefited from Dolly's death, but she was no closer to clearing her aunt's name.

As she continued her march down the sidewalk, she looked around her and studied her surroundings. Snowberry Creek was a pretty town with lots of nice people living in it. But she shivered as she passed each neat and tidy house, because, despite the warmth of the sun overhead, she had to wonder which one sheltered a cold-blooded killer.

Chapter Fourteen

That cheery thought made her want to go straight home and barricade herself inside, but there was still one pressing item left on her agenda. At least it should be relatively simple to take care of, since she only had three questions. Had Troy ever found the quilts? Did he have contact information for his wife? And had Julie ever photographed any of the quilts?

Not that she held out much hope for that last one. But on the off chance Julie had taken pictures and then left her camera behind, there might be a picture of the quilt Sybil had chosen to put in the calendar. Not that it mattered now, but it would be interesting to learn for sure which one her aunt had thought was special enough for the calendar.

And if, as she suspected, it was the one they'd made together, how had it ended up buried in the backyard with Dolly Cayhill?

After turning the corner onto Troy Tolbert's street, she paused to study the addresses. If she was counting correctly, his place was the small rambler about halfway down the block on the right—the one with a man pushing a lawnmower back and forth. Great. He was not only home, but he was also outside, meaning she had no excuse not to stop and chat.

"Lady Luck, you're sure ticked off at me for some reason. The only thing that could make this day any worse would be for me to run into Frank Jeffries again."

She gave her companion a pleading look. "Zeke, if I let myself get suckered into volunteering for any more committees or secret missions for the guild, bite me. I know I'm asking you to practice some tough love, but if it saves me from doing this kind of stuff, I would really appreciate it."

Zeke slurped his tongue up her hand and part way up her arm, leaving behind an impressive trail of slobber in the process.

She ignored the sticky mess and gave him a quick hug. "I love you, too, big guy. Now let's get this fiasco over with."

It took far too little time to reach Troy's house. From what she could see, he was a nice-looking man in his early forties. Maybe a shade under six feet tall, he was in reasonably good shape, physically fit without packing on a lot of muscle. Just an average guy dressed in jeans and a black polo shirt with what looked like a pink logo of some kind embroidered on the pocket.

She stopped in front of the house and waited for him to turn back in her direction. When he finally spotted her, he gave her a puzzled look but turned off the lawnmower. He took off the black baseball cap he was wearing and wiped the sweat off his forehead before heading in her direction. There was a steep slope along the front edge of the yard, leaving him standing several feet above the sidewalk.

He offered her a friendly smile as he looked down at her. "Hi, were you wanting to talk to me? I don't believe we've met."

Okay, this was proving to be far more awkward than even she had expected it to be. "No, you don't know me, Mr. Tolbert. My name is Abby McCree, and I'm the new head of the local quilting guild."

His smile immediately dimmed. "I'm sorry, but I've already told those women that their quilts aren't in my house."

"I know, and I hate to bring up what must be a difficult subject for you. To be honest, I had hoped to avoid bothering you at all. I even tried looking at your wife's Facebook page to see if I could track her down that way. However, it doesn't look as if she's posted anything on her public page since Christmas."

He looked at her as if she were spouting pure gibberish. "I didn't even know she had a Facebook page. I can't imagine why she would bother with such nonsense."

What could she say to that? Considering Julie had run off with a new lover, it was obvious the woman had been keeping multiple secrets from her husband.

Rather than point that out, Abby went back on point. "Anyway, the ladies from the guild were wondering if you have any current contact information for your . . . wife. They'd really like to talk to her about the missing quilts, some of which are quite valuable."

For a minute, she didn't think he was going to answer. God knows the question had to feel like a hot poker on a barely healed wound. He flexed his hands several times before finally speaking.

"I'm sorry, but I have no idea where she is. Like I told them ages ago, she emptied our savings account and took a bunch of our personal possessions that could be sold for some quick cash. All I got was a note saying she was leaving me."

"And her family hasn't heard from her either?"

"They told me that she emailed them right after she left

to say she'd let them know where she finally settled. I know they've heard more since then, but the last I heard she only said she was fine and not to worry."

He stared over Abby's head for several seconds before once again looking straight at her. "I tried to email her myself several times, but they bounced. Maybe she's got a new email address or something. If so, I don't know what it is."

He shifted from foot to foot, clearly finding the conversation upsetting. "Look, I don't talk to my in-laws very often. It's just too painful. I feel guilty because I had no idea she was so unhappy, and they feel bad because she ran off like that. They're people of deep faith who take things like marriage vows pretty seriously. However, they also feel obligated to protect their daughter's privacy."

Another dead end. Abby didn't hold out much hope that the answer to her next question would be any more positive.

Zeke whined and stirred restlessly. She didn't blame him. She was ready to bolt down the street herself. "One last thing, and then I'll let you get back to mowing the lawn. Is there any chance that Mrs. Tolbert left her camera behind? If she did, then maybe the data card would still have any JPEGs she might have already taken of the quilts. She promised to take the pictures as soon as the ladies delivered them to her."

She offered him what she thought was a sympathetic smile. "I really am sorry to bother you with all of this. The only reason we're asking is that several of the members are trying to duplicate the quilts they lost, and it would help if they had photos of the originals to use as patterns."

Okay, that last part was a stretch, but it was the best explanation she could come up with on the spur of the moment.

A flash of pure fury swept over his face, only to disappear as quickly as it had come. If she hadn't looked up from petting Zeke at that exact moment, she would've missed it altogether. For that brief instant, his entire demeanor changed from affable to something far different. Even Zeke noticed. His big body tensed, and a deep growl rumbled in his chest. She tightened her hold on his leash although she wasn't sure she'd be strong enough to hold him back if he really did feel the need to defend her.

Troy's eyes narrowed as he briefly stared down at Zeke before turning his attention back to her. "Okay, just how many times do I have to repeat this? I don't know anything about those quilts. I never saw them. And as far as I know, my wife lost all interest in photography years ago. If she even still had a camera other than the one on her cell phone, it's probably up in the attic somewhere, covered in dust."

Then he shook his head, looking thoroughly disgusted. "No, actually, on second thought, she probably hocked it along with everything else she stole from me when she ran off."

Despite what Jean and Louise thought of this man, Abby was starting to empathize with why his wife might have left him. It would be really hard to live with someone who blew so hot and cold with no warning. On some level, she realized her reaction to him probably had a lot to do with her own recent divorce. However, Troy accusing Julie of stealing some of their joint possessions really rubbed her the wrong way. Whatever Julie had taken with her had belonged to her, too, just like when she and Chad had owned and built their business together. It hadn't belonged to him any more than it had to her, and she had the divorce settlement to prove it.

And thanks, Troy, for sending her on another lovely trip down memory lane.

Yeah, it was definitely time to get moving.

"Again, I apologize, but I had to ask." She ran her fingers through Zeke's soft fur to comfort them both. "I'll be going now, and I'll ask the ladies not to bother you again."

Troy's slick smile was back, but she didn't trust it.

"Look, Abby, was it? I'm sorry for being so curt, but all of this has really taken a toll on me. Did you know that one of those old ladies threatened to report this whole mess to police? I told her if she or any of the others bothered me again, I'd be the one to call the authorities. All I want is for people to respect my privacy. Every time somebody asks about Julie, it just stirs up a lot of pain all over again."

Once again, she felt some sympathy for his situation. "Thanks again for talking to me, Mr. Tolbert. As I said, I just took over the board, so I've been playing catch up. Enjoy the rest of your day."

She walked away without waiting for any further response from him. Zeke lagged behind her. It was impossible to know if he was getting tired or if the big guy was still in protection mode and wanted to stay between her and any perceived danger. At the end of the block, she used the pretense of adjusting his collar to glance back down the street. Just as she feared, Troy Tolbert was standing right where she'd left him, watching her every move. When he realized she'd caught him staring, he turned away and stalked into his house.

"You're so smart, Zeke. I think you're right about that guy. I'm just sorry that I'm on his radar now. I'll have to find some tactful way to warn the ladies to stay away from him." She leaned down to kiss Zeke on the head. "He's not somebody I'd want mad at me."

The dog whined as he stared up at her with his soulful eyes.

"You're right, boy. It might be too late for that."

With that unhappy thought, she headed back home.

* * *

Dinner wasn't anything to brag about, but that was her fault. It wasn't as if she'd put any effort into it. Cooking for one had gotten old within weeks of leaving Chad behind, but she usually did better than a grilled cheese sandwich and a handful of potato chips. Not exactly a balanced diet, but she'd do better tomorrow. Maybe. She'd have to go to the store again since pickings in the pantry had gotten pretty slim.

Right now she didn't have the energy to even think about it. She'd had a headache by the time she and Zeke returned home from their walk. No surprise there, considering how that particular expedition had gone. What made it all especially frustrating was the fact that she had remarkably little to show for all the aggravation. Maybe she'd feel better about it if she made a list of what she'd learned. If nothing else, it might spawn some idea of where she could go next in her two investigations: Dolly's death and the missing quilts.

She'd met Dolly's heir and learned enough that she no longer included her on the suspect list. Allison had seemed clearly surprised by the sudden windfall from her aunt's death, and Abby was inclined to believe her. She also now had firsthand knowledge that the old woman's closest friends were both angry and unhappy.

Then there was her conversation with Troy Tolbert. He claimed to have never seen the quilts at all. She might have believed him, but the ladies of the guild were adamant that all twelve had been delivered to his wife at their house. If she had to choose who to believe, the ladies of the guild would win hands down. Not only that, she'd seen the sample pictures Julie had taken of Louise's quilt at a meeting. Why would Troy think his wife's camera was packed away if she'd been using it? That was definitely a puzzle, one she was too tired to solve right now.

Abby ate the last bite of her sandwich and then set her plate in the sink along with the small skillet she'd used. Her aunt wouldn't have approved of leaving dirty dishes overnight. Too bad.

Now that she was done eating, the rest of the evening stretched out ahead of her with nothing to fill the lonely hours. Normally, she'd call her mother for a quick chat, but she'd gone out of town with two of her friends. Something about a girls' weekend at a nearby casino and hotel. She'd been excited about the trip, making it sound as if they were planning to have a really wild time of it. Considering her mom's two-drink limit and preference for the nickel slots, her idea of getting crazy wasn't actually a call for concern.

That didn't mean Abby wasn't a bit jealous. She couldn't remember the last time she'd gone out on a date or even just hung out with friends. Of course, somehow the majority of their friends had been something else Chad had ended up getting in the divorce. She was starting to rebuild her life, but most of the ladies she'd spent time with since moving to Snowberry Creek were from her aunt's generation. They were lovely, but she missed spending time with people her own age. She had met some women here in Snowberry Creek who might eventually become the kinds of friends she could call at the last minute to see if they wanted to go out for drinks, but they weren't quite there yet.

And wasn't this the most pathetic self-pity party she'd ever been to?

The chime of the doorbell gave her hope. Maybe whoever was out there would save her from herself. Zeke beat her into the foyer, his tail going a mile a minute. Good, that meant it was a friend, not a stranger.

But when she opened the door, she knew it wasn't going

to be good news, even though Gage was wearing jeans and
a sports shirt instead of his uniform.

"Hi, Gage. Come on in."

He stepped inside but made no effort to go any farther
than the foyer. His actions didn't bode well at all. That
didn't mean she wouldn't try to be a good hostess.

"I could make coffee if you would like a cup."

"Sorry, but my daughter, Sydney, is waiting out in the
car. I'm taking her and a couple of her friends to the mall."

He shifted from one foot to the other, clearly not happy
to be there. "Listen, I got a call from Troy Tolbert this afternoon. He said you'd been there asking him questions about
his wife." Then he grinned just a little. "Actually, he said it
was someone named Abby, although he didn't remember
her last name. All things considered, I figured it had to
be you."

Once again, here she was, having to confess her sins to
Gage. "Yes, it was. I didn't mean to upset him. Heck, I
didn't want to bother him in the first place."

"I've heard his side of the story. Now I want to hear
yours. Why were you there?"

She didn't much appreciate Troy calling Gage in the
first place, especially when she'd already promised not to
bother the man again. Regardless, he had made the call,
so she was going to have to deal with the fallout.

"As you've already heard, I took over Aunt Sybil's position as head of the quilting guild, and I'm doing my best to
play catch-up on the status of the organization. When the
other board members and I were going over the budget for
the coming year, they mentioned a shortfall in the projected
income for the guild. They'd planned to make calendars
using some of the groups' favorite quilts as the theme. The
cover would've been the completed mystery quilt project
that they all worked on together."

When she paused, Gage waved his hand in the air, saying without words that he needed her to pick up speed. Fine. "From what they indicated, Julie Tolbert was a relatively new member to the group. I don't know how long she belonged, but I could probably find out if you need that information."

"Good to know, but I don't need it right now."

"The ladies said they were discussing getting a professional photographer to do the actual work when Julie offered to take the pictures. She did some sample shots of one of Louise's quilts to show them what she had in mind. I've seen the JPEGs, and they were really good. In fact, Louise liked them so much that she had them framed for her wall at home."

"So why would that land you on Tolbert's doorstep?"

She drew a deep breath. "According to the ladies, the plan was to keep the quilts secret until the pictures were done. Each of the twelve members who bought one of the months in the calendar were instructed to wrap their quilts so that they couldn't be seen. Aunt Sybil and Glenda personally delivered them to Julie at her house. According to Glenda and Louise, Julie said she needed to take the pictures right away and then would return the quilts immediately afterward."

Gage looked puzzled. "You're making it sound as if it was a rush job. Did it have to be? You know, to make a deadline?"

"I have no way of knowing that for sure, but I don't think it was a deadline issue on the part of the guild. Julie apparently led Glenda to think she and Troy were leaving on a trip or something, and she wanted to finish the pictures beforehand. As it turned out, she was the one leaving."

Gage checked his watch. "I'm guessing the ladies had already talked to Troy about some of this stuff."

She nodded. "They asked for their quilts back, but he swears he never saw them. They thought that since I was new to the situation, he wouldn't mind if I stopped by to see if he had any new contact information for his wife. They were wrong about that. He minded a lot, not that I blame him. I told him I tried to track her down through social media before coming to him, but he didn't even know Julie had a Facebook page. He said her parents have heard from her, but he doesn't talk with them very much."

"Under the circumstances, I can understand that."

Abby felt the same way. "Anyway, he sounded sincere when he said every time someone asks about Julie, it rips open the wounds all over again. Jean and the others believe he really had no idea that she was unhappy enough to take off with someone else with no warning at all."

Something she understood all too well. The pain of Chad's betrayal had all but destroyed her. The memory still had the ability to sucker punch her at the oddest moments. Like now, for instance.

"I also asked him about any possible pictures she might have taken. I thought that, if she'd left in a hurry, she might not have taken the camera with her. However, he insisted Julie had lost interest in photography years ago, and that if she had still had a camera other than the one on her phone, it was probably buried up in their attic somewhere. That, or it might have been among the things she took with her when she left. That's likely what happened to the quilts, too. We may never know for sure." Finally, she shrugged. "The bottom line is, I apologized to Troy for bothering him and made it clear that I would tell the guild members that they shouldn't contact him again. I meant that."

Gage studied her for a second or two. "Okay, that's good." The sound of a car horn had him grimacing. "Looks like

I'm being summoned. Thanks for the information. I needed to know what had set him off."

She followed Gage out onto the porch. "Do you know if one of the ladies actually reported the missing quilts to the police?"

"You know I can't answer that."

"Sorry."

For the first time, he smiled. "No, you're not. You're disappointed. Now, I'd better get moving before Syd comes to drag me back to the car."

She waited until he was pulling out of the driveway before she locked the door, still thinking about what he'd said—and what he hadn't. If Gage hadn't heard about the quilts, wouldn't he have simply said so? More likely, he'd meant just what he said—that he couldn't discuss police matters with her. Right now, she didn't much care either way. The day hadn't gone well at all, and her reward was a crushing headache. For now, she wasn't going to think about anything more complicated than what flavor of tea would go best with ibuprofen.

"Come on, Zeke. Let's grab you a quick snack while I make myself a cup of tea. Then I'll read while you take your evening nap."

Considering naps and treats were two of his favorite things in the world, it came as no surprise when he charged past her toward the kitchen with his tail wagging a mile a minute. She stuffed his favorite chew toy with peanut butter and tossed it toward him. He chased it down the hall, slipping and sliding on the wood floor in his haste to enjoy his goodie in the living room.

After washing down two ibuprofen with water, she followed behind with her mug of Earl Grey. The sun was already disappearing to the west, casting the room in deepening shadows. She tried reading, but quickly gave up when the book failed to hold her attention. Her mind kept going back to the missing quilts. What had Julie done with them?

She set her book aside and reached for her laptop. After booting it up, she considered her options. Finally, she checked several online sites to see if anyone had recently posted any quilts for sale. The results were pretty mixed. No one seemed to have more than one or maybe two for sale, but maybe that wasn't too surprising. Julie had to know the ladies would want their quilts back. Posting them all in one location would make it far more likely that someone might notice. Even listing one or two at a time could be risky if she did so in this same geographical area.

Had Glenda or any of the others thought to keep an eye on some of the more popular sites? It was hard to know how tech savvy any of them were. She'd have to ask Glenda the next time she talked to her.

"Zeke, this is so frustrating. While I'd love to get the quilts back for the ladies, the problem is that I have no idea what any of the quilts look like. I don't suppose you have any great ideas."

Zeke gave that comment all the attention it deserved— none at all. While she continued to poke around online hoping for inspiration, he kept his toy trapped between his paws and continued to lick the peanut butter. By the time she set the computer aside, he was clearly having trouble staying awake. She understood just how he felt.

Finally, they both drifted off to sleep.

Chapter Fifteen

The sharp stab of Zeke's teeth on her arm was too real to be a dream. It stung a little, but that didn't mean Abby was ready to wake up. Then he barked right in her face, blasting her with peanut-scented doggy breath. Her eyes popped open, or at least she thought they had. It was hard to tell if the room was dark or if she was still trapped in a dream.

Zeke's growl definitely sounded real enough. Something had him upset, and that something had him in full-on protection mode.

She rubbed her arm. There was a hint of slime, making her ask, "Why did you nip me, boy?"

He woofed again and then growled, his attention focused on the front window.

"What's wrong?"

Like he could actually answer questions. There was only one way to find out what had him all riled up. Night had fallen big time, so it was too dark to see much of anything. Before she could stand up to get a better look, the window behind her chair shattered and sent her diving for the floor. Landing hard on shards of glass hurt like crazy, but she needed to get out of the line of fire.

Zeke went crazy, barking and scrambling to reach the window. She ignored the pain in her hands and knees as she made a grab for his collar. If he tried to jump through the broken window, he could get badly hurt. Even if he suceeded without mishap, he'd be in danger from whoever had just lobbed something through her front window.

"Come on, boy, we need to get to the kitchen."

It was hard to crawl while dragging an angry dog in her wake, but she managed to reach the relative shelter of the hallway. Once there, she risked standing up and then bolted the rest of the way to where she'd left her cell phone on the counter. Who should she call first? The police or Tripp?

The decision was made for her when the man in question suddenly appeared on the back porch as if she conjured him out of thin air. How had he gotten there so fast? Had the sound of the glass breaking carried all the way to his house?

"Come on, Abby, let me in!"

She almost tripped over Zeke in her rush to reach the door. Her hands were shaking badly enough that she had trouble turning the lock, but finally she managed it. As soon as the door swung open, Tripp charged inside.

"What happened? I was taking out the trash when I heard glass shatter, and then a minute later a car tore off down the street."

She held up her bleeding palms. "I was napping in the chair by the bay window when Zeke started pitching a fit. Before I could figure out what was going on, the glass broke right behind me. I dove for the floor and then grabbed Zeke to keep him from jumping through the broken window to go after whoever was out there."

All of that poured out in one breath, leaving her gasping for air. Tripp set something down on the counter and then pulled out a chair at the table and gently shoved her toward it. "Have you called the police yet?"

Abby shook her head. "I was debating whether to call you or them first when you got here."

"I'll make the call, and then we'll see how badly you're hurt."

It would be the second time that he'd stepped up to call the cops on her behalf. While she was appreciative of his willingness to help, this was her problem. "I'll make the call if you'll hand me my phone."

He stared at her for a second and then did as she asked. "Where's your first aid kit?"

"In the linen closet in the bathroom."

While she made the call, he disappeared down the hallway, presumably looking for first aid supplies. By the time she hung up, Tripp was back.

"They're on their way. They reminded me not to touch anything until they get here."

She started to get up to wash her hands. As soon as she put weight on her right foot, a stabbing pain shot up her leg. "Ow, that really hurts."

Tripp grabbed her arm to steady her. "Sit back down. You must have gotten glass in your foot. If you insist on walking around on it, you'll drive the sliver in deeper."

The pain was only starting to register. "I hadn't realized I was hurt."

"Well, I did." He pointed to the floor. "You left bloody prints on your way in here. Now, are you going to let me assess the damage or would you rather wait for the paramedics to get here?"

Considering she hadn't told the operator she was hurt, Tripp was her best choice. She plopped back down in the chair and held up her foot. "If you don't mind."

He tossed her a warm washcloth. "Clean up your hands. I'll look at them next."

Then he knelt in front of her. His big hands were amazingly gentle as he studied her injury and then rooted around in the first aid kit. When he pulled out a pair of tweezers, he grinned. "Your aunt kept this well stocked."

"How did you know it wasn't me?"

His answering snort was less than flattering, but he obviously knew her better than she'd thought. She turned her attention to wiping the blood off her hands, once again wincing when she put pressure on a sliver still stuck in her right palm. She pulled it out herself while Tripp was busy slathering antibiotic ointment on her heel and then covering it up with a large bandage.

She picked another small shard out of her hand. "I think that's it. Everything else is okay, but we should check Zeke for injuries, too. He was right next to me when the window broke. Even if he wasn't hurt at the time, he's probably got pieces of glass stuck in his fur. I'm not sure what would work best to get it all out."

They both studied the dog. Trip called Zeke to his side. "Think he'd let me vacuum him?"

Now that was an image worthy of posting on social media. "I'm not sure, but we can try."

She hobbled to the hall closet and got the small upright vacuum she kept there. "I'll hold his head for you."

Amazingly, Zeke sat perfectly still as Tripp quickly ran the brush over his fur. Once he'd gone over every inch, he turned off the machine and then ran his hands over the dog head-to-toe and back again. Next, he lifted Zeke's paws to check them for damage. They were both relieved that the dog had been luckier than Abby had been.

A blast of sirens preceded a knock at the front door by a minute, tops. Great. The neighbors were going to be thrilled to have their quiet evening disturbed by the arrival of the police for the second time since Abby had moved in. Neither occasion was her fault, but she doubted that would make much of a difference. Even if she wasn't a troublemaker, she was obviously a lightning rod for it lately.

She had started toward the living room when Tripp barked a one word order. "Shoes!"

Yep, good idea. She slipped on the pair she kept by the back door before hobbling down the hallway to let the police in. To her surprise, she found Gage standing on her front porch. "I thought you were at the mall."

"I was, but I've let it be known that I wanted to be notified immediately if there was any further trouble at your house."

She stepped back to let him in. "You were expecting something to happen?"

"Not exactly, but I thought it was a possibility."

He looked past her to where Tripp stood holding Zeke by the collar. "I'll want a statement from both of you after I have a chance to look around."

For the first time since the window shattered, Abby felt safe enough to turn the lamps on in the living room. Bits and pieces of glass sparkled like frost on the carpet. There were large, jagged shards still stuck in the window frame centered around a huge opening right in the middle. The hole was roughly the same shape as the brick lying on the floor right beside the chair where she'd been sitting.

The two men flanking her stared down at the mess. Gage looked grim while Tripp was clearly furious.

"That brick could have only missed her head by inches. Do you think he knew right where she was sitting?"

She waited for Gage to deny that possibility. When he didn't, she backed out of the room. With the window open to the night air, the threat lurking outside suddenly became more real.

"You don't think it was a bunch of kids screwing around?" Abby crossed her fingers that Gage would say yes to the possibility. She'd be a lot happier knowing there were juvenile delinquents on the prowl in Snowberry Creek than thinking someone out there had it in specifically for her.

Gage shook his head. "Maybe, but I doubt it. Were the lights on in here when it happened?"

"No. Zeke and I were both tired and fell asleep before it got dark in here."

"And then?"

She rubbed her arm. "Zeke must have heard something because he nipped at me to wake me up. When that didn't work, he barked in my face. Before I could figure out what was wrong, the window shattered. I hit the deck and dragged Zeke down the hall to the kitchen. I was going to call Tripp, but he came running when he heard the window break. After he came inside, I called 9-1-1."

"Were you hurt?"

She held up her hands and then balanced on her good foot while she took off her other shoe long enough to show him the bandage covering her heel. "Both are minor cuts, but we got the glass out. We also checked Zeke over to make sure he wasn't hurt and to remove any glass from his fur."

If anything, Gage only looked more grim. "So, you didn't handle the brick?"

"No. I didn't want to hang around in here any longer than I had to."

She started toward it, but Gage stopped her. "No, don't touch it. It's doubtful we'll get any usable prints, but it's still worth a shot to check."

He pulled out his cell phone and made a quick call. "Would you send a technician to meet me at Abby McCree's place? Thanks."

She hadn't forgotten that Gage had had other plans for the evening. "Don't you need to get back to Sydney?"

"Nope, I called my mom to come cover for me." If Abby wasn't mistaken, he looked relieved as he continued to explain. "She has more patience with teenagers than I do. I was just drinking coffee at the food court while the girls prowled through all of their favorite stores. There are only two things I'm good for on these kinds of outings: providing transportation and forking over my credit card on demand."

His eyes crinkled at the corners, making it clear he really didn't mind providing those services for his daughter. "I told Mom Syd's spending limit for the evening and that I would pay her back when I see her."

"You're a good dad."

She meant that even if she was a bit jealous of his relationship with his daughter. Her mother had been awarded primary custody when Abby's parents had divorced. Although she'd spent summers with her father, they'd never regained the closeness they'd shared before he'd moved out of state to be with his new wife.

That was neither here nor there. Right now, she was cold and a whole lot scared. Tripp must have picked up on it, because he tugged her down the hall to the kitchen.

"Sit down while I fix a cup of tea for you."

Her conscience pointed out that this was her house, and she should be the one playing hostess. The truth was, right now she simply wasn't up to it. "Can we have mocha hot chocolate instead?"

Tripp switched gears with his usual efficiency. "Gage, how about you?"

"I'm good." Gage joined Abby at the table. Just that quickly, she was flashing back to the morning when the goats had discovered the dead body.

She shivered. "Do you think this has something to do with Dolly's murder?"

"It's too soon to jump to that conclusion." He pulled out the same little notebook he'd used the last time the three of them had gathered around this table to discuss a crime. "Once you've got something hot to sip, we'll go over everything again."

Recounting the events that had occurred since he'd left didn't take all that long. Although Gage remained calm, cool, and collected, the same couldn't be said for Tripp. She kept expecting him to explode, but at least he waited until she reached the part where he'd come charging up to her back door.

She knew full well how gentle his hands could be, but right now they were clenched in tight fists and ready to do battle. When he finally spoke, his deep voice sounded more like one of Zeke's growls. "When I find out who did this—"

Gage slowly set his pen down and pegged him with a hard look. "You won't do anything, Tripp. I'll handle it."

"You'd better, or I will."

"Just because we're friends doesn't mean I won't throw your ass in jail. Remember that."

The two men glared at each other, neither one willing to back down. Maybe she could distract them long enough for their tempers to cool off a bit.

She set down her empty mug. "How will you figure out who it was if there aren't fingerprints on the brick? Or if you only get a couple of partials? Even if there are usable prints, what are the chances they're in the system?"

Gage's mouth quirked up in a small grin. "I take it you're a fan of crime shows."

Not since she'd uncovered a murder victim in her own backyard, but at least she'd gotten his attention off of Tripp. "I've watched my fair share."

"I'll admit getting anything useful is a long shot, but you never know."

He flipped to a new page in his notebook. "Next, I need a list of people you've talked to in the past week or so, especially anyone you might have had words with or who might have ties to Dolly Cayhill."

This time it was Tripp who looked amused. "Yeah, Abby. How many people have you pissed off lately?"

Jerk.

When she didn't immediately respond, Gage tapped his pen on the paper. "Why don't I start with the ones I know about and then you can fill in any gaps. There's Frank Jeffries, Troy Tolbert, and that group of ladies out in front of Dolly Cayhill's house. Did I miss anyone?"

Tripp let out a low whistle. "Wow, I'm impressed, Abby. That's quite a tally for just one week. Personally, I don't normally piss off that many people in an entire month. You must have a real talent for it."

Gage fought to hold back a grin but failed miserably. "Actually, that's just today's list."

Enough was enough.

"All right, you two. Do I need to remind you that I'm the victim here?"

"No, but clearly you need to be more careful about who you talk to these days." Then Tripp frowned and pointed toward the list. "Who's this Troy Tolbert? And what did she do to make a bunch of women so mad at her?"

She waved her hand in front of Tripp's face to remind him she was sitting right there and could answer any questions for herself. "The ladies were friends of Dolly's. They're convinced my aunt had something to do with her death. Not to mention they still think you were part of the conspiracy." Glancing at Gage, she said, "I'm guessing they're the ones who told you about the bad crab dip episode in the first place, trying to cast blame on Aunt Sybil. It's not the first time they've taken their anger out on me. I'd never even met them before when they gave me the cold shoulder at the coffee shop the other day. Ask Bridey. She'll tell you I didn't do anything to them at all."

Gage wrote down something in his notebook. "I will talk to her and them, as well. However, somehow I don't remember any of them looking strong enough to toss a brick through a window that size."

She tried to imagine that happening but couldn't picture it. "I haven't seen Frank Jeffries since that day in the store. One thing, though, is he doesn't strike me as someone who would do something sneaky like breaking windows if he was mad. He certainly didn't hesitate to confront me in public."

"Maybe, but you never know. Is there anyone else you can think of who had connections to Mrs. Cayhill?"

"After you left me this afternoon, Allison Samuels invited me into Dolly's house. Evidently, her aunt left the quilting guild both her fabric stash and a sizeable cash donation. Mrs. Cayhill also left a quilt to Aunt Sybil, but Allison hasn't been able to find it. I suspect it was the one that was supposed to be in the calendar."

While Gage took notes, she wondered if she could avoid

bringing up the conversation she'd had with JB Burton on the day of the garage sale. The last thing she wanted to do was cause the boy any problems. Whatever trouble he'd had with Dolly had been resolved months ago.

Unfortunately, Gage picked up on her hesitation. "Abby, don't hold back on me now."

"Fine, but if I give you the name, promise you won't bother him."

Gage looked as if he'd just sucked on a lemon, but it was Tripp who didn't appreciate her putting conditions on her willingness to cooperate. "You know it doesn't work like that, Abby. You can't tie his hands so that he can't do his job."

Tripp was right. That didn't mean she had to like it. "Fine, but it's really nothing. JB Burton Jr. was one of the teenagers you recommended to help us set up the garage sale. He asked me about finding the body."

Tripp looked puzzled. "What's his connection to Dolly Cayhill?"

Gage didn't seem inclined to answer, so she did. "JB and his buddies were celebrating him getting appointed to West Point. They were parked someplace near Dolly's yard. When she threatened to call the cops on them, the kid who was driving panicked. Evidently his tire blew out, and he drove into her prize roses. The boys involved were given community service rather than being officially charged, which she didn't think was punishment enough. From what I heard, JB's dad didn't take it well when she threatened to notify the academy and tell them why JB didn't deserve to go there."

"I can see why he'd feel that way. What happened then?"

"Besides his assigned community service, JB also

offered to do a bunch of work for Dolly herself, several hours a week for a month or so."

Gage looked up from his notes. "I didn't know he did that."

"Yeah, he said they'd end up looking at her photo albums, and she even baked cookies for him. It doesn't seem likely that she would've carried through on her threat to write a letter to the academy. It was clear he was genuinely upset about her dying that way."

Tripp asked, "How did his father feel about it, though?"

"I don't know. I've never met the man."

Gage didn't answer right away. Finally, he sighed and put his notebook away. "My best guess would be that JB Sr. would've been proud of his son for spending time with Mrs. Cayhill. That kid has always been mature for his age."

"So, you see why I don't want to stir up any unnecessary trouble for him."

For the first time in a while, Gage grinned. "And I was so looking forward to kicking in their front door and dragging the whole family out in chains. I was even going to invite Tripp along. It's been a while since he's helped clear a house."

"Yeah, but all my combat gear is in storage." He gave Abby a sly look. "Except for my hand grenades. I keep those handy because I never know when my landlady will need me to run off a reporter or something."

Both men cracked up big time, clearly enjoying themselves.

"All right, you two have had enough fun at my expense."

Gage quickly sobered. "Sorry, Abby. Don't think I'm taking this situation lightly."

"I know that, but where does this leave us?"

"The only one we didn't talk about is Troy, but I know it

wasn't him. He told me he was leaving on a four-day run this afternoon. I saw him driving his rig out of town about an hour before I stopped by to see you earlier."

When the doorbell chimed, Gage said, "I'll get it. It should be our tech."

After he disappeared down the hallway, Tripp asked, "You want a refill on the hot chocolate?"

"No, I'm good. Thanks again for coming to my rescue." Her smile felt a little wobbly as she gave voice to her fear. "God, I'm scared, Tripp. First, someone buries a dead body in my yard, and now this. I can't imagine being able to sleep in this house tonight."

"I promise no one will get to you, Abby. They'd have to go through me first, and that's not happening."

Her sometimes affable, sometimes grumpy tenant disappeared in a heartbeat. In his place sat a battle-hardened warrior, a man she hardly recognized. For the first time, she noticed he hadn't shaved, and the shadow of his beard only emphasized his capacity for violence if the occasion called for it.

He must have picked up on her reaction, because he quickly banked the fires and looked away. No longer able to sit still, she stood up to put her empty mug in the sink. That's when she saw the gun lying on the counter. She had no experience with weapons of any kind and had no desire to start now. Regardless, some part of her was relieved to know Tripp had come prepared for anything.

Once again, he saw too much. "It won't bite. The safety is on."

"I figured as much."

She meant that. He wasn't the kind of man who would be careless with his weapons. He picked the gun up and stuck it in the back of his waistband. "While Gage is still here, I'm going out to the garage to see if any of the old lumber out there is big enough to cover the window."

"Good idea. I'll call the glass company first thing in the morning."

He started to walk away but then turned back and yanked her into his arms for a quick hug. "Try to stay out of trouble while I'm gone. You've caused enough excitement for one night."

She was still sputtering when he disappeared into the darkness.

Chapter Sixteen

Sharing breakfast with a man made for a strange start to her day. In fact, Abby couldn't remember the last time she'd made pancakes, bacon, and eggs for anyone other than herself. Looking back, Chad avoiding meals at home had been one of the first indications that all was not well with her marriage. If she'd been more perceptive, maybe she would've picked up on the fact that although he claimed to be trying to drop a few pounds by skipping breakfast and sometimes dinner, he never lost any weight.

That was then, and Tripp was nothing like her ex-husband. From the way he was chowing down on the pancakes, he wasn't worried about his boyish figure. Oddly enough, she liked that about him. Of course, he'd probably go out and bench press his truck to work off the extra calories.

"Did I thank you for sleeping over last night?"

Tripp nodded. "Yes, twice, and you're welcome."

After he and Gage had done a patchwork job of covering the broken window with old plywood, he'd refused to leave her alone in the house. Pointing out that she had Zeke for company hadn't gotten her very far. Both men insisted she needed someone to keep an eye on things. Her choices were a deputy parked out front all night or Tripp sacked out on her couch. In the end, it was no contest.

"More coffee?"

"No, I'm good." He pushed his plate back. "That was great. Thanks for cooking."

She put the butter and eggs back in the refrigerator. "It was the least I could do."

"Are you going to be okay by yourself today? I've got classes, but I can skip them if you want me to stick around."

"I can't ask you to do that. Besides, I won't be alone all day. The window guy promised to be out here before ten to take measurements. After that, Glenda is coming by."

"If you're sure."

She managed a reassuring smile. "I am. Besides, I wouldn't be surprised if Gage checked on me, too."

He carried his dishes over to the sink. "Let me know if he's learned anything."

"I will."

"No more thoughts on who might have been behind this?"

She'd stayed awake for hours trying to answer that exact question. "Not that I can think of, and I think we pretty much eliminated everyone on the list Gage made. He clearly didn't think it was a teenage prank, so I don't know where that leaves me."

There was a strong hint of Tripp in warrior mode when he turned to face her, maybe because he still hadn't shaved and was wearing yesterday's clothes. "It leaves you being real careful about who you talk to for a few days."

She did her best imitation of a teenage girl dealing with an overprotective parent. Batting her eyes, she said, "Yes, Father."

Tripp didn't seem to find that as funny as she did, but

she was pretty sure he was fighting the urge to grin on his
way out the door. "I'll be back by three at the latest."

She followed him out onto the porch. Thanking him
again didn't seem like quite enough of a payment for sticking by her last night. Offering him another break on his rent
wouldn't be right, either. He'd signed on to mow the grass
and do a few odd jobs around the place, not to come running with gun in hand whenever she ran into problems.

"I don't want to interfere with your homework or anything, but I'd really like to take you out to dinner tonight.
You know, for everything you've done."

He studied her for a few seconds before finally nodding.
"Only if we go to the Creek Café."

Exasperated, she crossed her arms over her chest and
cocked her hip to one side. "I can afford a more expensive
restaurant, you know."

Tripp mirrored her stance, which looked pretty cute on
him. "Yeah, but they won't serve Frannie's coconut cream
pie, will they?"

He had her there. While she hadn't lived in Snowberry
Creek all that long, she was well acquainted with Frannie's
dessert menu.

"It's a deal. I can be ready any time after five. Give me
a yell when you want to leave."

"Will do."

Normally, Abby would've had no problem picking out a
shirt to go with her best jeans. There was an entire closet
full of perfectly good possibilities hanging right there in
front of her, but it might as well have been filled with rags
for all the appeal anything in it had right at the moment.
She would've started getting ready earlier if she'd known it

was going to be this hard. How should she dress to have dinner with a friend as opposed to what she'd wear on a real date? If she could answer that one question, then she'd know what to wear, because this definitely wasn't a date.

Simply put, she owed Tripp for the help he'd given her. That was all. Nothing more than that. A friend thanking a friend. He wouldn't care what she wore. It wasn't like he was a clothes hound himself. So why did she think that putting on her forest-green silk blouse instead of the more practical red cotton-knit shirt would convey an entirely different message? Telling herself not to be ridiculous, she grabbed the green silk and put it on. Then she tossed her jeans back on the bed and slipped on a pair of black slacks and then a pair of black booties with silver buckles on the side. A pair of silver earrings and a matching necklace added the final touches.

She studied her reflection in the mirror. The color of the blouse definitely brought out the green in her eyes and the reddish highlights in her dark hair. "Okay, it's not a date, but there's nothing wrong with looking my best."

That was her story, and she was sticking to it.

"Miss McCree? Can I borrow you a minute?"

She ran over to the staircase. "Sure thing, Mr. Pinkly. I'll be right down."

Abby checked her appearance one last time before joining Mr. Pinkly downstairs in the living room, where he and his assistant were replacing her broken window. Earlier that morning, he'd stopped by to measure the glass. To her surprise, he had the right size in stock and had time in his schedule to install it that afternoon. Right now, he was frowning at the piece of paper in his hand like something had gone terribly wrong. Considering his assistant was doing a final polish on the window, it couldn't be that.

"What's up?"

He glanced at the paper one more time and then reluctantly held it out to her. "We found this outside. Normally, I would've thrown it in the trash, but considering how your window got broken in the first place, I thought maybe you'd want to see it."

"Thank you, I . . ." She gave the wrinkled paper a quick glance. Then she blinked and read it again, her heart falling into a ragged, syncopated rhythm as the words typed on the page slowly started to sink in.

Remember, there's plenty of room for you in the back-yard, too.

Her hands trembled, rattling the paper. "Where did you find this? I mean specifically?"

He motioned for her to follow him outside. Pointing toward one of the large rhododendrons that flanked the front porch, he said, "It was caught deep in the branches of that bush. We were cleaning up the broken glass underneath it when we spotted it. No telling for sure how long it's been there."

He ran his hand over his balding head. "Now, truth be told, we often find bits and pieces of stuff when we're sweeping up after a broken window. Most of the time, we just pitch it all in the trash. However, all things considered, I thought someone ought to see that one. If you think it's nothing, we'll just get rid of it."

She wanted to think that. Yeah, she really did. It wasn't nothing, though, and they both knew it. Her first thought was that she needed to show it to Gage, and sooner rather than later. Maybe he'd take one look at it and scoff, saying just what Mr. Pinkly had said about no one knowing how long it had been hiding in that bush. God knows, she hoped that's what he would say, but Tripp had recently pruned all of the bushes in the front of the house. Wouldn't he have seen it?

Trying to sound far calmer than she felt, she said, "Thanks for finding this, Mr. Pinkly. I'm leaving to go out to dinner with a friend in a few minutes. We'll drop this by the police station on the way. If you're not quite finished with the window when I have to leave, can you make sure the front door is locked?"

He followed her back into the house. "No problem. We should be gone before then. If we're not, though, I'll double check the doors myself."

"Thanks."

After he went back to helping his assistant fold up the tarps they'd put over her furniture, she went down the hall to the kitchen with the paper still clutched tightly in her hand. What should she do to preserve it? It had already been exposed to the elements overnight, and both she and Mr. Pinkly had handled it. Finally, she settled for stuffing it into a gallon freezer bag and sealing the top shut. At least that way it wouldn't pick up any more fingerprints along the way.

Chances were the only ones on it were hers and Mr. Pinkly's, but she could always hope. After setting it by her purse, she sat down at the table and waited impatiently for Tripp to text her that he was ready to go. Staring at the clock did nothing to make the time pass any more quickly.

"Zeke, did I mention I was going out to dinner tonight?"

His only response was a soulful look and a big sigh as he heaved himself up off the floor to lay his big head in her lap. She stroked his soft fur. "We won't be gone all that long. I promise. I'll even fix your dinner before we go."

That earned her a quick lick of his tongue and two wags of his tail.

"Have I ever told you how much I appreciate your calm nature?"

She meant that. It took a lot for him to get all worked up about something. A new batch of his treats, hot out of the oven, did the job. On the other end of the spectrum, so did a brick through the window.

With no one else handy to listen, she whispered her fears to him. "I'm scared, Zeke. I was only worried about Aunt Sybil's reputation up until that brick came flying through the window. I got upset when Mr. Jeffries and then those awful old women yelled at me, but I wasn't scared. Not exactly, anyway. I am now."

It took a lot of effort to keep her eyes focused on Zeke and not the plastic bag over on the counter. "I'll show that to Tripp and then give it to Gage. I'm not sure how much he'll learn from it, if anything at all. Maybe he has some super-duper lab techs who can figure out what brand of printer it was made on and who in town owns one, but I figure that's a longshot at best."

Zeke's tail did another long sweep to show he agreed with her assessment of the situation.

Mr. Pinkly appeared in the doorway. "Miss McCree, we'll be heading out now. Let me know if you have any problems with the window. Remember, it's under warranty."

She stood to shake his hand. "Thanks again for coming on such short notice this morning. I never expected you would be able to fix it today. You and your helper definitely went above and beyond. I gave your office my credit card number to take care of the bill. I'll also leave five-star reviews on the major websites for you, too."

He beamed at her. "I do appreciate that. It's amazing how important that has become to all of us small businesses these days."

She locked the front door behind him and watched from her brand new window as he drove away. Her phone buzzed to tell her she had a new text message. Tripp was ready. Good. She texted back that she would meet him at her car. Zeke followed her back into the kitchen, probably to make sure she made good on her promise to feed him on her way out.

After filling his bowl halfway with kibble, she added an extra treat of his favorite canned dog food. He immediately dove right in as she picked up her purse and keys along with the plastic bag with the note in it.

"Be good, Zeke. I'll be back soon."

To her surprise, he actually stopped eating long enough to look up at her, which warmed her heart. Normally, nothing distracted him from food. She patted him on the head and let herself out, locking the deadbolt behind her.

Tripp stood leaning against the front fender on her car. One look at him and she knew the green silk and black slacks had been the right choice. By this time of day, he was usually sporting a pretty serious five o'clock shadow. Instead, he looked freshly showered and shaved, and he was wearing khakis and a dark blue sports shirt, which set off his tan rather nicely. Too bad Edith and the other ladies weren't there to see him.

She stopped just short of where he stood and smiled. "You clean up well, Mr. Blackston. Pretty dressy, though, for the Creek Café."

"You've got no room to talk." His cheeks flushed a bit as he shrugged. "Besides, everything else was dirty or had holes in it."

It was tempting to stand there and maybe see just how rusty her flirting skills really were, but now wasn't the time. She didn't want to ruin their evening out, but neither Tripp nor Gage would thank her for waiting until tomorrow to turn over the note.

"I'm sorry, but we need to make a quick stop on the way to the restaurant."

It was hard to put on a brave face, but she tried. Evidently, her best effort wasn't all that good, because Tripp immediately pushed away from the car to stand right in front of her. "What's wrong?"

She held out the baggy. "Mr. Pinkly, the window guy, found this stuck in one of the rhododendrons out front. The one right under the window that was broken last night. There's no telling how long it's been there, though."

He took the note from her and read it out loud. "Remember, there's plenty of room for you in the backyard, too."

Hearing the words again did nothing to calm her already frazzled nerves. His temper didn't help, either. His anger grew by the second as he studied it. "How on earth did Gage miss finding this last night?"

"I don't know. Like I said, all we know for sure is that it was there today."

Tripp handed her the note back. He did a slow visual sweep of the yard as if searching for the enemy in and among the shrubs. Finally, his dark eyes snapped back to look directly at her. "Have you called Gage? Because he'll be furious if you've been sitting on this."

"I haven't had a chance to tell him." She slipped the note into her purse for safekeeping. "Mr. Pinkly found it just as they were finishing up out front. They left just as you texted me. I thought we'd save Gage from having to make another trip out here by dropping it off at the police department on our way to dinner."

He tamped down his temper. "I'm sorry this is happening, Abby."

"Yeah, me, too."

This time her attempt to smile felt more natural. "But let's not let this ruin our evening. I've been looking forward to Frannie's pie all day."

At least he let her change the direction of the conversation. "Do you want me to drive?"

She was feeling pretty fragile right now, so maybe that was a good idea. Tossing him her keys, she said, "Sure thing."

He snatched them out of the air and walked around to the passenger side to open the door for her. It wasn't the first time he'd demonstrated such old-fashioned, good manners. True, she could've opened the door for herself, but she still appreciated the small gesture.

With luck, Gage wouldn't be in and she could just leave the note with whoever was manning the front desk at the police department. She'd let the officer know that she'd be home later in the evening if they needed to talk to her. Otherwise, she would be home most of tomorrow.

For now, she was going to do her best to ignore that somehow she'd managed to draw the attention of a killer.

Chapter Seventeen

Unfortunately, the desk sergeant insisted on calling Gage about the note before he'd let her and Tripp leave. After briefing his boss, the officer handed the phone over to Abby. It took only a minute for her to bring Gage up to speed.

"Like I said, Mr. Pinkly found it. I hadn't been near that part of the yard all day, so I can't say one way or the other how long it had been there."

Gage sighed, his frustration coming through loud and clear. "I'm really sorry I missed seeing it last night."

"We don't know that it was even there then."

Not that that would lessen the threat implied in the note. Besides, the thought of whoever had heaved the brick through her window sneaking back later to drop off a threatening message was creepy times a hundred. Maybe even a thousand.

"Are you going to be okay? The offer of having someone parked outside of your house still stands."

"I'll be fine. Tripp and I are headed over to Frannie's for dinner. After that, I plan to stay home with the doors locked and Zeke close at hand. And I'm thinking a bottle of wine might be a nice way to cap off the evening."

She paused briefly and then added, "All things considered, maybe even two."

He laughed a little. "I hear you. Now let me talk to Tripp for a minute. Enjoy your dinner, and I promise we'll get to the bottom of this, one way or the other."

"I know you will, Gage. Here's Tripp."

She handed over the phone and then walked to the other side of the small lobby, allowing the two men some semblance of privacy. They were talking about her, no doubt, but she really didn't want to know the details right now. She trusted Tripp would fill her in on anything she needed to know. Besides, she suspected she already knew what they were planning. Zeke wouldn't be the only personal body-guard she'd have tonight.

Tripp joined her at the door. "Ready?"

"Yeah, let's go. I want to get there before Frannie runs out of pie."

He looked horrified by that possibility. "That actually happens?"

"I've heard rumors to that effect. I'm planning on ordering mine as soon as we're seated."

"I like a woman who thinks ahead."

His grin brightened her spirits. For now, she wasn't going to think about broken windows, threatening notes, or the fact that a killer was still walking the streets of Snowberry Creek.

The café was packed. No surprise there. It might not be the fanciest place within easy driving distance, but it definitely had the best home-style cooking around. They found a booth in the far corner next to the front window, which had just been vacated by a young family.

When they were settled in, Tripp asked, "Are you really okay?"

There was a lot of gruff concern in his question. She looked up from her menu long enough to nod. "I am for now."

Evidently Tripp took her at her word, because he immediately turned his attention back to studying tonight's offerings at the café. "It's hard to decide what to order."

"Are you talking about the pie or the entrées?"

"Yes."

She understood just what he meant. If there ever was an occasion that called for comfort food, this was it. Tomorrow would be plenty soon enough to worry about all the excess calories she planned to consume tonight. The daily special of pot roast and mashed potatoes and gravy, along with whatever vegetable came with it, would do nicely. Add in a piece of chocolate cream pie, and what more could she ask?

Tripp must have been thinking along the same lines. When the waitress arrived to take their orders, Abby watched wide-eyed as he asked for a double order of the roast beef and three pieces of pie. While they waited for their food to arrive, she tried to think of a topic of conversation that wouldn't send them looping back to the broken window and that hateful note.

"How were your classes today?"

"Fine. The history class is pretty much a slam dunk. But as it turns out, my high school calculus is rustier than I thought."

She toyed with the napkin on the table. "I'm impressed. I never had calculus, rusty or otherwise."

He angled himself in the corner of the booth, stretching his long legs out under the table. "What did you major in?"

"Business, with an emphasis on human resources and management. My ex majored in marketing. Our two different skillsets made for a good combination when we decided to start our own import business."

"I take it you aren't part of the company anymore."

He wasn't really asking a question, but she found herself explaining anyway. "We knew going in that a lot of start-up companies don't survive, but ours did. It was our marriage that failed. He bought me out as part of the divorce settlement."

"So that makes two of us figuring out what comes next." Tripp's grin was surprisingly playful as he lifted his water glass up to offer a toast. "Here's to all the new possibilities life has to offer."

She smiled back at him and clinked her glass against his, once again her mood doing another upswing. "To the possibilities."

It was pretty clear that Tripp was talking about his future employment when he finished college. On the other hand, she was pretty sure it wasn't the job market that had her pulse racing. Luckily, the waitress arrived with their salads, giving her something else to concentrate on other than the handsome man sitting across from her.

An hour later, she followed Tripp out of the diner. She was stuffed almost to the point of being uncomfortable. If *she* felt that way, she couldn't imagine how Tripp could even walk.

"I can't believe you ate a double order of the roast beef, several pieces of pie, and then got another one to go. You said it was"—she paused to do air quotes with her fingers—"'for later,' but we both know that pie won't last the night."

Tripp didn't look the least bit ashamed of pigging out

like that. It wasn't as if she minded the higher cost of the meal. The total bill was far less than what she would have had to pay at the steakhouse in the next town over, but darn it, she would've liked more pie, too. If she'd eaten as much as he had, they would've had to roll her out of the restaurant in a wheelbarrow.

"I owe you for the extra entrée and the second and third pieces of pie."

When he reached for his wallet, she waved him off. "No, you don't. Dinner was my treat. I didn't put any limits on the offer."

They walked around the corner to the parking lot. "I'm just trying to figure out how you stay totally ripped like that and eat like you do." Okay, she had not meant to let the part about how well he was built slip out. "Forget I said that."

Tripp's grin turned wicked. "Which part? The part about me eating too much or the part about me being totally ripped?"

They both knew there was no way for her to win this discussion. "Never mind. Let's go home."

As she rounded the back of her car, heading toward the passenger door, the headlights from a truck pulling into the lot washed over her. It stopped as if waiting for them to pull out, but then suddenly the driver gunned the engine and drove to the far end of the row. It seemed odd, but maybe the driver had seen another spot farther down the line. She climbed in as soon as Tripp pushed the button to unlock her door. Seconds later, they were pulling out onto Main Street.

Still, something about that truck bothered her, but she couldn't quite put her finger on what it was. She looked back over her shoulder to see if she could see the driver. He was just pulling back out onto the street. Although he only gave them a very brief glance before turning away, there was something vaguely familiar about the man's profile. Then it hit her. If she didn't know better, she might have thought it was Troy Tolbert. There was no way to know for sure without a better glimpse of his face, but he'd driven off in the opposite direction.

"Everything okay over there?"

"I'm good."

More or less, anyway. Between the note and everything else, she was on edge. That wasn't Tripp's problem; it was hers. She briefly considered asking him to turn around and follow the truck until she could get a better look at the driver but then rejected the idea. Her mind had to be playing tricks on her, because Gage had said Troy had left town on one of his long-haul jobs. There was no way he could be back already.

They made the rest of the trip back home in silence. When they pulled into the driveway, Tripp turned the engine off but made no effort to get out of the car. He rested his hands on the steering wheel, his fingers beating out a soft rhythm for several seconds.

"Should I camp out on the couch again tonight?"

Rather than answer immediately, she gave the matter some thought. It was tempting to accept, but asking him to babysit her at night for the long term wasn't reasonable. Besides, if someone was really intent on doing her harm, daylight wouldn't guarantee she was safe. He couldn't stay with her twenty-four seven.

"Thanks for the offer, but I'll be fine. Like I told Gage, I've got Zeke and a cell phone. At the first sign of trouble, I'll call in the cavalry."

He nodded. "Do you want me to come in and make sure the house is secure?"

"Just walk me to the porch. If there's been any problem,

Zeke will let us know as soon as I open the door. After that, I will be fine."

And she would, too. No way she was going to let some person, or persons, ruin living in Aunt Sybil's house for her. It had been hard enough to walk away from the condo that she and Chad had called home for so long. She wouldn't be driven out again.

Tripp followed her as far as the porch and watched as she turned the key in the lock. Zeke bolted past her to greet his buddy as soon as she opened the door. He then bounded back up the steps to her, long enough to say hello. Before she could grab his collar, he was off and running again.

He did a quick circle of the backyard, stopping long enough to do his business. When he came trotting back, Tripp patted him on the head one last time.

"Thanks again for dinner, Abby."

"It was little enough to do for you sacrificing your back by sleeping on the couch last night."

"A price I'd willingly pay again for three pieces of Frannie's pie." He shooed Zeke up onto the porch. "Sleep well, you two. Call me if you need anything at all."

Oh, boy, he really shouldn't make blanket offers like that. It was definitely time to walk away. She offered him one last smile, hoping it didn't reveal any of her wayward thoughts. "I will."

Once inside, she considered her options for what was left of the evening. As much as the bottle of wine was calling her name, it probably wasn't a good idea to indulge herself with anything alcoholic. She hoped and prayed that the brick-throwing vandal wouldn't pay her a second visit, but she would need her wits about her if he did.

Maybe a bath and then spending time with a good book and a cup of herbal tea made more sense. The only problem was that the only books she had to read right now were all murder mysteries. Not exactly entertaining when she was living right smack in the middle of one of her own. Rather than dwell on it, she checked to make sure all the doors and windows were locked before heading upstairs. The entire master suite had been remodeled a few years back, and the bathroom now had all the bells and whistles, including a huge walk-in shower that she loved.

That wasn't where she was headed, though. Instead, she was going to enjoy the one original feature that Sybil had kept—a huge, old-fashioned clawfoot tub. She turned on the water and tossed in a double handful of her favorite lavender-scented bath salts. Next up, she lit the row of candles on the windowsill and the two on the vanity, filling the room with their soft flickering light. Already the tension she'd been fighting all evening was starting to fade. By the time she adjusted the volume on her favorite playlist and slipped into the steaming water, her mood was much improved.

But as her mind drifted, her thoughts kept coming back to everything that had happened since the day they'd first found Dolly Cayhill's body. Abby had moved to Snowberry Creek to give herself time to find a new direction for her life. Thanks to Aunt Sybil and the divorce settlement, she didn't have to be in a big hurry to pursue a new career. She'd looked forward to living at a much slower pace than she had in the years that she and Chad pushed hard to get their business off the ground.

But lately, her days and nights had been anything but the peaceful lifestyle she'd been looking for. Sure, she could put the house up for sale and move back to the city, but that idea held little appeal. She liked the majority of the people she'd met in Snowberry Creek, and right now she had commitments that required her continued presence in town. After all, she'd promised to serve out Aunt Sybil's terms of office on both the quilting guild and that senior affairs committee for the town.

She'd given her word, something she took seriously. That didn't mean she wouldn't spend the time until her current commitments ended figuring out what came next for her. If she couldn't find something she found satisfying to do with her life here in Snowberry Creek, then maybe it would be time to look farther afield.

But that would only be as a last resort. She loved this old house and had friends here in town who had come to mean a lot to her in a short time. Glenda and the ladies in the guild. Bridey and her husband at the coffee shop. Tripp. And finally, Gage Logan, even if she'd really rather not have to deal with him in his professional capacity again.

Yeah, she'd already put down some roots, ones she would really hate to rip up anytime soon. Now, if only they could figure out what Dolly Cayhill had seen or done that had gotten her killed. It would be so nice if life could go back to normal again. It was exhausting to worry about who might be lurking out there in the shadows.

Feeling chilled by that unhappy image, she ran more hot water into the tub in the hope it would chase away the darkness in her thoughts. If it didn't, she could always crawl into bed and pull the covers up over her head. That might not work, either, but desperate times called for desperate measures. If all else failed, she'd coax Zeke up onto the bed with her, even if he took up way more space than was comfortable. Heck, maybe she would do that anyway. At least then she wouldn't feel quite so alone.

Chapter Eighteen

One of the many things she didn't miss about her old life was having to wake up to an annoying buzz every morning. She leaned over Zeke and picked up her cell phone to check the time. Yeah, she was pretty sure she hadn't set her alarm to go off at eight-thirty. Must have been a dream. She started to put the phone back down on the bedside table when it started ringing.

Okay, her sleep-fogged mind had incorrectly translated the obnoxious noise as her alarm clock, when the reality was that someone was trying to call her. She squinted at the phone to see if she really wanted to answer the summons. When she saw Glenda's name on the screen, she dropped back down on her pillow and resigned herself to answering.

"Hi, Glenda. What's up?"

"Abby, are you okay? You don't sound right."

She rested her forearm over her eyes, trying to block out the bright sunshine streaming in through the window. "I'm fine. Just groggy. Not really awake yet."

Or actually at all.

After a slight pause, Glenda said, "Oh, I've been up for hours."

The woman didn't sound at all apologetic for dragging

Abby out of a sound sleep. In fact, Abby suspected she was a little shocked that someone might still be asleep at this hour. It was so hard not to accidentally disconnect the call and then mute the phone so she wouldn't hear it ring a second time. She was pretty sure her conscience could live with the guilt over ignoring her friend for another hour, maybe even as long as two.

Unfortunately, Glenda's next words hit her like a double shot of caffeine. "Abby, I just had to share the wonderful news. I'm getting my quilt back."

Abby bolted upright in bed. "The one you made for your niece? Did Troy Tolbert finally find them at his house?"

"Yes, it's the one I made for my niece. But, as it turns out, Troy didn't have it after all. A friend called me last night to ask me why I would sell my quilts for so little at a swap meet. All I can figure is that Julie really did take the quilts to sell for cash. I'm awfully disappointed in that girl."

Abby's brain still wasn't firing on all cylinders as she struggled to make sense of it all. "Did your friend tell you where she got it?"

"Like I said, Ruth spotted it at a swap meet and snapped it right up. She always did have an eye for a bargain. She didn't realize it was one I'd made until she got it home and saw where I'd embroidered my name and the date on the back. She agreed to sell it back to me for the same price she paid for it."

It was a shame that Glenda would be out the money, but Abby suspected that wasn't as important to her as getting the quilt back. "What I really meant to ask was if she told you where the swap meet was being held and if it would still be there."

"I didn't think to ask, but I can call her back and find out. Why?"

Abby would've thought the answer to that would be

obvious. "Because we're still missing all those other quilts. There might be a chance that we could track down more of them if we talked to the vendor who'd bought yours from Julie."

"I'll make the call right now."

"Good. Also ask her if she remembers the name of the person she bought the quilt from, or even a shop name if there is one. Meanwhile, I'm going to hop in the shower and then grab a quick breakfast. If the swap meet is open today, I'll go talk to the people to see if I can learn anything about the other quilts."

Except, considering she'd never seen the quilts, recognizing them would be problematic. Evidently, Glenda had the same thought. "I'll come with you, Abby. I might be able to recognize some of the other quilts if they are there. In fact, why don't I contact the other people who had bought a page in the calendar and get a description if I can."

"Good thinking. I should be ready to go in an hour. Will that give you enough time to check in with everyone?"

"Yes, it shouldn't take long. In fact, several of them might even have pictures they can send me. A lot of us keep notebooks for our patterns and pictures of the quilts we've made using them."

All of that would be really helpful, but still, Abby hesitated. "I'd really hate to get their hopes up too much. Even if Julie sold more of the quilts to the person at the swap meet, chances are they're already gone."

Glenda sighed. "I realize that it's a long shot. We wouldn't have even known where my quilt ended up if my friend hadn't happened to find it. I can't speak for everyone, of course, but I'd want to know one way or the other."

"And if we locate any of the quilts, should I buy them back?"

Before Glenda could respond, Abby answered her own question. "Yes, of course I should. And if any of the ladies involved can't afford what I paid for them, that's all right. In fact, we can consider the money a donation to the guild in my aunt's memory."

"Sybil would be so proud of you."

Abby would really like to think Sybil would feel that way. "I'll be there to pick you up in just over an hour. If you need to change the time, just leave a message if I don't pick up."

"I will."

Abby dropped the phone back down on the bed. It was so tempting to grab a few more minutes of blissful slumber, but there wasn't enough time. She threw back the covers and climbed down over the foot of the bed to avoid disturbing Zeke, who showed no inclination to move out of her way.

When she finished her shower and got dressed, he finally jumped down off the bed and led the parade downstairs to the kitchen. She let him outside and then fixed a quick breakfast for both of them. Zeke wolfed his down and then whined at the door.

She patted him on the head. "I have to go out for the morning, big guy. Unless Tripp's going to be around, I'll have to leave you in the house."

Before she could call the man in question, she spotted him out in the backyard. In case he was getting ready to leave, she blocked Zeke's frantic efforts to escape when she stepped out onto the porch.

"Tripp, would you be up for letting Zeke hang out with you for a while? I have to take Glenda somewhere this morning, and he's not happy about being shut inside."

"No problem. I'll be here until my afternoon class. I'll put him back inside before I leave if you're not back yet."

"That would be great. I'm not sure how long we'll be gone."

She opened the door and jumped back out of the way as

the dog bolted past her to join his buddy over near the garage. She topped off Zeke's water bowl and set it out on the porch. She also put several of his favorite treats in a baggy to hand off to Tripp on her way out. They both spoiled Zeke rotten, but she didn't care. By all reports, he'd had a rough time of it before ending up at the shelter. He deserved to know that not all humans were horrible, and the snacks were organic and healthy for him.

Tripp was waiting by her car. "Going anywhere special?"

Maybe he asked out of idle curiosity, but somehow she doubted it. Granted, the way things had been going for her lately, maybe he had good reason to worry. She handed him Zeke's treats. "If you must know, Glenda called to let me know one of the guild's missing quilts turned up at a swap meet. We thought we'd go check the place out in case some of the other ones are there, too."

"How did it end up there?"

"We don't know. A friend of hers bought the quilt and then realized it was Glenda's creation. The lady was willing to sell it back to her, but she had no idea how the people at the booth got it in the first place."

"Interesting." He moved out of her way.

Before getting into the car, she just had to ask one question. "So, tell me. Did that third piece of pie make it through to breakfast?"

"Nope." The jerk actually looked proud of that fact. "Heck, it barely made it in the door last night."

"That's what I figured."

Again, if she'd eaten like that, she wouldn't have been able to fasten her jeans this morning. "See you later. Zeke, behave."

As she started to back out of the driveway, Tripp motioned for Abby to lower her window. "Did you need something, Tripp?"

He grinned at her. "Yeah. Stay out of trouble and try not to tick off anyone else today."

She didn't dignify that with a response. She also didn't miss the fact that he was still laughing as she drove off. Regardless of what the big jerk thought, she had a reputation for getting along with all kinds of people, even former soldiers.

Well, at least sometimes.

It took longer than expected to get to the swap meet. Since they were passing close by the area where Glenda's friend lived, they'd stopped there first to pick up the quilt. The woman was sorry to lose such a bargain, but, under the circumstances, she was only too glad to sell the quilt back to Glenda. She'd also been able to give them a description of the person at the swap meet who had sold it to her. She didn't remember seeing any other quilts of similar quality, but space in the booth was pretty limited.

Glenda sighed. "I'm sorry Ruth wasn't more help."

Abby was, too, but it wasn't her fault. "There was no reason for her to have grilled the vendor on where she got the quilt. Neither of them had any idea that it was stolen goods."

"I just hope that we can recover the rest of the quilts. It doesn't seem likely, though, since Ruth doesn't remember seeing any others like it."

Hoping that they'd recover the other eleven quilts so easily was probably wishful thinking, but maybe they'd get lucky. After all, who would have guessed that of all the people who frequented the swap meet, the one who'd spotted the quilt had been a friend of Glenda's.

There was no use in giving up on the possibility that they'd find more of the quilts at the same location. "That doesn't mean they aren't there. It could be that the proprietor was only putting out one at a time if the booth is small."

"We'll just keep our fingers crossed."

Glenda pointed at a building sitting off to the side of the road. "There, that must be the place. Ruth said it was nothing fancy."

That was an understatement. Abby eyed the ramshackle structure. The center of the building looked as if it had originally been a small house with wooden siding. There were longer additions jutting out from both sides and the back that were covered in corrugated steel, some of it rusty. Classy.

They had no problem finding a parking spot right by the door. It was the kind of place that probably did the majority of its business on weekends, so they were lucky it was even open.

Once inside, Abby stopped to give her eyes a chance to adjust to the dim interior.

Glenda looked around and then asked, "How do we figure out which way to go?"

Before Abby could answer, a man standing behind the first table on the left held out a sheet of paper. "Hi, there. Here's a map for you. We try to group merchants with similar wares together to make it easier for customers to find their way to what they're looking for. Maybe I can point you in the right direction if you're looking for something in particular."

That would certainly make things easier for them. "A friend bought a lovely quilt while she was here yesterday. The woman who sold it to her was named Rowena. We thought we'd take a peek to see if she had any more like it."

He laid the map down on the table and drew circles in three different spots. "This first one is Rowena's booth, but there are a couple of other possibilities if Rowena doesn't have what you're looking for. She does sell a lot of textiles, but these other two also carry some."

Abby took the map. "Thanks for the help. We appreciate it."

If he had sold something besides car parts, she would've made a small purchase as a way of showing her gratitude in a more tangible form. But as they walked by, she spotted one item that drew her interest. "How much for that toy army Jeep? It looks the right size to go with a friend's G.I. Joe collection."

He held it out so she could get a better look at it. "It's not that brand, but it is the right size. I'm asking twenty dollars for it."

When she hesitated, he grinned and winked at her. "But for two lovely ladies, I'll take ten."

He probably would've taken five, but Abby didn't bother to haggle since he went out of his way to help them. "You've got a deal."

As they walked away, Glenda gave her a knowing look. "I'm guessing that's for Tripp. How do you know he has a G.I. Joe collection?"

Abby wasn't about to admit that this wasn't the first present she'd purchased for her handsome tenant. The ladies from the guild already had too much fun teasing Abby about him. Nothing good could come from giving them more ammunition.

To change the subject, she pointed down the aisle ahead of them. "I know we'll walk right by the other two places on the way to Rowena's, but let's start with her and work our way back."

"Fine with me, but I know you're trying to distract me, young lady." She patted Abby on the arm as they continued on down the aisle. "I just think it's sweet that you'd buy that toy for Tripp. I bet he'll think so, too."

Maybe he would, but the man was anything but predictable. Right now, she had other things on her mind. "I'm trying to decide how best to approach this woman. I have to wonder why she didn't question why someone would be selling such a beautiful quilt for so little, especially if it wasn't the only one she bought."

Glenda's eyes widened. "I didn't think of that. Aren't there severe penalties for dealing in stolen goods?"

"I'm sure there are, but then most of the stuff in this place is secondhand. They could have the best of intentions and still occasionally end up buying something from a person who had no right to sell it in the first place."

Abby coasted to a stop while she thought things through. "No, I think the smartest thing to do is to play it safe. I don't think we should mention the quilt Ruth bought was actually yours. Instead, we'll tell Rowena that your friend told you about the lovely quilt she purchased here. We came to see if she had any more of the same amazing quality, which is more or less the truth."

The older woman immediately nodded, no doubt all too glad to let Abby take point. "I'll trust your judgment."

They each drew a deep breath and took that last step forward into the booth. If Abby had to describe the place in one word, she would call it cluttered. There were heaping piles of doilies on one counter, and crocheted baby blankets, hats, and mittens on another. The shelves on the right wall were lined with plastic crates on their sides to form a row of cubbies. Each one was stuffed full of different yarns, but not very many of any one type. Enough for a small project, perhaps, but not for anything that required more than two or three skeins of the same color.

Glenda was studying a stack of linen tea towels and

fancy pillowcases. "My mother had this same kind of towel in her kitchen. I did some of the embroidery on them myself. I also made the lace edging on a lot of pillowcases. I probably still have some tucked away somewhere. They made for a pretty bed, but I really hated ironing them."

Abby laughed. "Aunt Sybil must have felt the same way about them. I found a bunch up in the attic that she and other members of the family had done over the years. I was going to ship a few off to some distant relatives of her late husband, but I decided to launder them first. They came out of the dryer looking like wadded up paper towels. I might eventually get around to pressing them. Well, provided I can remember where Aunt Sybil kept the ironing board."

Before Glenda could respond, a lady stepped out of the storeroom behind the counter. "Can I help you ladies find anything in particular?"

Glenda took a half step back to let Abby take charge of the conversation. "You have a lot of interesting things here in your shop, but what we were hoping to find is a quilt like the one you sold our friend yesterday. It was such beautiful work, and we were wondering if you had any more like it."

"If it's the one I'm thinking of, I can understand why your friend loved it so much. It was beautifully done."

"Do you know if the person who sold it to you had any more to offer?"

"I actually bought three quilts from him."

Him? It had been a man who had sold the quilts? That fact left Abby feeling a bit stunned.

Meanwhile, Rowena was still talking. "I have two more in the back."

Abby let a little of her excitement show. "I'd love to see them."

Glenda waited until Rowena ducked back into the storeroom to whisper. "I'm so tense right now I can hardly

breathe. Julie must have let her new man handle the sale
for her."

"It sounds like it. Now, take a deep breath, and you'll be
fine. If they're our quilts, we'll pay the lady and return them
to their owners."

The two of them had studied the pictures that Glenda
had received from her friends before coming to the swap
meet. Neither of them had thought it would be a good idea
to walk into the place flashing photographs and demanding
to know if anyone had seen a bunch of stolen quilts.

Rowena was back. She carefully unfolded the first quilt
and laid it out on the counter. One look was all it took to
know it was another of the quilts Julie had taken. Meanwhile, Rowena made room to spread out the second quilt.

Abby traced the minute stitching with her fingertip.
"They're both quite beautiful. Don't you think so, Glenda?"

"They are. You can tell a lot of hours and love went into
the making of these."

Bracing herself for some serious sticker shock, Abby
asked, "How much do you want for the pair?"

Rowena wrinkled her nose. "Actually, I sort of promised
two of my regulars first crack at these."

Abby wasn't sure if she believed her, so she let the
games begin.

"Only *sort of* promised?" She looked around the booth.
"Because it looks like we're the ones standing right here
with money in hand. Well, depending on what you're asking
for them."

Which Abby was willing to bet would be far more than
Ruth had paid for the other quilt. Sure enough, Rowena
hemmed and hawed a bit before naming a figure that had
Glenda gasping in shock.

Ignoring her friend's distress, Abby counteroffered with a number only slightly higher than what Ruth had paid.

Rowena sighed heavily. "You see, I really hate to disappoint my regular customers."

Yeah, right. Abby recognized a shark when she saw one. Rowena would screw over her best friend if it meant a profit. "Again, they're not here, and there's no guarantee they would buy the quilts anyway."

Again, if those regulars actually even existed. The negotiations continued for another minute before they finally agreed to meet in the middle.

Abby handed over her credit card. While waiting for the payment to go through, Rowena refolded the quilts. "I'll get these wrapped up for you. I hope you enjoy them for years to come."

Glenda finally rejoined the conversation. "By any chance, did the guy who brought them in say if he'd be coming in with more things?"

Good question, but Rowena's answer was disappointing. "Nothing specific. As I recall, he mentioned that he'd just started cleaning out his mother's house and wasn't sure what all he'd find worth selling. He did say that if he came across anything else I might be interested in, he might stop by the next time he was in the area."

That didn't sound very promising at all. "I take it he wasn't local."

"It didn't sound like it."

Abby handed the bag with the first quilt off to Glenda. "Any chance you could tell me his name?"

Rowena was already shaking her head. "No, I make it a policy to protect the privacy of the people I do business with."

Abby tried one more time. "Can you at least tell us what he looked like?"

Rowena went on point. "Why? What does that matter?"

Good question. What excuse could she give for wanting to know? "I just thought it might help other vendors know who we were asking about. I understand that you want to respect his privacy."

"He came in right at closing, and the booth was really busy. I didn't have a chance to talk to him for long. He was just an average guy. The only thing about him that stood out at all was that he was wearing sunglasses, even though it's not all that bright in here."

Then she looked around the booth. "If there's nothing else I can show you, then I need to get back to doing inventory. I'm sorry I couldn't be of more help."

Abby picked up two of Rowena's business cards off the counter. She stuck the first one in her purse and then scribbled her own name and phone number on the back of the second one and gave it back. "If he brings in any more quilts, please give me a call."

The other woman studied the information and frowned. "Are you a collector, or are you buying them to resell?"

"Neither, actually. I recently inherited a large Victorian house that I'm redecorating. These quilts will be perfect for the guest bedrooms."

"If I see him again, I'll call. But like I said, he was a little iffy about whether he'd be back by here or not. He didn't give me any contact information other than his name."

From the way Rowena's gaze slid off to the side with that last part, she wasn't being completely honest about what she knew. Maybe she suspected there was something hinky about the guy but didn't want to admit it. Regardless, it was pretty clear that they'd gotten as much out of the woman as they were going to without resorting to direct threats. Maybe Gage could've convinced her to reveal the guy's name, but maybe not. This wasn't his jurisdiction, and they'd already recovered the only quilts the woman had at the moment.

They'd barely walked out of the door when Rowena came charging out behind them. "I don't know that it means anything, but I just remembered there was something distinctive about the cap that guy was wearing. It was black, and the logo was a fuchsia-colored, lady's high-heeled shoe. I've never seen that particular logo before, and it struck me as odd."

Every little bit of information helped. "Thanks again."

Glenda waited until they were some distance away before speaking. "Do you think there's any chance that she actually already has more of the quilts?"

After pondering the thought, Abby shook her head. "No, I don't. She had no reason not to show them to us if she did. My gut feeling is that it played out just as she said. The guy waited until she was busy, offered her a deal on the three quilts, and then left just as quickly as he came in."

"It would be useful if we knew something about the guy Julie ran off with. Maybe then the police could track them down."

Abby hated to burst her bubble, but the truth was there wasn't much the police could do about the situation. They had no solid proof that Julie had the quilts, especially with her husband swearing he'd never seen them in the house at all. "We can talk to Gage about it, but he wouldn't have much to go on."

"Well, we might as well check out the other two booths while we're here. I want to be able to tell the other ladies that we tried our best."

They stopped to study the map. "Looks like we need to

turn left just ahead. The first place should be right around
the corner and the second just past that one."

It didn't take long to learn that the mysterious man
hadn't been in either booth. They had no quilts for sale at
all, which was disappointing but not surprising.

Glenda took the news pretty hard. "Well, at least it
wasn't a complete failure. It was too much to hope for that
we'd find all of the quilts."

"I know you're disappointed, but at least we know a
little more than we did before. I'll tell Gage about what
happened. Who knows, maybe he'll have some ideas about
how to proceed from here."

"I'll let the two women who made these quilts know that
we have them back. Everyone else will be disappointed,
but at least I'd warned them we weren't optimistic about
our chances for success."

As they walked out into the bright sunshine, Glenda
seemed to shake off her gloomy mood. "If you're not in a
hurry to get back home, why don't we stop for lunch? You
pick the place, and it will be my treat."

She looped her arm through Glenda's. "Lady, I love the
way you think. Let's forget all about missing quilts and
gloomy thoughts, and just enjoy ourselves."

If nothing else, she could celebrate the fact that she
hadn't pissed anyone off today. Tripp would be so proud.

Chapter Nineteen

Gage sipped the iced coffee that Abby had brought him and set it aside. "It's a longshot, Abby, but I can make some calls."

She fought to hide her disappointment. After all, she'd known when she walked into his office that there probably wasn't much he could do to help recover the quilts. "Anything you can do will be appreciated. Glenda and the other two ladies were thrilled to get theirs back, but they also feel bad about the ones that are still missing."

He paged through the stack of five pictures she'd brought him. "These will be helpful to help identify at least a few of the missing ones."

Abby nodded. "The other three ladies are still looking to see if they have any photos. If nothing else, they both said they can provide samples of the fabrics they used and a description of the pattern."

Gage set the pictures aside. "So three quilts have been recovered, and we have pictures or descriptions of eight more. If my math is correct, that still leaves one unaccounted for."

"Yeah, that would be Aunt Sybil's quilt. Since the ladies

didn't tell each other which quilts they were submitting for the calendar, no one knows which one she gave to Julie, including me."

"She didn't keep an album like these other ladies did?"

"To tell you the truth, I haven't had a chance to check. I've barely started going through everything in the house." She offered him a rueful smile. "Somehow going through her things in the quilting room seems a lot more invasive to me than going through her closet and dresser. Added to that, it never crossed my mind that she might have maintained files of her past work until Glenda mentioned that it was a common practice among the members of the guild."

He studied her for a few seconds. "Are you going to check now?"

She hesitated, but then finally nodded. "I will, but I'm not sure how much good it will do. I have no idea how many quilts she made or what she did with them all. It could take time to match any pictures she may have kept to the quilts still in the house. Any that are unaccounted for could be ones she did for gifts or donated to various charities over the years."

"Well, at least we have this much." He pulled out a folder and carefully placed the pictures inside. "I'll keep you posted if I learn anything, good or bad."

"I appreciate it, and now I should let you get back to work."

"One more thing before you go."

A sick feeling settled in her stomach. What had she done this time? "What's that?"

"I just wanted to make sure you haven't had any more problems at home. No sign of anyone sneaking around the place or anything."

"Not that I know of. No more broken windows or threatening notes."

"You'll tell me if anything happens, won't you?"

"Sure thing."

Did he think she was a complete idiot? Well, maybe he did have some grounds for thinking she might not be fully forthcoming if something minor happened. She finished the last of her own drink and tossed it in the trash. "I only saw Tripp for a second last night, but he didn't mention any problems. I'm thinking the whole thing with the window might have been some teenage prank after all."

Gage wasn't buying it. "I might have accepted that some idiot kids went on a brick-throwing spree, but no one else has reported anything like that happening. To me, that means you were specifically targeted. Then there's the note. I know you don't want to hear it because it's big-time scary, Abby, but that note was clearly a threat."

She sank back in her chair, his words hitting her hard. "I just can't figure out what I did that would stir up that kind of anger in someone. Yes, I asked a few questions, but I backed off doing that when you told me to. I haven't crossed paths with Dolly's friends again, and I haven't talked to her niece since the other day. I've also stayed away from Frank Jeffries."

Was that everyone who might hate her? No, there was one more. "And finally, I have no desire at all to tell Troy Tolbert that Julie did take the quilts. She must have hidden them from him until she was ready to leave."

"Yeah, talking to him about anything to do with his wife probably wouldn't go over well. I can't imagine coming home from a long business trip to find my wife had taken off with another man."

Speaking of Troy's business trips. "Gage, about Troy. Didn't you say that you personally saw him leaving town on a run?"

"I did. From what he said, he makes that same trip a couple of times a month. Why?"

She grimaced. "I saw someone who reminded me of him as we were driving out of Frannie's diner the night after the window got broken. Obviously, I was mistaken."

And now she wished she hadn't brought it up. She might not have appreciated Troy complaining to Gage about her, but she did understand the pain he must have gone through over his wife's decision to end their marriage with no warning. Chad hadn't run off with no warning, but the end results of his actions were the same.

She hadn't realized that she'd said that last part out loud until she noticed the sympathy in Gage's expression. She found it harder to take than anger would have been.

"That must have been hard for you."

Luckily, he returned to the topic at hand. "Back to the window and note. My guess is that you stepped on someone's toes without realizing it. Maybe he or she thinks you know more than you're letting on. We also can't assume that whoever killed Mrs. Cayhill thinks like a normal person would. Even if it turns out that killing her was done on impulse, that doesn't change the fact that the disposal of her body showed a lot of careful thinking. Look how long it went undiscovered. You would have thought waiting around for months for the body to be found would've taken its toll on the killer. Instead, provided the guilty party is still in the area, he or she is going about their daily life as if nothing happened at all."

That had occurred to her. "Do you have any leads at all?"

He hesitated, making her think he wasn't going to tell her anything. Finally, he said, "We know she had an airline ticket she never used. That narrows down the date she died to somewhere between December twenty-third, the day she argued with your aunt, and December twenty-eighth, which was when she was supposed to fly to Florida. There are a couple of other things we're still looking at, but nothing definitive yet."

That's what she was afraid of. Well, this was a conversation she didn't want to continue. It was definitely time to leave. She picked up her purse. "Like I said, I'd better let you get back to work. I'm going home to hole up in Aunt Sybil's quilting room for the afternoon. If I figure out which quilt is missing, I'll let you know."

"Sounds good." Then he surprised her with a smile. "I heard through the grapevine you got roped into helping with the city-wide cleanup day that the mayor's office organized."

She sighed. "Yes, somehow they realized I hadn't signed up to help. Connie called me personally to see if I'd mind working the dessert table during the lunch break. When I couldn't figure out a way to get out of it, she then pointed out that since I was going to be there anyway, they could use some help replanting some of those huge flower pots along Main Street."

Gage laughed. "The woman is crafty that way. If it's any consolation, she's got me, Seth, and a couple of other guys spreading bark in the flower beds at the park."

As they talked, he ended up escorting her all the way out to the parking lot. Maybe he just wanted a breath of fresh air, but she suspected he considered it his duty to make sure she made it to her car safely. She blamed it on the fact that he was in law enforcement, but she'd noticed Tripp had also taken to doing the same thing. He would casually ask where she was going and when she'd be back. At first, she didn't think anything of it, figuring he was simply making neighborly conversation. But lately, whenever she was heading for her car or returning from an errand, he would just happen to be working in the yard.

Any other time in her life, she might have resented their hovering, but the threatening note combined with the broken window had given her a serious case of the heebie-jeebies. Having Tripp around helped calm the waters for her. And sure enough, when she turned into her driveway, he stepped out onto his porch. Did he have that pistol stuck in his waistband? Not that she was going to ask him.

She still hadn't given him the toy truck she'd bought for him. It was tempting to leave it by his front door when he was gone to class, but that seemed cowardly. Well, no time like the present. After grabbing the bag out of the backseat, she got out of the car and headed straight for him. "Do you have a minute?"

There was a brief hesitation before he finally moved closer to the front step. "Yeah, but that's all. I'm working on a paper and needed a break before I start in again."

She stopped just short of the porch. "You know Glenda and I went to that swap meet yesterday to buy back any of the quilts."

He slowly nodded, his eyebrows riding low over his dark eyes, clearly wondering what that had to do with him.

Abby tried to explain. "Well, there was a man there who went out of his way to help us, and I wanted to buy something from him. You know, as a way to thank him."

Another nod, this one slower still. "Okay."

"Well, he mostly sold car parts. Even if I recognized what they were, I wouldn't know what to do with them if I had them. Long story short, I bought this from him."

She stepped close enough to shove the bag into his hands before retreating to a more comfortable distance. "It's for you."

As if that hadn't been obvious.

He peeked inside the bag, his look of confusion morphing

into one that was much harder to read. A second later, he pulled the small vehicle out and held it up to inspect it in detail. Was he angry?

"Thanks, I think?"

At least he didn't immediately try to give it back. "I thought it would go with the action figures. The guy who sold it to me said it wasn't the same brand, but it was the right size."

"It is." He put the truck back in the bag. "I'll add it to the collection."

She couldn't help but tease him a little. "Up in your closet out of sight?"

Not that she'd ever seen him entertaining any guests of either gender since she'd moved into Sybil's house. He'd been looking straight at her, but now he was staring at some point past her right shoulder. Before she could turn to see what he was finding so fascinating, he answered her question.

"Actually, a couple of them are sitting out on the desk. I like to have something to fiddle with when I'm thinking."

She would've bet her last dollar he wouldn't have admitted to that. Rather than jerk his chain about playing with toy soldiers, she changed the subject. "I promised Gage we'd let him know immediately if there were any more incidents. You know, like the window and the note."

His gaze did a slow sweep across the yard before coming back to her. "I haven't seen anything new, but I have been keeping an eye out."

"Me, too." Well, that had pretty much exhausted the last topic of conversation she could come up with. "Well, I'd better go let Zeke out for a while."

"I took him for a walk about an hour ago."

That was a relief to hear. She enjoyed their strolls, but

she wasn't in the mood at the moment, and had been dreading it. Maybe it was all the talk about the potential threat still lurking out there somewhere.

"Enjoy yourself studying."

He rolled his eyes. "Yeah, there's just nothing more fun than writing an essay for an English lit class."

"I remember those days." She forced herself to back away, making her intentions to leave clear. "I'll be gone a good part of tomorrow. I got volunteered to help out at the mayor's cleanup party."

The big jerk snickered. "I repeat—you're really going to have to get better at saying no, or you're going to be sucked into helping out on every project or serving on every committee in town."

He wasn't wrong about that, not that she'd admit it. "I can say no when I want to."

Tripp arched an eyebrow, his smile all superior and irritating. "So you're saying you really do want to be on the senior affairs committee and heading up the quilting guild, although, as far as I can tell, you haven't even threaded a needle since I met you?"

Rather than continue an argument she couldn't win, she walked away. "Thanks again for walking Zeke."

He was still laughing when he walked inside and closed the door.

The next morning, Abby woke up to a bright sunny day, the perfect weather for the town's cleanup event. After a quick breakfast, she headed off to help get everything set up to feed lunch to the volunteers. Just before noon, Connie Pohler cruised by the food tent to make sure everything was set for lunch. "Thanks again, Abby, for volunteering to help with serving lunch and then with the flower pots."

Shanghaied was more like it, but Abby kept the snide remark to herself. For one thing, she actually liked the mayor's assistant a lot and didn't want to offend her when the woman was only doing her job.

"Not a problem. I'm enjoying myself."

Surprisingly, that was true. She'd been assigned to the crew serving lunch to the volunteers. Although she hadn't met all of her coworkers before, a couple of the women belonged to the quilting guild. Better yet, Bridey was manning the dessert table with her.

Connie looked up and down the serving line and nodded in approval. "Everything looks great. I need to check on a few other things, but you have my number if something comes up that you need my help with." She flashed another smile and then she was off and running again.

Bridey turned back to cutting the large pans of brownies she'd brought from her shop into individual servings. "That woman makes me tired just watching her. She and the mayor accomplish more in a day than I do in a week."

Abby laughed. "I'm not sure I believe that. You run your own business with all that entails and still have time to make desserts to feed the entire town."

Bridey looked pleased with Abby's assessment. "I didn't make all of this stuff. Frannie donated several of the pies, and one of the local churches baked the cookies. The other churches combined efforts to provide the salads and side dishes. The town had the sandwiches catered."

"I'm impressed how everyone pulls together to do things like this. I've never lived in a place where things like this happen."

But maybe she was wrong about that. Looking back, she and Chad had been so incredibly focused on their business to the detriment of everything else, including their marriage. "I don't know if it comes from living in a small town, or if I simply never took the time to get to know my old neighborhood."

Bridey handed her a small spatula. "Let's get a bunch of these plated up before the crowd hits this end of the table." Once they had fallen into an easy rhythm, she picked up the conversation where Abby had left off. "When I was married to my first husband, we both worked at his family's restaurant. It definitely ate up every minute in our day and all of my energy. It wasn't until I walked away from the job and my marriage to move back here that I remembered how much I enjoyed days like this. He would've never understood the appeal."

Bridey nodded toward a group of men making their way toward the food line. Her husband waved as he walked by, deep in conversation with two men Abby didn't know. "Seth gets it, though. He's made good friends here in town, but he also moves in the high-end art world just as easily. It's one of the things I love about him."

Abby set down several brownies in a row and was about to turn back to get the next load when she realized all of the men in the group, including Seth, were wearing black baseball caps with a bright pink stiletto heel on them. That had to be the same logo Rowena had described, the one the man who'd sold the quilts to her had been wearing. Her best guess was that one of the sponsors for the day's activities must have donated the caps for the volunteers. But which one?

Unfortunately, with the huge crowd of people working their way down the buffet in her direction, now wasn't the time to abandon Bridey. After lunch, though, she'd go on the hunt. Once she figured out the source of the distinctive caps, she'd tell Gage what she'd learned. With luck, they would be one step closer to learning who had sold the stolen quilts. If they succeeded, at least she would have solved one of the two big mysteries in her life. She'd rather clear her aunt's name, but right now she'd take any progress she could.

Chapter Twenty

The crowd plowed through the food line, consuming everything in sight. Good thing the woman in charge of the whole meal had advised all the helpers to fix themselves a plate, including desserts, before they started serving everyone else.

Abby carried her plate as well as Bridey's over to a table where two seats had just opened up. Her friend followed with their drinks. "Whew, it feels good to sit down."

Bridey agreed. "I'm on my feet a lot during the day at the shop, but I move around a lot. I'm definitely feeling the burn from standing in one place for so long."

"At least you know your brownies were a major hit. If I hadn't grabbed a couple early on, I would've had to go without."

"I'm glad you like them. Personally, I scored a piece of Frannie's blueberry pie."

They'd just started eating when a deep voice spoke from right behind her, making her jump. "Hey, how come you rate two brownies?"

She twisted around in her chair to glare up at Tripp.

"First of all, I've asked you not to sneak up on me like that. And second, I got two because I volunteered to help serve the desserts. Besides, Bridey likes me better than she likes you."

Bridey almost choked on the bite she'd just taken. After swallowing, she held up her hands. "Hey, you two leave me out of it. I just baked the brownies. I didn't set the rules on who got how many."

Tripp walked around to the other side of the table and sat down across from them. "Sorry, Bridey. I didn't mean to put you on the spot. I'm just pointing out that Abby here took advantage of her position to sneak extras."

As he spoke, he tossed a cap down on the table, the exact kind Abby was looking for. "Hey, where did you get that?"

He picked it back up and twirled it on his finger. "This? What's the answer worth to you?"

Abby rolled her eyes. "Okay, let me guess. The price of an answer is a brownie."

He nodded, his grin somewhere between wicked and hopeful. "Or two."

She tugged the small plate holding the brownies closer to her side of the table. "One, and that's my best offer."

He tossed her the cap and snagged a brownie. "It's a deal."

She tried to hand the cap back. "I don't need this. I just want to know where you got it."

"Keep it anyway. It's not exactly my style."

Bridey gave him an appraising look. "I'm guessing the high heel image isn't manly enough for you."

Tripp winked at her. "Not at all. I could totally rock the stilettos. It's the wrong shade of pink for my coloring."

After finishing off the last of his brownie, he finally answered Abby's real question. "Some of the sponsors of today's festivities were giving away freebies. The hats were donated by a local trucking company."

She pushed the other brownie across the table. He eyed it and then gave her a suspicious look. "Why are you being so generous all of a sudden?"

"No reason, but if you don't want it . . ."

"I never said that." He grabbed the brownie and took a big bite before she could change her mind. While he finished it off, she ate the last few bites of her own lunch.

Tripp stood up. "I'll take your trash, and then I'm heading back to the house before that lady from the mayor's office figures out we've already finished up all the projects at the park. A bunch of guys from the local veterans group showed up to help, so it didn't take as long as she thought it would. I wouldn't put it past her to have a list of other stuff she'd like done around town."

"You could help me replant the flower pots on Main Street."

He held out his hand for their empty plates and cups. "Nope, if I'm going to do stuff like that, I'd rather work in your yard. Besides, one of us should let Zeke out for a while."

"Fine, be that way. Before you go, though, have you seen Gage anywhere?"

At the mere mention of the police chief's name, Tripp tensed up and immediately did that scan-the-perimeter-thing he was always doing with his eyes. "He was still over at the park right before I came here. Why? What's wrong now?"

Now Bridey was looking worried. "Abby, has something else happened?"

Evidently word about the broken window hadn't made it as far as the local coffee shop. "Someone tossed a brick through my front window the other night, and it's left me a little jumpy. As far as we know, it was some teenagers on the prowl."

Abby shot Tripp a quelling look before he could contradict her. Yes, she knew that both he and Gage thought there was more to the incident than mere high jinks. Now wasn't the time to rehash that discussion, even though she suspected they were right. Pointing to the cap, she explained, "But to answer your question, Tripp. I need to talk to him about the guy who sold those quilts to the lady at the swap meet. From what she told us, he might have been wearing a cap just like this one."

Tripp relaxed, but only a little. "Do you want me to help you find Gage?"

Nice of him to offer, but she really didn't need a security detail to escort her through town, especially in broad daylight with so many people out and about. "No, that's okay. I'll go look for him at the park, but then I've got to get back to city hall to help with the flower pots. After I'm done there, I'll head back home."

She made a show of scoping out the area and dropped her voice to a whisper. "Because I think you're right about Connie having that big to-do list."

"See you at the house, then. Bye, Bridey, and I loved the brownies."

Abby watched as Tripp disappeared into the crowd. When he was gone, Bridey gave her an assessing look. "Don't take this wrong. I like Tripp, but he can be awfully intense at times. Do you find him hard to deal with?"

He was also very private and wouldn't appreciate being the topic of conversation. On the other hand, she felt compelled to defend him. "Not at all. He's a great tenant and not just because he does so much work around the place. That's part of the deal he struck with my aunt, but he's really conscientious about it."

She managed a small smile. "But beyond that, I don't know how I would have gotten through the day we found Mrs. Cayhill buried in the backyard without him. And on the night when someone threw the brick through the window, he insisted on sleeping on the couch in my living room so I wouldn't have to be alone in the house."

Reminding herself that he deserved to have his privacy protected, she added, "Although I wouldn't like that to get out. Gage is still investigating both the murder and the vandalism, so we're not supposed to talk a lot about what happened in either instance."

Okay, even though that was true, Tripp sacking out on her couch wasn't exactly part of the investigation. She was just hoping that it would give more weight to her request that Bridey keep that particular detail to herself.

"Don't worry. I won't tell anyone. Now, I'd better get my baking sheets back to the shop and see how things are going there. My assistant is great, but the other barista just started working for me about a week ago. They might need a little extra help this afternoon with all these people working around town.

Bridey headed back to where the cleanup crew was starting to break down the tables that had been used to serve the food. Meanwhile, Abby picked up Tripp's cap. Rather than leave it behind, she put it on. It wasn't exactly her style either, but at least it would help protect her from the sun for the time being. As she adjusted the strap in the back to fit her better, she checked the immediate area to see if she could spot Gage anywhere close. When she didn't see him, she walked toward the park.

About two blocks down, she spotted a familiar-looking pickup truck driving down the street. She slowed to watch it, almost sure it was the same one she'd seen the other night in the café parking lot. Unfortunately, the sun hit the windshield at just the right angle to make it difficult to see the driver clearly. It was a man, but that was about all she could tell for sure. Right before he would've pulled even with her, he gunned the engine and did an abrupt right turn into a narrow alley between two buildings, without bothering to signal first. The driver right behind him had to slam on his brakes to avoid running into the back end of the pickup. He honked and flipped off the truck driver before continuing on down Main Street.

She didn't blame the guy in the car for his actions, but the truck peeling off into that alley was a bit odd. If she was right about it being the same truck, then that was the second time the driver had done something strange in her vicinity. Maybe she was getting paranoid, but either he was a lousy driver all the time, or he was trying to prevent her from getting a good look at him for some reason.

Why would he feel that way? Not that she was going to hunt him down and ask. If she was wrong about the situation, she'd look like a fool. If she was right, then she'd probably only make the guy even madder at her. And, after all, she'd promised Tripp she'd try not to aggravate anyone new for a while.

Rather than dwell on the subject, she hurried on down the sidewalk. Connie had told her that everyone who was supposed to work on the flower pots should meet in the parking lot behind city hall in about twenty minutes. That didn't leave her very long to find Gage and get back to where she needed to be.

When she reached the park, she didn't see Gage anywhere, but one of his deputies was driving through the parking lot. She'd met him on the day they'd discovered Dolly's body, but so much of that day was still such a blur in her memory that she couldn't remember his name. No matter. She waved him down anyway.

He stopped and rolled down his window. "Hi, Ms. McCree. Is there something I can help you with?"

She stepped close enough to his cruiser to talk without having to yell. "I was wondering if you might know where Gage is right now."

"It's actually his day off. The last I heard he and his daughter had plans for this afternoon. Is there something I can do for you?"

It seemed unlikely that Gage had informed his staff about the missing quilts. It wasn't as if it was a major case, and they no doubt had more important matters to deal with. "No, that's fine. I wanted to tell him something, but it can wait."

Although he was still smiling, the deputy definitely had his cop face on now. "Does it have something to do with either the murder investigation or the broken window?"

"Nope, neither of those things. I'll catch up with him on Monday."

He seemed hesitant to leave, but finally he said, "If you're sure . . . enjoy your day."

She backed away from the car. "Thanks, I will."

As he drove away, she had to wonder if all the deputies would always think first of Dolly's death whenever they looked at her. Was that one of the unexpected hazards of their job? Did they see past case files instead of individual citizens? For their sake, she hoped not.

Now wasn't the time to dwell on such things. She had dirt to dig and plants to stick in pots. Once she was done with that, she could finally go home. Once there, she'd fix something light for dinner and then spend the evening up in the quilting room looking for pictures of Aunt Sybil's quilts. If she found them, she'd spend tomorrow inventorying the quilts in the house, matching them with the pictures.

Maybe, eventually, she'd finally be able to figure out which one Sybil had dropped off at Julie's house. The chances of getting it back were pretty low, but then she really hadn't expected to get back the three they'd already recovered.

Her evening planned out, she reported for flower pot duty.

Chapter Twenty-One

"Come on, boy, let's go outside and work in the yard."

The big dog pushed his back end up off the floor and did a long stretch. Abby grinned as he held the position for a surprisingly long time. "You know, Zeke, my old yoga instructor would be most impressed with your form doing that downward-facing dog pose."

He took the compliment as his just due, continuing his stretch another few seconds for good measure before trotting over to stand by the door. She let him out and grabbed her sunglasses and water bottle off the counter before following him out onto the back porch. It was tempting to curl up in one of the rattan chairs and read for a while, but she was restless and really needed to do something more active.

She'd spent most of Saturday evening and a good part of Sunday rooting around in the quilting room. Her intent had been to look for any records that her aunt had kept of the quilts she'd made over the years, but everything had gotten so dusty that she'd started sneezing like crazy. It was almost embarrassing that she'd let the room that was so quintessentially her aunt's get so dirty. After hours of dusting, vacuuming, and scrubbing, the room was finally back up to Sybil's exacting standards.

At least in the process, she'd finally found the files she'd been looking for. Matching the pictures to the quilts in the house had taken a surprising amount of time. In part, it was because the quilts were scattered all over the place. The easiest ones to find were in use on the various beds in the house, and a few more were displayed on quilt racks. Several more were in the cedar chests in the master bedroom and one of the guest rooms.

Sybil had also noted which quilts had been donated to charity or that she'd made as gifts for specific people. While all of that had helped, there were three pictured in the files still unaccounted for. They could be packed away up in the attic, but Abby wasn't in the mood to wade through all the clutter up there to look for them right now.

Besides killing off the dozens of dust bunnies that had threatened to take over the quilting room, the only good thing that came from all the work was that she'd found a picture of the quilt she and Sybil had made together. Eventually, she would have the print enlarged before having it matted and framed as a reminder of that special summer with her aunt.

Granted, she'd rather have the actual quilt, but that one was lost for good. Not that she wanted it back now, but Dolly Cayhill's makeshift shroud was locked up with the rest of the evidence the police had gathered the day her body had been recovered.

Too many dark thoughts. She definitely needed to spend time out in the sun. After getting her yard tools from the shed, she walked around to the front of the house to work on deadheading the hanging baskets on the front porch and the roses planted along the far edge of the yard. Zeke wandered around on his own before finally seeking out another favorite napping spot in the shade of a vine maple tree. It afforded him a clear view of the rest of the yard and allowed him to keep an eye on her.

She appreciated his nondemanding company. "You know, Zeke, having you around is like having my very own furry guardian angel."

He woofed softly, acknowledging her praise, before settling in for a nap. While he dozed, she started on the flower baskets, dropping the dead and dying blooms into a bucket. Next up, she watered and fertilized the baskets to keep them blooming for a while longer. When that was done, she started on the roses. She'd had to do a lot of reading on gardening to figure out how to take care of her aunt's most prized flowers.

Zeke's low growl was the first warning she had that she was no longer alone. She tightened her grip on her pruning shears as she slowly turned around to face her unexpected and definitely unwelcome guest. What on earth was Troy Tolbert doing standing in her front yard? Whatever his reason was for being there, she wasn't happy to see him.

"Sorry if I startled you, Ms. McCree. I happened to be passing by when I spotted you working in the yard."

She hadn't checked to see if Tripp was home, but at least she had Zeke. The dog had left his place in the shade to sit beside her. Troy glanced at him and took a half step back. She appreciated even that small difference in the distance between them. Odd that she felt so uncomfortable in this particular man's presence, when everyone else thought he was such a great guy. Judging by the tension in Zeke's stance, she wasn't the only one who wasn't a fan.

"Is there something I can help you with, Mr. Tolbert?"

Although she couldn't imagine what it might be. Good

to her word, she hadn't gone near him or his house since their one encounter. She wondered what Gage would think about the man seeking her out after he'd reported her to the police for bothering him.

He shifted from side to side as if uncomfortable with the situation, too. After giving Zeke another worried look, Troy finally answered her. "I happened to run into Mrs. Unger at church, and she mentioned that she'd gotten her quilt back."

It was hard not to sigh. She'd really hoped that Glenda would've kept that little tidbit to herself. At the very least, Abby would've preferred she not talk to Troy about it, but there was no use in denying it. "Yes, she did."

He looked at her expectantly, maybe hoping she'd be more forthcoming. Finally, he said, "Evidently, it was just stupid luck that the woman who bought the quilt from some secondhand dealer happened to be a friend of hers."

"Yes, it was an amazing coincidence."

He ran his fingers through his hair as if finding the entire discussion frustrating. "See, here's the thing. Like I told you before, I never saw the quilts. However, I realize now that doesn't mean that Julie didn't take them. I can't believe she'd steal from her friends like that, but then I still have trouble believing she would walk out on me, too."

If he'd been anyone else, Abby would've felt sorry for him. God knows she'd had her own bad experience along those same lines. But for some reason, she didn't quite believe him, even if she couldn't pinpoint the reason why. Maybe he really was the innocent party and was genuinely shocked that his wife had deserted him, but she still had to wonder if he'd done something to drive Julie to take such extreme measures to get away from him.

She aimed for sounding sympathetic. "I'm sorry this is all so hard for you, Mr. Tolbert."

He flashed her a boyish smile. "Thank you, but please call me Troy."

Considering she had no intentions of ever being friends with the man, what she called him didn't really matter. "Why did you want to talk to me specifically?"

"Mrs. Unger said you had also managed to buy back two more of the quilts at the same place. I was wondering if the vendor could tell you anything about the man who sold them to her."

"Why?"

His expression hardened. "I would think that would be obvious. If it was the guy who Julie ran off with, maybe I could get his name. If so, I might be able to track her down through him, since my in-laws haven't been any help. I get that she doesn't want to come back home, but we have some legal stuff that we need to work through. I can't do that as long as I don't know where she is. She might be moving on with her life, but I'm stuck here spinning my wheels."

Okay, that was a legitimate enough reason for asking, but Abby was still reluctant to go into much detail about their discussion with Rowena. No way she wanted to send an angry man in that woman's direction.

"The only description she could give us was that he was an ordinary guy just like a bazillion others who passed by her place in any given day. I asked for details, but there was nothing about him that stood out to her. Evidently, he came in when the booth was crowded, so she didn't have much time to talk to him."

"Did she happen to catch his name?"

"Not that I know of. To be honest, her place does a brisk business in textiles of all kinds. It's doubtful this one transaction would stand out from all the others."

Troy frowned. "Did she think there was any chance he'd be back with more quilts to sell?"

Abby shrugged. "No way to know. As far as she knew, he was just passing through the area. Besides the booths at the swap meet also come and go with no notice. There's no telling if the same booth would be there even if he does come back."

Once again, something about Troy's reaction to her answers seemed off somehow. If Troy was really hoping to learn the man's identity with the hope of tracking down his missing wife, Abby would've expected him to look frustrated or at least disappointed with the few details she'd been able to provide. Oddly enough, she got the impression that he was relieved. For sure, a lot of the tension in his body language had faded considerably.

On the other hand, Zeke's hadn't. He still watched every move Troy made, no matter how small. What was it about the man that put the normally friendly dog on edge this way? She trusted the dog's instincts, though.

"I'm sorry I couldn't be of more help, Mr. Tolbert." When he frowned, she tried again. "Sorry, I meant Troy."

He shrugged "Well, there are still more quilts missing. Maybe we'll have better luck if more turn up for sale."

When Troy took a step forward with his hand out, Zeke lurched to his feet with a deep growl rumbling in his chest. Abby immediately grabbed him by the collar, not that she'd be strong enough to stop him if he really did go on the attack.

Troy staggered back several steps. "What's his problem? I was just going to shake your hand. You need to keep that dog chained up before he hurts somebody."

It wouldn't help the situation to point out that Troy was the only person that Zeke had ever threatened that way.

"I'm sorry, but I don't know what's gotten into him today. I'll put him in the house after you leave."

And not a second before. She'd also give him several treats for forcing Troy to keep his distance, but she kept that part to herself.

Troy didn't respond to her apology. Instead, he stalked off down the sidewalk in the direction of his own neighborhood. She had to wonder how he'd happened to pass by her house. It was a little out off the beaten path from his place. Not that that meant anything. After all, she'd also sort of happened to pass by his house when she'd wanted to talk to him about the quilts.

"Zeke, my boy, I think I'm chasing shadows when it comes to the quilts, not to mention the matter of Dolly's death."

Patting him on the head, she turned her attention back to the roses. "Funny, though, that both mysteries involve a quilt. How odd is that?"

She poked and prodded that idea while she cut a bouquet of roses for the kitchen table. By the time she'd put away her gardening tools and dumped the dead flowers in the yard waste bin, she finally decided that, all things considered, the quilt connection was pretty darn odd. But try as she might, she couldn't figure out what it meant. Standing in the backyard staring at nothing wasn't going to accomplish anything, either.

For now, she'd give Zeke his promised treats and then fix herself a cup of tea and read out on the porch for a while. With luck, her subconscious would continue to tug on the loose thread and eventually unravel the mystery. She could only hope. But if all else failed, she'd mention it to Gage and see what he thought.

* * *

Sleep didn't come easily as Abby's thoughts waltzed in circles, chasing an elusive idea that remained just out of her grasp. Normally the soft patter of rain on the roof would have lulled her to sleep, but not this time. She had tried hard to relax, but her mind kept spinning and spinning and getting nowhere. Any other time she would've put it off to too much caffeine, but the tea she'd had after dinner had been an herbal that was supposed to help people sleep.

Right before midnight, she finally gave up the fight and went back downstairs to read a little more, hoping that going through her bedtime routine one more time would hit her reset button and let her catch some shut-eye. It was a little after one before she went back to bed. After settling in, she stroked the soft cotton of the patchwork quilt and took comfort from the connection to the past and the special times she'd shared with her aunt in this house.

Evidently, her plan worked, because that was the last coherent thought she had until Zeke suddenly jumped on the bed and started barking like crazy and jarring her out of a sound sleep. The hot blast of doggy breath as he gave her face a quick lick chased the last filaments of sleep from her mind. Sitting up on the side of the bed, she shoved her hair back behind her ears.

"What's got you all upset, Zeke?"

Then she heard it for herself. Someone was pounding on her back door. Grabbing her cell phone, she considered calling the police before venturing down to the kitchen, but all she'd able to tell them was someone wanted her attention. Fearing she might be starring in a scream-queen movie as the ingénue who runs back into the house, she grabbed her robe and crept down the steps in the darkness.

Her tension eased up a little when she reached the hallway downstairs that led to the kitchen. It was clearly Tripp bellowing out there on her back porch, in between bouts of

pounding on the door. She ran down the hall, stubbing her
toe on the leg of a chair as she rounded the table on her
way to let him in. Hopping on one foot and muttering
words that would've horrified her aunt, she unlocked the
door and jerked it open. He stood there, fist raised and
blood dripping down the side of his face.

Her own pain forgotten, she stood back to let him stumble inside. Pushing him into a chair, she grabbed a clean
towel out of the drawer and pressed it to his forehead.

"What happened to you?"

Tripp shook his head and winced with the motion. "Call
the cops first before he gets away."

"Who?"

But she didn't wait for him to answer before dialing the
three numbers that would once again bring the cavalry
rushing to their rescue. While she waited for the emergency
operator to answer, she went from window to window on
the lower floor, looking out into the darkness for any sign
of the intruder. She didn't see anyone, but that didn't mean
much. He could be long gone, or he could be crouching in
any number of places, hidden by the deep shadows under
the trees.

After telling the emergency operator the bare bone facts
that there'd been an intruder and her neighbor was hurt, the
woman promised the police would be on their way. Tripp
glared at Abby when she also requested the EMTs come as
well, but she didn't care. Rather than argue with him, she
went through the house to turn on the porch light. The flash
of red and blue lights in the distance meant help was already heading their way. She scurried back to tell Tripp the
good news.

Besides, if it turned out that he didn't need medical treat-
ment, she'd apologize to all concerned. She was no expert
in trauma care and had no idea how badly he was hurt. She

wasn't going to assume this was a minor head wound, which she knew could still bleed like crazy. Case in point, she grabbed another towel and tossed the blood-soaked one into the sink.

"You promised answers."

His cheeks flushed hot as he adjusted the towel to peer up at her from behind the crimson terrycloth. She might have thought it was due to his injury, but he looked more embarrassed than anything.

"I have trouble sleeping some nights, and the walls close in on me. When that happens, I walk the perimeter of the yard. I spotted someone sneaking up on your back porch."

For the first time, she noticed he was wearing flannel pajama bottoms and a white T-shirt, both of which were soaking wet from the rain. Not only that, he was barefoot. The meaning of what he was telling her finally sank in and sent waves of fear burning along her nerves. Regardless, she would not—could not—give into the terror, not with Tripp cold and hurt. There'd be time for that later. For now, she hustled back down the hall and grabbed an afghan out of the hall closet and wrapped it around his shoulders.

"Thanks."

His complexion now looked ashen. Rather than press him any further for answers, she decided to wait until the police were with them so he'd only have to go through it once. The sound of the doorbell chiming came as a relief.

She patted Tripp on the shoulder. "I'll be right back."

Before opening the door, she peeked out through the curtains at the two men on her porch. Only one was in uniform, but the other was all too familiar. The emergency operator had obviously also called Gage, dragging him from bed in the process. She sighed and unlocked the door. "Sorry to drag you out in the wee hours of the morning."

He ignored her apology. "What's happened now?"

She tightened the belt on her robe. "I'll have to let Tripp do the honors, Gage. I was upstairs asleep when he came pounding on the back door to say there was an intruder. That's as much as I know at this point. Right now he's in the kitchen nursing a head wound."

Gage looked around the front yard before responding. When he did, it was to give his deputy orders. "Wait until the second officer arrives and then do a full yard sweep. If some guy managed to take down Tripp, I don't want either of you out there on your own."

By that point in the discussion, the aid car from the fire department was pulling up out front. "Send them on in. Tell them the kitchen is straight down the hall."

"Will do, sir."

Abby let Gage go first, needing that half second of extra time to bring her badly jangled nerves under better control. When she finally reached the kitchen, she noticed Tripp was on his third towel and would likely be needing a fourth pretty soon. Stubborn man might not think he needed the EMTs, but she was glad they were there to make sure he was going to be all right.

Gage looked at his friend with rough concern. "You okay?"

"I've had worse headaches after a bar fight." Tripp pulled the towel away from his forehead to look at it and then pressed it back in place. "But not many. The bleeding is slowing down, though."

Abby wasn't so sure about that, but the front door had just opened again.

A woman's voice called out, "Fire department!"

Gage answered for them. "Back here, Angie!"

He and Abby stepped back out of the way and let the EMTs do their thing. They managed to stop the bleeding, but both of them thought Tripp should be transported to the local hospital to be checked out at the emergency room. Although the bleeding was scary enough, Abby's fear about the severity of Tripp's injuries skyrocketed as soon as they started throwing around words like concussion.

He wasn't having it, though. "Just put a few butterfly bandages on the cut, and I'll be fine."

She wanted to hit the stubborn man. Stepping between her hardheaded tenant and the EMT, she put her hands on her hips and got right in his face. "Tripp Blackston, knock off the macho crap and get your stubborn backside to the hospital. I'll pay the bill, whatever it takes. Right now, you're covered in blood, you're half frozen from getting soaked out in the rain, and your hands are shaking. Don't tell me you're okay. I don't want to hear it."

Someone in the room muffled a laugh, most likely Gage. Tripp ignored their audience, his dark eyes more worried than mad. "Fine, but I want you to drive me. No ambulances."

Clearly, there was no winning this argument. "It's a deal."

Abby smiled at the woman Gage had called Angie. "I'll go throw on some clothes, and then the two of us will head straight to the hospital."

"We'll bandage his wound while you do that." Then Angie stepped closer. "Are you sure you're up to driving him? You're looking a little shaky, too."

No surprise there. "I'll be fine."

Maybe she was fooling herself, but she evidently didn't fool anyone else. Gage intervened. "I'll drive him there as soon as you've got him patched up a bit. I need to take his statement, anyway." Then he looked at Abby. "You're coming with us, too."

Both she and Tripp started to protest at the same time,

but Gage cut them off with one look. "Until I know what is going on around here, I don't want her here alone."

What could she say to that? "I'll . . . go get dressed."

As she headed up the stairs, holding on to the railing for support, she realized one thing. If she hadn't been scared enough already, she sure as heck was now.

Chapter Twenty-Two

Abby had been prepared to wait hours in the emergency room for Tripp to be seen, but evidently there was nothing like having the local chief of police as a personal escort to speed things up. She was still on her first cup of coffee when they called her back to the examination room where Tripp sat perched on the side of a hospital bed.

He looked only marginally better now than he had when they'd brought him in. The bandage on his forehead was different, and someone had given him a surgical scrub shirt to wear in place of the bloodstained T-shirt he'd had on when they'd arrived.

"Are you doing all right?"

He winced as he nodded. "Pretty much, other than my head feels like it's an anvil and someone is banging on it with a ten-pound hammer. They decided I needed a few stitches, so I'll have an interesting scar as a permanent reminder of why I shouldn't go prowling without being fully armed. Wearing shoes would have been a smart idea, too."

While she wasn't particularly comfortable around weapons of any kind, under the circumstances she could certainly understand why he felt that way. "I'm so sorry this happened, Tripp."

If anything, her comment only made him crabbier. "Unless you were the one sneaking up on your own back porch with a club in your hand, what do you have to be sorry for?"

She bit back the urge to snap back at him. He was tired. Well, they both were, but he was hurting. There was also a distinct possibility that he was beating himself up over letting the intruder get away. Then the meaning of what he'd just said cut through the fog in her mind.

"Dear God, he hit you with a club?"

By this point Tripp looked even more disgusted. "No, he didn't. When he saw me coming, he took off running toward the trees along the back of the yard. I'd almost caught up with him when I stubbed my stupid toe on a root and took a header into one of the Douglas firs. First thing tomorrow, I'm cutting that stupid tree down and turning it into firewood."

It was tempting to laugh at the image of Tripp taking revenge on an innocent tree, but she couldn't really blame him for wanting a little payback.

"Where's Gage?"

"He's checking in with his deputies to see if they learned anything useful at the house. He said he would be back to update us in a few minutes."

"When can we go home?"

"Soon. The doctor is still waiting for the results on the scan they did to make sure I didn't crack my skull on that tree. I tried telling them I was too hardheaded for that to happen, but they said they'd heard that story before."

She smiled only because he expected her to. She was too angry at the sneaky creep who had caused Tripp to get hurt to think anything was funny about the night's events. "Did you get a good look at the guy?"

"Gage asked me that, too. On top of it being the middle

of the night, the porch light wasn't on, and it was raining. I'm ninety-nine percent sure it was a guy, but I couldn't pick out any details. He was wearing dark clothes and could haul ass when he wanted to, which makes me think he's in pretty good shape and probably not all that old. Best guess, he could be anywhere from fifteen to fifty."

Gage walked back into the room. "The doctor says he'll be right in to go over your results with you. After that, I'll drive you both back home."

Abby tossed her empty coffee cup in the trash. "Any news from the deputy?"

Like maybe the guy had come back and surrendered peacefully. Yeah, like that was ever going to happen.

"They found some footprints in one of the flowerbeds in the backyard. They covered the area with plastic to protect them from the rain."

Tripp shifted a bit as if trying to find the one position that didn't hurt. "Could be mine. I worked in that part of the yard this week."

Gage pointed at Tripp's shoes. "Not unless those clod-hoppers of yours have recently shrunk a few sizes. The one complete print they found measures between a ten and an eleven."

Tripp held out one of his feet for her inspection. "In case you're curious, I wear a thirteen. But half the men in town probably wear a ten to an eleven, so that's not particularly helpful."

Gage didn't argue the point. "No, it isn't, but every bit of information helps."

Then he picked up two of the molded plastic chairs from the far corner and set them down right in front of Tripp. "Have a seat, Abby. I've already taken Tripp's statement, but I need yours as well."

God, this was getting old. She felt like she should be

earning frequent flier miles with the Snowberry Creek Police Department. She plunked down in the seat. "I didn't see the guy, so I don't know how much help I can be."

Tripp snickered, wincing as he did so.

"What's so funny?"

"I'm guessing Gage wants to update the list of people you've talked to or aggravated lately. He needs to make sure it's current."

"Not funny, Tripp."

"Yeah, it is. You just have no sense of humor."

All right, that was insulting. "I'll have you know, I have a great sense of humor. I just don't find any of this amusing."

His expression immediately sobered. "Sorry, Abby. I understand why you're upset and scared. Blame it on the pain meds, which are at long last kicking in. Not sure what they gave me, but the buzz is really kind of nice."

She managed a small smile. "If they're that good, share some with me, and we'll call it even. In fact, I'll even throw in a dozen cookies as payment."

Gage made a pretense of covering his ears. "Would at least one of you remember that I've sworn to uphold the law? I can't hear that kind of stuff."

It was her turn to apologize even though she knew he was mostly kidding. "Sorry, Gage. If I act a bit punchy, I promise it's lack of sleep and not chemically induced."

"Good to hear it." He got out his little notebook and opened it to a new page. Boy, she was really learning to hate that thing.

"Start at the beginning and tell me what happened."

She gave him a brief replay of the events from the minute Zeke had started throwing a hissy fit and ending when Gage and his deputies arrived. He asked a few questions, but the events were pretty cut and dried.

"Now, like the man said, help me update the list of anyone you've talked to over the past few days."

It didn't seem fair to point the police in the direction of people who were obviously innocent. Maybe he'd let her be a little more selective. "How about just the men? We know it wasn't a woman on the porch tonight, and it's doubtful many women could throw a brick through my window like that."

He considered her question briefly before finally shaking his head. "No, I'd rather have everyone's name just to make sure we've got all the bases covered. Just because it was a man on your porch tonight doesn't mean there isn't a woman involved, too."

Sending a silent apology into the cosmos to the ladies on the list who she knew had to be innocent, Abby rattled off all the names she could think of. First, she named the women from the quilting guild she'd talked to recently. "Then there's Ruth, the friend of Glenda's who bought her quilt at the swap meet, and Rowena who owns the shop where it was sold. I don't remember her last name, but I have her business card at home. I talked to a bunch of people at the town cleanup event the other day, but that was mostly to do with serving food or potting a bunch of plants. I had lunch with Bridey that day."

She waited until he caught up with her before continuing. "After lunch, I talked with one of your deputies to see if he knew where you were. I wanted to tell you that I think the guy who sold Rowena the quilts might have been wearing one of the hats from the trucking company that donated a bunch to the volunteers on Saturday. Considering how many of them were given away, though, that's probably not going to be much help in finding the guy."

"You're probably right about that, but I will add the info to my file."

"Is that everybody?"

She almost said yes, but then she remembered the odd conversation she'd had with Troy Tolbert. "No, there's one more although he's already on your list—Troy Tolbert."

Before she could explain the circumstances, Gage looked up from his notepad with a frown. "You promised you'd stay away from him."

"And I have. This time he found me, not the other way around. He stopped by yesterday afternoon. He said he happened to be passing by and saw me working in the yard. He had run into Glenda at church and heard about how she'd gotten her quilt back. He wanted to know if the store owner knew the name of the guy who'd sold her the quilts."

That had Gage sitting up taller. "Why?"

"Troy is hoping if he can identify the guy, he might be able to find his wife. He said he's accepted she's not coming back, which means there are legal things they need to get started on so they can both move on. That much is true. I know from my own experience, there's no way to untangle their lives completely until the lawyers and courts have settled everything."

"What did you tell him?"

"That the booth owner didn't remember much about the guy. He came in when the shop was busy, so she didn't spend much time with him. Even if she did have his name in her records, she wouldn't give it to me. All she did say was that he was of average appearance. The only two specific details she mentioned were that he wore sunglasses and a black hat with a pink high heel on it."

Might as well tell him the rest even if she had no idea how he'd react. "By the way, I didn't share any of that description with Troy. I also pointed out that the booths at the swap meet probably change all the time. Even if the guy does come back with more quilts, chances are the same booth might not be there."

Tripp blinked several times as if having a hard time following the logic of her comment. "Why did you tell him that?"

"Okay, I know everyone seems to think Troy is a great guy, so this might sound crazy. There's just something about that man I don't trust." She held up her hand to forestall whatever Gage was about to say. "Having said that, the ladies of the quilting guild really like him and feel bad about how his wife left him. Even though it's been months since that happened, at least a few of them still take him casseroles and baked goods on a regular basis."

Tripp perked up. "Are you talking about the dreaded tuna casserole?"

When she nodded, he shuddered.

"That poor fool." He gave her a narrow-eyed stare. "By the way, you promised to make Jean stop, but she showed up with another one just yesterday."

Did she really want to know? Yeah, she did. "What was her special ingredient this time?"

"Anchovies." Tripp's expression was pretty bleak. "Lots and lots of anchovies."

Gage gave up trying not to laugh, and she couldn't help but join in. Tripp clearly didn't think it was funny and muttered under his breath that there would be retribution at some point.

Dragging herself back to the matter at hand, Abby tacked on one last item to her reasons for not trusting Troy. "I know this is going to sound stupid, but in my defense, I'm not the only one who doesn't care for the man. Zeke doesn't like him, either. Not at all. In fact, both times we've crossed paths with him, Zeke has growled at Troy. To my knowledge, he's never done that to anyone else."

At least neither man laughed at her, although it was difficult to tell how much weight Gage gave to a dog's opinion.

"Did Troy say anything else?"

"Not that I remember other than I needed to keep Zeke chained up. He left right after that, and I went back inside."

Gage made a few more notes and returned the spiral book to his pocket. "I'll let you know if we learn anything more about who was on your porch tonight, but we don't have much to go on."

"I know."

Which made it all the more scary. She was getting tired of being afraid. Right now all she wanted to do was go home and hide from the whole world. Her two companions were looking pretty haggard, too. At the sound of approaching footsteps, they all looked in unison toward the door. She hoped like heck it was the doctor back with Tripp's test results.

Luck was with them. The doctor peeked around the curtain that afforded the room some privacy from the constant stream of people passing by the glass wall that faced the nurse's station in the middle of the emergency room.

"Mr. Blackston, looks like you were right about your hard head. No fractures." He softened the comment with a smile. "The nurse will be in to discharge you in a few minutes. Follow the list of directions she'll give you and check in with your family doctor in a week to get the stitches out. If your symptoms change or get worse, see him sooner or come back here."

He glanced at Abby. "He really shouldn't be alone for the next twenty-four hours. Will you be with him?"

Before Tripp could protest, she nodded. "I will keep an eye on him."

"Good. Take care, everybody."

The nurse came in right after he left and made quick work of Tripp's discharge instructions. That he didn't protest when they brought in a wheelchair for him to ride in on the way out to where Gage could pick them up, was clear evidence of just how bad he was feeling by that point.

The ride home was uneventful, and Gage helped her get Tripp inside and settled in the bed across the hall from her own room. He promised that one of his deputies would be parked out front for the rest of the night and that he'd stop back by in the morning to see if they could find any more evidence to help identify the intruder. She suspected he didn't hold out much hope. At least it had finally stopped raining, which would make any investigation easier to do.

She locked up once Gage left and trudged back upstairs to get ready for bed for the second time in one night. It felt like heaven to crawl back under the covers. Meanwhile, Zeke seemed unsure which human needed his company more. Finally, he flopped down on the rug in Tripp's room. She wished he was closer to her but didn't begrudge him for wanting to stay near his injured friend.

The way things had been going lately, tomorrow would probably bring a whole new set of problems, but right now she didn't care. She turned on her side to face the open door, which afforded a view of the man sleeping across the hall. Poor guy, he never signed on for this kind of trouble when he'd moved into the cottage out back. She'd have to think of a special way to thank him yet again.

She drifted off to sleep thinking about apple pies and chocolate cakes.

Chapter Twenty-Three

The next morning Tripp insisted on heading off to class despite Abby's best efforts to convince the stubborn idiot to stay home and take it easy. At least he'd let her drive him and promised to call her if he got to feeling worse. One of Gage's deputies was parked out front when she returned. She walked Abby to the door and made sure everything was okay before returning to her squad car. She also promised that she and the other deputies would maintain a high profile in the neighborhood until further notice.

Once the woman left, Abby left Zeke to stand guard and went upstairs to continue hunting for the last few quilts pictured in Aunt Sybil's notebook.

She found two in one of those plastic storage bags with all the air sucked out, so at least some progress was being made. As she continued her search, it occurred to her that she hadn't mentioned the odd coincidence to Gage or Tripp that both mysteries she was dealing with involved quilts. It was probably better that she hadn't, considering how both of them felt about her asking too many questions.

Right after lunch, she was debating if she wanted to dive into another one of the closets upstairs when the phone rang. Seeing that it was Gage calling, she sat back down at the kitchen table as she swiped her finger across the screen to answer. She was starting to think she should give him his own ring tone.

"Hi, Gage. What's up?"

"I tried to call Tripp first, but he didn't pick up. How is he doing today?"

No use in sugar coating the situation. "In my opinion, not all that well. I think his head was still hurting, but he insisted on going to class. I drove him, and he said he should be able to hitch a ride home with a classmate. I told him to call me if he got to feeling worse and needed to come back early, but we both know that's not going to happen."

There was a thread of amusement in Gage's voice when he responded. "Soldier Boy might not let you fuss over him, Abby, but I'm willing to bet that he appreciates the fact that you care enough to try."

Did men ever make sense? Not that she'd noticed recently, but they didn't seem to understand her all that well, either. "Any news on our intruder?"

"Sorry, but not so far."

She couldn't help but be a little disappointed by that even if she wasn't surprised. "Well, it was a long shot considering the rain and everything."

"We'll keep trying, though. I know you've already talked to my deputy this morning, and my nightshift guys will be driving past your place on a regular basis for the next few days. You know, just in case."

"That's good to know. Thank them for me. I'll definitely sleep better knowing they're out there."

After a brief silence, Gage let out a slow breath. "I debated telling you about this next part, but I think you should know. I would also appreciate it if you'd keep it to yourself. Well, you can tell Tripp if you feel the need, but otherwise no one else. Okay?"

She hated to make promises without having all the facts first, but she trusted Gage enough to do as he asked. "Mum's the word."

"I drove out to talk to Rowena out at the swap meet. She gave me the same basic description she gave you, so nothing new there. However, she did show me the name and address the guy gave her. Since it was a cash transaction, she didn't ask for any identification. When I ran the name and address, they both turned out to be bogus. Under the circumstances, I can't say I was surprised."

"Yeah, that makes sense if he and Julie are trying to stay under the radar."

The whole situation gave her the creeps. Why did they feel such a powerful need to hide? Unless Julie was afraid of being found for some reason. Stealing a bunch of quilts didn't seem like a good enough motive.

"I can understand why she might be hiding from Troy. From what he said, she practically emptied their savings accounts before she left, not to mention she took a bunch of stuff that could be easily sold for cash. Of course, the guy could be the one who's on the run. There are all kinds of reasons that could be in play. Maybe he's wanted for back child support or something."

Gage picked up the conversation from there. "Here's the thing, though. As far as I can tell, no one has actually talked to her at all, not even her parents. They have gotten a few emails saying she's okay and promising to let them know when she gets settled someplace, but that's all. It's been months now, so they're worried and understandably upset about her behavior. Oddly enough, they're siding with Troy. I get the impression they're pretty conservative and disapprove of a wife deserting her husband."

Abby couldn't help but express her opinion on that subject. "That all depends on the reasons she left. When I found out Chad was cheating on me, there was no way I could stay with him, so I'm not exactly impartial on the subject."

"I can see why. Anyway, I wanted to let you know that we're pretty much at a dead end on the quilt situation. And for what it's worth, I'm inclined to trust Zeke's impression of Troy. I don't have to tell you to avoid him if at all possible."

"No, you don't. And if he comes around again, I'll either lock myself in the house or find Tripp if he's home."

"Good thinking. Take care, Abby. And why don't I call Tripp and offer to pick him up from school? That will save you driving out there again, and I'll be out and about anyway."

"If you're sure, . . . or is that your way of telling me that I have to stay locked up in the house all the time?"

After a few seconds of silence, he finally answered. "No, but it would be smart if you stick to public places with lots of people around."

"Okay, I will. Talk to you later."

She sat staring off into space for several moments, her thoughts going nowhere fast. Finally, Zeke padded into the room to sit beneath the hook that held his leash.

"Subtle hint there, Zeke. But you're right. It's time for both of us to get some fresh air." She considered their options. "For a change of pace, let's drive over to the park and walk along the river. That should be okay. There's always a lot people hanging out there, and we can even stop at Bridey's on the way. A latte for me and one of her doggy treats for you."

Zeke stared up at her with those soulful dark eyes of his, as if telling her that one just wasn't enough, not for a guy his size. Okay, she was probably imagining things, but maybe not. Either way, it wouldn't hurt to indulge him a bit.

"Okay, big guy, I'll still get a latte, but I'll throw in two treats for you and maybe one for me. How does that sound?"

He barked in response as his tail beat out a syncopated rhythm of pure joy. She laughed at the way his jowls wobbled when he barked to hurry her along. After patting him on the head, she took down his leash and opened the back door. "Okay, jowly boy, let's hit the road."

She lucked out and scored a parking spot right in front of Something's Brewing and ran inside to get the goodies while Zeke waited in the front seat. She didn't bother locking the car. Who would mess with it while a ninety-pound dog with big teeth was on guard duty? After stowing her drink and Zeke's treats out of his reach, she drove down to the park where the two of them sat at one of the picnic tables and basked in the warmth of the sun.

Afterward, they did an extra lap along the trail that followed the river, so she could work off the extra calories from her peach muffin. By the time they reached the car, they were both happily tired and ready to go home.

The only question was which way they should go. The most direct route would take them right by Troy's house, and she'd promised to stay away from him. On the other hand, she didn't plan to drop by for a visit, and she would be safe in the car with Zeke there to protect her. Danged if she'd spend the rest of her time living in Snowberry Creek driving blocks out of her way to avoid one man.

Regardless, she'd drive straight past without slowing down or paying any attention to his house. If he was in the front yard and saw her passing by, well, she'd deal with that prospect if it came up. As soon as she turned down his street, she regretted her decision. Not only was he outside, but the truck parked in his driveway was all too familiar.

Without a doubt, it was the same one she'd seen in the parking lot at the Creek Café and again the other day when the driver had done an abrupt turn to avoid driving past her.

And if it really was Troy who'd been at the café that night, then he hadn't been out of town on the night her window was broken like Gage had thought. As far as she was concerned, that zoomed him right to the top of the list of possible suspects who might have thrown that brick through her window. When Gage brought Tripp home, she'd tell them both her suspicions.

Meanwhile, what was Troy doing? Even from a distance, his body language screamed anger, loud and clear. Not wanting to be spotted, she pulled in between two parked cars a half a block away but left the engine running just in case. As far as she could tell, he remained unaware of her presence, which was a huge relief. She stroked Zeke's soft fur, taking comfort from the contact as she kept an eye on the man down the street.

He carried two plastic bags over to the truck and started to toss them in the back end. One caught on the side of the truck and tore, revealing a brief flash of the contents before he pulled it free and shoved it inside the bed and out of sight. Her pulse kicked up to a higher gear as she tried to make sense of what she'd just seen.

"Zeke, I might be crazy, but I think that was a patchwork square I just saw." She wrapped her right arm around the dog's strong shoulders. "If I'm right about that, what's he going to do with that quilt?"

Well, duh! The answer was obvious. He was going to get rid of it. From the size and weight of those two bags, it wasn't the only one. Why would he do that? If he'd found the quilts, all he had to do was say so. Of all people, he had the perfect reason to have them. She doubted any of the ladies they belonged to would question him if he simply said he'd uncovered them somewhere in the house where he hadn't looked before. The attic, the garage, and even the crawl space under the house were all believable locations.

Which made her wonder why he hadn't taken the easy way out and returned them. Or did those quilts pose a threat to him in some way?

Meanwhile, he'd started the truck and was backing out of his driveway. Without hesitation, she made the decision to follow him at a discreet distance. Again, as long as she stayed in her car with the doors locked and kept the engine running, she was safe. If she saw him do anything else suspicious, she'd be on the phone to Gage in a heartbeat.

Troy made a right turn at the next intersection, probably heading over to Main Street. Where he would go from there was anyone's guess, but she needed to avoid being seen following him. Rather than turn at the same spot, she kept going for another block and then turned. When she reached Main Street, she looked in both directions for any sign of his truck.

There—he was headed west toward the outskirts of town. At this time of day, there should be enough traffic on the road to provide adequate cover for her. She drove the first two blocks on Main Street a little above the speed limit to narrow the gap between her car and the truck. After that, she slowed down to keep pace with the rest of the cars around her.

It didn't take long for them to reach the two-lane highway that led out of Snowberry Creek. Traffic picked up speed, but she had no trouble keeping him in sight. When he slowed to turn right onto a secondary road, she debated whether to keep following him. Luckily, the two cars ahead of her went the same direction, which would continue to give her some cover.

This was a dangerous game to be playing, and she knew

it. By this point, her hands ached from the tight grip she had on the steering wheel. Even Zeke was picking up on her growing tension. He whined softly and alternated staring out the windshield and looking at her for reassurance.

"Don't worry. We're fine, boy. Just out for a drive."

Okay, that was a lie, and not even the dog was buying what she was selling. She patted him on the head. "I promise we'll call in the big guns at the first sign of trouble."

Another mile had passed when Troy suddenly cut across the center line into a large parking lot on the left side of the road. He took the turn so fast that his tires kicked up a huge cloud of dust and gravel as he hit the brakes and came to a stop at the end of a row of semitrucks. Abby drove on by, slowing just enough to risk a quick glimpse at the company name on the side of the trucks. The logo jumped out at her immediately—a bright pink high heel. Step Fast Trucking, the company name, was written underneath in a flowery font.

Her mind struggled to make sense of all the information coming at her. Why hadn't it occurred to her before now to wonder which trucking firm Troy worked for? She drove into a busy gas station and mini-mart across the street and parked where she could keep an eye on him. He was out of his truck with the two trash bags in his hand. After putting them in the cab of the nearest rig, he headed into the small building that must serve as the office for the trucking company.

If he was leaving on a cross-country trip, there was no telling where those quilts would end up. It made her furious that he would treat other people's hard work with such casual disregard. Not only that, he was pointing the blame in his poor wife's direction and letting her friends think she'd betrayed their trust. What a jerk!

"Well, mister, you wait to see what Gage Logan has to say about all of this."

She reached for her cell phone to make the call when the door of the office slammed opened again and Troy came stomping out, yelling at the top of his lungs at someone behind him. Abby quickly rolled her window down to see if she could make out what he was saying.

Unfortunately a string of cars passed by, which prevented her from hearing anything. By the time they were out of her line of vision, a woman had followed him outside with her own phone in hand. She was clearly angry as she shouted, "Don't you walk away while I'm talking to you, Troy. It's your own fault you lost your run again this week. I warned you that's what would happen when you show up late. Regardless, I've had it with your attitude in general. And for threatening me, you're fired, effective immediately."

Even from a distance, the quietly pleasant demeanor that Troy normally showed the world was nowhere in evidence. His face was flushed red, his chest working like a bellows. As soon as the woman spoke, he spun back around with his fists clenched. "Just shut up, lady. You really need to learn your place."

The woman realized she was in jeopardy and backed away. "Come near me, and I'll call the cops!"

To Abby's horror, he slapped his employer hard enough to send her stumbling backward. Before he could do more damage, the woman caught her balance and bolted back inside the building. Abby was afraid he'd try to follow, but he didn't. Instead, he ran back to the semi to retrieve the garbage bags. This time, the already damaged one split open, and quilts spilled out onto the ground. He snatched them up and tossed them and the other bag back into his truck. Seconds later, he peeled out of the parking lot.

What should she do?

First, she needed to call Gage. No doubt the police were already en route, but she wanted to make sure he knew what was going on. Besides, the cops would come to the trucking office first. By the time they got there and found out what was going on, Troy could be anywhere. If he had time, he'd probably ditch the quilts someplace, and they'd never find them. Her mind was still struggling to put all the pieces together, but somehow she knew that it was paramount that they not lose track of the quilts. That he had them in his possession meant something.

She dialed Gage's number as she started her car, determined to follow Troy until the police could close in on him. The call went to voice mail.

"Gage, it's Abby. I just saw Troy Tolbert hit a woman in the face at the Fast Step Trucking Company. Sorry, I don't know the address. I'm sure she's already called 9-1-1. The trouble is, Troy has the quilts and is going to get rid of them. If he's the one who sold the quilts to Rowena, it makes me wonder why he tried to make it look like his wife took off with them."

She had no idea how much room was left on the recording. "I'm following him at a distance. We're headed north. Call me."

"Zeke, this is either the craziest or the bravest thing I've ever done. We won't know which it is until it all plays out."

She concentrated on her driving. It didn't take long to get far enough down the road that she could see Troy's truck in the distance. She hadn't gone more than a mile when her phone rang. She hit the button on her console, routing the call through her car radio. "Gage?"

"What on earth do you think you're doing, Abby?"

She tightened her grip on the steering wheel. "I'm trying to keep track of Troy until the police get here. I have no intention of doing anything that would allow him to get his hands on me."

"First, I'm only a few miles out from where you are. I just picked up Tripp from school, so he's with me."

It was amazing what a relief it was to know the cavalry was already on its way even if both men were likely to be furious with her. "That's good, Gage."

"Does Troy know you're behind him?"

"Not that I can tell. I've made sure to keep several cars between us the whole time."

"Smart girl for doing that much to keep yourself safe, but we're going to have a talk when this is all over. It will be long and unpleasant."

She shouldn't laugh, but she couldn't help herself. Maybe it was a touch of hysterics, but at least it helped ease the knot of fear lodged in her chest. "He's turning onto another side road. There's a sign pointing to a county park."

Gage spoke up. "Thanks for the update. I'll let the county police know what's going on. They may get to you before we do. I'm going to have Tripp call you on his phone so I can keep this line open."

"Okay."

She disconnected the call and counted the seconds until the phone rang again. "Tripp?"

"I've got you, Abby. We're coming."

Even Zeke perked up as Tripp's deep voice filled the car. "And just so you know, when Gage is done talking to you, I get a turn, and it's not going to be pretty."

His grumpy statement made her smile. "Duly noted."

She crested a hill, which afforded her a clear view of the road for at least a mile or more ahead. No sign of Troy's truck anywhere. "He must have driven into the county park."

"Then you keep going, Abby. Let the cops handle this."

Before she could respond, Troy's truck shot back out

onto the highway about half a mile ahead of her from a different entrance into the park. "He's back on the road, Tripp, still headed north. There's no shoulder on this road, so I'm going into the park long enough to turn around and head back toward town."

"Do that."

The road into the park was narrow and wound through a stand of tall Douglas firs. She followed it around to the parking lot, the only place where she could turn around. As she pulled in, she saw why Troy had risked stopping here even knowing the police were looking for him.

"Tripp, there's a Dumpster in the park. I'm betting he's already ditched the quilts in it."

"No, Abby, leave them right where they are. Just get out of there."

"I'm already here, Tripp. It will only take a second."

She pulled up in front of the huge trash bin and got out, leaving her car door open just in case she needed to make a run for it. Meanwhile she was going to need both hands free.

"I'll be right back with you, Tripp."

After stuffing the phone in her pocket, she lifted the lid of the Dumpster and was relieved to find two quilts lying right on top. There was a bag right below them that contained at least one more quilt. After pulling those things out, she spotted a second bag like the ones Troy had been carrying. With some heavy duty maneuvering, she managed to drag it out of the depths of the Dumpster and drop it on the ground. As far as she could tell, she'd managed to retrieve everything he'd thrown in there.

"I hope the ladies at the guild appreciate everything I've gone through to get these back for them."

She sure hoped they also knew how to get the stench of park garbage out of cotton. No way she wanted something that smelly in the car with her and Zeke. The distant sound of sirens was comforting as she dragged the bags around to the back to put them in the trunk. But before she could get it open, another vehicle came tearing into the parking lot. She glanced back over her shoulder, praying that it was Gage and Tripp, but the gods weren't listening.

Troy pulled to a stop right behind her car, blocking her in. As he climbed out, she retrieved her phone from her pocket. Hoping Tripp would know to stay quiet, she spoke loud enough that she hoped both he and Gage could hear what was going on. "Troy, imagine running into you here."

He sneered at her. "You stupid fool, you just couldn't leave well enough alone, could you?"

Acting wide-eyed and innocent probably wasn't going to save her, but she had to try something. "What are you talking about?"

He picked up one of the trash bags and flung it through the air into the bed of his truck. "What I'm talking about is you not knowing what your rightful place is in this world. I've had it up to here with being disrespected by a bunch of women who have no business talking to any man that way, much less me."

When he edged closer, she automatically retreated, only to find herself backed up against the side of her car. She sidled a little toward her left, hoping to reach the front end of the car and give herself more room to maneuver. His crazed eyes tracked her every move like a cat toying with a mouse.

"Well, this is your lucky day. I'm going to teach you some manners. While I'll enjoy it, I can pretty much guarantee you won't." His hands flexed as if he could already feel the crack of his hand against her face.

"I've never been anything but polite to you, Troy."

"Yeah, right. You're just like my wife and that nosy old

woman who kept coming around asking about her and those ridiculous quilts."

The truth about what he'd done snapped into pure clarity, and it was far worse than anyone had suspected. The quilts were only the tip of the iceberg.

"You killed Dolly Cayhill, didn't you?"

His shoulders straightened up in obvious pride. "Of course I did."

"And you wrapped her in one of the quilts before you buried her in my aunt's backyard."

"I did." His laugh was death personified. "Did you appreciate the irony of her being wrapped in your aunt's quilt? I loved hearing all those old ladies wondering if she'd finally done away with her archrival."

Abby didn't know what was scarier, the fact that he had just matter-of-factly admitted that he'd killed someone, or that he sounded so proud of what he'd done.

And he wasn't finished bragging. He held up one finger. "First, I choked my wife with my bare hands, because I'd had it with her whining. Maybe I would have let her live, but she defied me one too many times. I told her she had better things to do with her time than hang around with that bunch of biddies, but she snuck around behind my back and did it anyway. If I hadn't come home early from a trip, she might have even gotten away with it."

Up went another finger. "Second, I hit good old Dolly in the back of the head with a shovel. I don't know what she and my wife were up to, but she showed up at our house and demanded to talk to Julie. When I told her to get lost, she was stupid enough to follow me into our backyard to tell me she knew I'd been using Julie for a punching bag. Obviously, I couldn't risk her calling the police. After all, a man has a right and a duty to discipline his wife. Besides, I hadn't finished burying Julie's body under our patio yet."

He shook his head as if amazed that any woman would've dared stand up to him. Then a third finger joined the other two. "And, Ms. McCree, they say good things come in threes. I guess that means you have to die to round things out."

Time stood still as Abby saw her death written in the depths of Troy Tolbert's hate-filled eyes.

Chapter Twenty-Four

Running was her only hope, even if a successful outcome was extremely doubtful. She had on the right kind of shoes, but there wasn't any clear sanctuary anywhere in sight. If he wasn't so close, she might have been able to get back into the car and lock the doors. But Troy had longer legs and was extremely motivated to get his hands on her. That didn't mean she was going to stand there and let him steal her life without putting up a fight. She was about to make a break for it when she felt the car behind her move.

It took every bit of self-control she could muster not to react. How could she have forgotten she wasn't alone with a killer after all? To give her would-be rescuer time to get into position, she attempted to reengage the enemy in conversation.

"Wouldn't it have been better to return the quilts when the ladies asked for them? They all believed your story about Julie running off. Once they had the quilts back, no one would've bothered you except to bring casseroles and desserts to your house."

"Why?" His lips curved into a sneer. "Because it

would've been difficult to explain the blood stains on some of them."

The sirens continued to grow louder, but Troy didn't seem to notice. Maybe he was too focused on what he planned to do to her to realize that the police were breathing down his neck.

"I can see where that would be a problem."

Okay, resorting to sarcasm wasn't her smartest decision. Unfortunately, her brain had run out of safe topics of conversation at the same time Troy finally noticed they had company coming. He cocked his head to the side as if trying to judge how far away the cops were.

"You might still be able to get away before the cops get here."

Doubtful, but it was worth suggesting.

He shook his head and offered her a chilling smile. "No, it's too late for both of us."

When he lunged forward to grab her, she threw her cell phone at his face to distract him. At the same time, she broke into a run straight toward the entrance of the park. Her ploy didn't slow Troy down much, but it was long enough for Zeke to enter the fray. The determined dog caught up with Troy within a few steps and threw all of his strength into knocking Troy to the pavement, his teeth bared and ready to do battle.

Troy might have been brave enough to use his brute strength against women, but one big dog was enough to have him curling up into a ball and screaming like a banshee. Zeke grabbed hold of Troy's sleeve and held on tight, growling every time the man tried to break free.

It was a few seconds at the most before the first police car roared into sight, even though it seemed like an eternity to Abby. Two more came in right behind it. Thank goodness Gage and Tripp were leading the charge. Right now she

wasn't sure she could offer up any coherent explanation of
how she came to be standing in a parking lot with bloodstained quilts, an angry mastiff, and a cold-blooded killer.

Gage looked deadly as he approached Troy with gun
in hand. "Don't make a move, Tolbert. It won't end well
for you."

Troy kept thrashing around on the ground and screaming, "Get this crazy dog off me."

While Gage held his position, Tripp approached Zeke.
"Down boy. Gage has got this, and Abby needs you."

Evidently that's all the dog needed to hear. All signs of
aggression immediately disappeared as he trotted over to
her side. Gage barked orders at Troy as the other officers
joined the party, but Abby couldn't make sense of a single
word. The afterburn of the adrenaline rush hit her with a
vengeance, and her legs buckled. She had lost count of
the times Tripp's strong arms had kept her from hitting the
ground since she'd met him, but she drew comfort from
the sound of his voice as she laid her head against his chest.

Zeke had nothing on Tripp when it came to growling,
but at the moment she didn't care. He settled her on the seat
of a nearby picnic table and sat down beside her while Zeke
laid his head in her lap. The three of them sat in silence as
the police cuffed Troy and stuffed him none too gently into
the back of a police cruiser.

Once Troy was out of the picture, Gage joined them.
"Are you all right?"

Her eyes were a bit blurry, but what were a few tears in
the grand scheme of things? "I will be."

"The EMTs will be here any second. After they check
you out, Tripp can drive you to the police station to give your
statement. Thanks to your quick thinking with the phone,
we already know most of what happened."

"He killed Julie and Dolly." She shivered and leaned in

closer to Tripp. "Then he went on with his life as if their deaths didn't matter. What makes a person do something like that?"

Neither man had an answer for her, and maybe there wasn't one to be had. But at least the truth would come out. She supposed that was a victory of sorts, if not a very satisfactory one.

Despite their earlier threats to the contrary, both Gage and Tripp treated her with great care. Gage had the EMTs check her over before he and the various other police agencies asked her a single question. None of them were overly happy with her answers, but they were unrelentingly polite through the whole process. She suspected that had something to do with Tripp standing beside her, glaring at anyone who pushed her a little harder than he liked.

Their next stop was police headquarters for more of the same kind of discussion. The owner of the trucking company was there to make her statement, too. According to her, Troy had been difficult to deal with from the moment she'd bought the company from her male predecessor. From everything they'd learned about him, no one was surprised to learn Troy had resented taking orders from a woman. Gage figured that might have been the final straw that resulted in Troy killing his wife and her elderly defender.

Hours later, Tripp finally drove Abby home. After escorting her inside, he pointed her toward her favorite chair in the living room and tossed her one of Aunt Sybil's quilts to cover up with.

"I'll feed Zeke, order a pizza for each of us for dinner, and make tea. Stay right where you are."

She considered saluting, but there was no use in throwing gas on his temper. He'd held it in this long, and she wasn't quite ready to face the lecture that was coming. She could hear him muttering to Zeke. She wasn't sure, but she thought he was pointing out to the dog that he had questionable taste in owners.

He had no room to talk. After all, didn't that mean he also had the same bad taste in landladies? Not that she had any urge to say that out loud. Who knows, maybe her common sense was finally putting in a belated appearance. The more she thought about her decision to chase down a murderer, the more scared she got.

Tripp returned with her tea. "Take it easy with that. It's not just hot, it's mostly brandy."

Bless the man. As she sipped the hot liquid, its slow burn immediately made some serious inroads into the chill that had settled deeply into her bones. The cold shakes had started when the full impact had hit her about everything that had happened, and what Troy had done.

"You doing all right now?"

She braced herself and nodded. The explosion wasn't long in coming. Tripp paced back and forth across the living room several times before launching into his lecture.

"We told you to stay away from the man. You knew he was dangerous if for no other reason than Zeke didn't like him. I swear, woman, you don't have the sense God gave a goat." He stopped to glare at her. "Do you have any idea what it was like for Gage and me trying to catch up with you before that jerk could get his hands on you? How were we supposed to live with the guilt if we hadn't gotten there in time to stop him?"

An apology wasn't enough. Not this time. She set her teacup on the table and tossed the quilt aside. It took two attempts to stand up, but she finally made it. When she was sure she wouldn't fall, she took three steps forward straight into Tripp's waiting arms.

His arms clamped around her like iron bands, holding her close and letting the warmth of his big body chase away the last vestiges of fear and cold. She pushed back enough to look up at him, meaning to offer a long overdue thank you and maybe toss in an apology or two for good measure. Before she could say a word, he kissed her hard, stealing her breath and curling her toes.

Then he took an unsteady step backward and stared down at her with his dark chocolate eyes. "Don't ever—EVER—scare me like that again."

Without giving her a chance to respond, he stalked out of the room. A few seconds later the back door slammed shut. Abby considered going after him but decided the man might need his space for a bit. She traced her lips with a fingertip, savoring the last tingle of that kiss.

At a loss as to what to do next, she sat back down to wait for dinner to arrive. After a bit, she realized she was smiling. Considering the day she'd had, how was that even possible? Well, maybe it could be the lingering effects of the brandy, but she didn't think so.

Then it hit her. Maybe Troy had been right about good things coming in threes. First up, Aunt Sybil's name and reputation had been cleared. Even more important, Dolly and Julie would finally get justice. And last but not least, she was alive and a handsome man had just kissed her senseless.

She picked up her tea and held it up in a silent toast to the cosmos. Yep, things were definitely looking up.

Connect with

Us

Visit us online at
KensingtonBooks.com
to read more from your favorite authors, see books
by series, view reading group guides, and more.

Join us on social media

for sneak peeks, chances to win books and prize packs,
and to share your thoughts with other readers.

facebook.com/kensingtonpublishing
twitter.com/kensingtonbooks

Tell us what you think!

To share your thoughts, submit a review,
or sign up for our eNewsletters, please visit:
KensingtonBooks.com/TellUs.

Grab These Cozy Mysteries
from
Kensington Books